THE MARQUESS'S ADVENTUROUS MISS

An Oxford Set Novel, Book One

AVA BOND

First published 2021.

This edition published 2022.

Copyright © 2022 by Ava Bond

Cover Art by: Forever After Romance Designs

The moral rights of the authors have been asserted.

ISBN: 9798421479734

All rights reserved. No part of this publication may be reproduced, stored or transmitted in any form or by any means, electronic, mechanical, photocopying, recording, scanning, or otherwise without written permission from the publisher.

It is illegal to copy this book, post it to a website, or distribute it by any other means without permission.

This novel is entirely a work of fiction and all characters and events are fictional. Any resemblance to actual persons, living or dead, events or localities is entirely coincidental.

This novel contains scenes of a sexual nature.

For my husband, thank you.
x x x

CHAPTER 1

B*rayton Manor, Cumbria, July 1810*
   Richard Cavendish, Marquess of Heatherbroke, sat in his family home in his father's one-time study, feeling overwhelmed by responsibilities. He wasn't sure it was acceptable for a marquess to be overwhelmed. But there was no getting away from it, he was. Papers cluttered his desk, whilst before him stood his slight, balding, and rather harried-looking lawyer, Mr. Forshaw. The man was reciting a long list of Richard's duties.

Just six months ago, none of these things had been a worry for Richard. He had been able to sail through polite society, playing the part of the feckless, but rather charming, younger brother of the Marquess of Heatherbroke. It had been a good life, filled with *ton* parties, balls, races, either on horses or by boat, with far too many hours idled away with his dear friends, the Oxford Set as they had been christened. It hadn't been chosen, more of a nickname that had stuck to the lot of them, the Marquess of Heatherbroke, Duke of Woolwich, Lord Lynde, Mr. Trawler, Viscount Silverton, and Baronet Verne, as well as Richard himself. Of course, they had enjoyed the notoriety that came with their arrival into the *ton*. Each of them was good looking, from well-connected families, and never long out of each other's company. They had gone to the races, the palace balls, to Almack's, too, but no more than once a month. On occasion, they had been mentioned in the scandal sheets or in the betting book at White's. In short, they had set London ablaze.

Richard had been a late addition to the Set, allowed in because of his older brother, but he nevertheless felt a great affinity with them. It had been a great deal of fun, "a lark," like life had been paused so that Richard could enjoy himself. But all that had changed with the death of his brother, the Marquess of Heatherbroke. Dear, dear George. Then all the responsibility had fallen to Richard.

"My lord?" Mr. Forshaw spoke with more volume, drawing Richard's attention back to the study. Mr. Forshaw stretched out his gloved hand and passed yet another sheet to Richard.

"And this is?" Richard asked. He had only had six months to adjust to being the marquess. To being Heatherbroke. George had had his whole life to prepare, had been raised to assume the title. Richard had not. There had been some talk of the law, or possibly setting up business with one of the other members of the Set. But Richard had fallen into the habit of putting it off. Looking back at his earlier self, Richard felt a curl of disgust at his own laziness.

Duty bound, he followed the lawyer's instructions and dropped his head to start looking through the new pages. The numbers and letters pooled this way and that, but Richard knew the estate needed to economise. The important thing now was protecting the Heatherbroke name and his numerous tenants.

"The Mayfair house. It's costing more than £800 a year, with everything included," Mr. Forshaw said. "I thought that might be unnecessary if you were to stay up here..."

Perhaps, Richard thought as he flicked through the pages, wondering how anyone sane ever tolerated a Season. Perhaps, he would have been able to manage this new role had he not been robbed of his family. George was all he had had left. His father and mother were gone. In this whole world, there remained only his grandmother whom he loved. Still, he told himself, self-pity wouldn't help. He had been an idle man, and there were people who depended on him to be more than that. He needed to rise to the occasion; it was expected of him. He could at least make his family proud. Going forward, that would be his aim.

"Close the place down, except for a skeleton staff. I will discuss with the dowager if she would like to visit in the next year."

"Very good, my lord," Mr. Forshaw said with great primness. He was at least twice Richard's twenty-four years. Richard had known the man since infancy and was grateful for his many years of loyal service, since he had worked for both of the last marquesses.

Getting to his feet, Richard moved across to a nearby dresser, sliding open one of the drawers. "I should have said earlier, but I wanted you to have this. It belonged to my brother. He valued you, as did my father." He handed Mr. Forshaw a bible, which had belonged to George and had a handwritten inscription in it.

Mr. Forshaw's pale eyes bulged in surprise, and he swallowed audibly. Richard turned away and looked to the mirror, giving Mr. Forshaw time to compose himself. Intense expressions of grief made Richard sure he, too, would break down. He glanced at his own appearance, one which had once been a matter of immense pride and a lot of time and care. Previously, he had spent hours every day with his valet, perfecting his look. The break from the city had brought a collection of youthful freckles over his nose and left his dark, curled hair too long, but otherwise he remained the same, a quirk to his lips, green-brown eyes, and the same haughty look he had learnt, despite how its everyday use gained him nothing.

Turning, Richard found Mr. Forshaw standing close by. "It might not be my place to say it, but I think both of the late

Heatherbrokes would have been proud of what you're doing. I believe you are setting their plans in motion."

"I never wanted it," Richard said. He needed Mr. Forshaw to know that. The older man nodded, wet his lips, and opened his mouth to speak but was stopped when there was a loud shriek of sound that retched through the halls of Brayton.

"Are the French coming—" Mr. Forshaw's sentence was cut off when the door of the study flung open.

On instinct. Richard went for the pistol but stopped short at the sight of the man in the doorway. It was Woolwich. He had always been the tallest of the Set, but today, he seemed to have grown even larger. His blue eyes were icy, and he resembled more of a marauder from centuries back than a dignified duke. Richard gazed back at the man, his brother's closest companion, his supposed friend, and from Woolwich's face, Richard knew. Knew with absolute certainty that his shameful secret had been discovered. Richard looked away in embarrassment. "God, you dog," Woolwich grunted and started across the study.

"Sir!" Mr. Forshaw was in his way and had not got out a word before he was shoved aside and thrown unceremoniously to the floor.

"Really," Richard began to say; it was fair that Woolwich try to take him apart, but it wasn't permissible for Forshaw to be attacked. No one else should suffer for his mistake.

Woolwich strode forward, his face livid, looking fully capable of murder. It wasn't normal for him to be like this; he was, or had always been, a good, generous man. A touch cynical but nevertheless thoughtful, kind... it was gone.

Behind him, the door was pushed wider, and Richard saw his grandmother and Silverton, Verne, and Lynde, enter the study. Before he saw anyone else, Woolwich slammed his fist in Richard's jaw. The sheer force of it knocked Richard back, but he managed to stay on his feet. He looked away from the door, back to the furious man before him. His grandmother shrieked, and one of the Set held her back.

"You know why I'm here, don't you?" Woolwich asked, his voice low.

It only took the raising of Richard's eyes up to Woolwich's for the duke to make a furious noise at the back of his throat and raise his fist again. This time Richard didn't try to stay up. He let his body relax, and the hit sent him to the floor. Woolwich was here for blood; he may as well let the man have it. Sprawled down on the carpet, Richard reflected that he deserved this. His mouth filled with the taste of iron.

"Get up," Woolwich said, and with great reluctance, Richard rolled onto his side to view the rest of the inhabitants of his study. It would have been bad enough if it had just been of them, but it was all the Set. *His friends, whose eyes were on him*. Which meant Woolwich must have told them what Richard had done.

"Woolwich," Verne's voice was calm and measured, his slight French accent peeking out, "If you kill him, it will cause a scandal. Aren't we here to ensure that doesn't happen?"

"If this is a matter of honour, have a duel," Richard's grandmother said. She looked almost as angry as Woolwich. The dowager had pulled herself out of Lynde's hold and moved over to help Forshaw up. Her grey hair was piled high on her head, and it wobbled as she moved, her cap at a rakish angle. Richard could not resist the idea that she would probably have to serve as his second, as no one else in the room would. He forced himself to his knees.

"This..." Woolwich's eyes travelled back to Richard. "This cur has no honour."

"I would like to know. I am entitled to know what you accuse my grandson of."

Richard braced himself for the revelation. Woolwich would say Richard was a seducer, a damned blaggard, for taking advantage of the angel-like, beautiful Annabelle, Duchess of Woolwich. He would be named and shamed; that was inevitable. How Woolwich had discovered their brief affair, or terrible mistake, as Richard thought of it, he had no idea. Annabelle's flowery romantic letters had been hidden away, stuffed into a drawer in his desk.

Had she been fool enough to send another one that had been intercepted?

"He tricked my wife to bed."

Richard, who had gotten to his feet in order to best face the embarrassment, turned in bewilderment to Woolwich. "That isn't true," he said, his voice hoarse. The accusation was even worse than he could have imagined. The humiliation more acute. But even to his own ears, he sounded childish.

He turned to his grandmother and grasped her hands. "I swear to you."

She nodded, although she was very pale. Richard looked past his grandmother, to his assorted friends who were watching the proceedings. None of them would meet his eye. It was a solid confirmation he had only ever belonged to the Set as an obligation to George, and now they cut him.

"Are you going to claim it was love?" Woolwich asked, scorn dripping off every word. He looked like he wanted to murder Richard and barely kept himself in check.

In his mind's eye, Richard saw himself go to the cabinet and withdraw Annabelle's letters. There were five in total, sent to him after their one fateful night together. Why he'd kept them, he couldn't even say. It wasn't supposed to be a way of holding something over Annabelle's head. More that he wanted to hold on to a reminder of the mistake. He could use them now to excuse himself, but then he would be throwing Annabelle into the path of Woolwich's fury. She would be ostracised if he did that.

"It was a mistake—right after George's death," Richard said. He could feel everyone's eyes on him. Part of him wished the rest of them would leave, let him confess to how drunk he'd been, how vulnerable, without everyone judging him. "I can only apologise for the grave error on my part."

Able to read his desperation, the dowager strode away from the recovering Mr. Forshaw and opened the study doors that looked over the stone steps and led down into the peaceful gardens to the rear of Brayton. The cool summer air rushed in, and the dowager grabbed the two of the men nearest to her, Silverton, and Trawler. "Out," she said. "This is a serious accusation between His Grace and my grandson. I don't see why this involves the rest of you." Her tone was firm, fully that of a dowager marchioness. The Set followed her out, with only Lynde lingering behind.

Lynde shot Richard a strained look of hurt disbelief. Nicholas Lynde was Richard's dearest friend amongst the Set. His clear-sighted and azure eyes were filled with disappointment. With a betrayed sigh, Lynde shook his head at Richard. He followed the rest of the Set out.

Woolwich had likewise watched the others leave. He sank into one of the armchairs close to the desk. He was still angry, but Richard could also see there was something else there too, an element of smug satisfaction. This had been part of his plan. *Humiliate me, cut me off from the Set. It is what I deserve,* Richard thought.

Letting out a sigh, Richard looked back at Woolwich. "Do you want to call me out?"

"I want no one beyond the Set to know of this." Woolwich leant forward in his seat, fixing Richard with his cold, hypnotic eyes. "I wish to avoid a scandal."

"I cannot go abroad."

In response to this, Woolwich smirked. "The idea of you, a useless wastrel, taking on George's mantel—" He cut himself off. "Enough. I tell you, you will stay away from London. You will never speak to my wife again."

"Are you going to divorce her?" The scandalous note that this added to the room made the guilt in his stomach writhe.

"Would you like that? So you could wed her?"

It would be the honourable thing to do in a terrible situation, Richard knew that. He knew, too, that whilst he cared for Annabelle, he was never going to fall in love with her. "If that is what you need me to do."

"No." Woolwich was on his feet. Once more, there was a furious glint behind his eyes. "You don't get to come in and destroy a marriage. She is to go into the countryside and remain secluded."

"If Annabelle—"

"Don't you dare use her name."

"I never tricked her."

The duke made a small tutting noise, and Richard leapt on it. "You know I didn't. You know she's in love with me."

A shadow passed over Woolwich's face. "It is my word against yours, the untried, unprepared son, nothing more than a wastrel. All the Set knows the story I have told them. If you try anything, you will be ruined by those in the aristocracy, those in trade, and those in the military. Don't our friends fill some important roles?" His joke was bitter, and Richard had no reply. Woolwich was right, the Set members had found powerful roles. They had influence and were prepared to blacken his name should Richard do anything to reveal the truth.

"Annabelle was given a choice," Woolwich continued. "A man who didn't want her or to stay with a duke whom she had fought so hard to win."

"You lied to them," Richard said, indicating the Set with a nod of his head towards the gardens, "so that you would not be labelled a cuckold."

"Do not think there was any advantage in this for me. I did this to protect my wife and her reputation."

"And in doing so, you get your revenge. You get to destroy me."

"You cannot..." The gleam vanished, and Woolwich smirked. He almost seemed to be enjoying the confrontation. "Come now, you must know how I discovered it."

Richard's brain had slowed down, so that everything he thought seemed to be laden down with treacle, until it finally clicked. "She is with child."

"It cannot be mine," Woolwich said.

His slow-moving mind whizzed forward, alive with the ideas, calculating it all and realising what had happened. Annabelle and he were together only one night. In January. The night George had died. A drunken night which he thought had been consigned to the past. Woolwich had been in Paris, unable to make it back, not even for George's funeral. It had been many weeks before the duke had returned to England. "You must divorce her, and I will wed her."

"That is not for you to demand. She will deliver the child." Here, the harsh, strict elements that Richard had suspected but never witnessed, poked out from beneath the duke's façade. "And you will forever wonder where your child is. Where I might have placed it and with whom. That will be your punishment. Shall I send your son off to some gambling hell? Your daughter to a brothel? What I have done with the baby... that can be the only fit punishment for you. It will not bear my name."

He had moved closer to Richard, and when he was finished, he spat in Richard's face before turning and leaving the study to stand outside in the fresh, cool air amongst decent men. His words burrowed into Richard's skull, chiming, and hurting with the implications.

"Richard?" His grandmother was moving through the study, her hand raised, and for a moment, he thought she would stroke his cheek. Instead, she slapped him. "What were you thinking?"

"I never forced myself on or misled Annabelle. She's... she's with child."

"Blast it," the dowager muttered. Her sharp eyes went round the room before she marched back to the study door. "Mr. Forshaw, a moment please." Sliding back into the room, the lawyer was looking worse for wear. "I trust you to keep silent on today's proceedings." The lawyer nodded; his face was still pink from where he'd hit his head.

"Woolwich said there will be a child," the dowager repeated.

He had ruined it all, even the poor child's life.

"He said he'd take it to a brothel," Richard replied, his stomach churning.

"Can we claim the child?" the dowager asked. "Better than letting the mite be shipped to god knows where."

The study looked wrong, with its elegantly kept books, polished oak furniture, Chinese carpets, and paintings by Kneller and Reynolds. The room had housed his father, and here was Richard, further spoiling his family's reputation. Distantly, he could hear the sounds of the Set leaving, their voices raised, and headed towards the stables. They had arrived to see his humiliation; they had believed Woolwich. A flare of anger ignited in his stomach. *Did they know what was intended for his baby?*

"It is not my area of expertise," Mr. Forshaw said, "but if the child is christened, and no one claims to be its parents... If the duke does not let it be christened with his name, then..." Mr. Forshaw flushed. "It would be named a foundling, rather like an orphan. Provided you could locate the babe, there would be no reason why you could not raise the child as your ward."

"At least I would be able to rectify that," Richard said. *It was only an idea, a glimmer of hope, his unborn child, a silver lining in such a wasted life. It is my chance, no, it is my only chance at salvation.*

LONDON, APRIL 1814

Richard was on a mission. His tight-lipped expression aged him past his twenty-eight years, adding gravity to his features and grit to his expression. He was returning to London in a high-speed chase, at the request of his recently hired Bow Street runner, Mr. Clifton. The runner's note assured Richard that there was finally news of his child. Clifton had some promising new leads that needed to be heard in person. In truth, over the last few years, Richard had heard so many different tales that he had almost lost hope. Since that fateful day, that *dark day* as he thought of it, there were only the Heatherbroke estates and the quest for the child. In a way, he told himself without much humour, the desire to locate the baby had replaced, or become a welcomed distraction from, the loss of his dear brother. An urgent, overwhelming desire to find the child at any cost.

Tightening his fists, Richard wished the carriage would go faster. He disliked returning to London, but needs must. Most of his business was contracted through Forshaw and his associates, but Clifton promised that the lead was genuine.

The child. His child was a girl. Hidden deep in his waistcoat pocket, was a sketch of the child, the mirror image of her mother. Years back, his hirelings had combed through foundling hospitals, but without much hope. Richard had had the recurring dream that Woolwich had thrown the child into the Thames.

"Drive on," Richard muttered as he fidgeted in his squab. He could have sworn he would have been able to drive the blasted thing faster. They must be nearing Oxford by now. They had stopped only to change the horses, the drive down lasting hours. It was getting dark, the cloudless sky blackening. *I will be there soon*, Richard promised. *If I am lucky, I could see my child within days.*

Leaning into the cushions of the chase, Richard allowed himself to relax. His obsession over the girl's safety had kept him going, had kept him sane almost to the extent of all else. With his eyes closed, he pictured a scene where they were all together, picnicking on the grounds, teaching her to read perhaps. Lord, he would need to get her a tutor. Richard was lulled into an uneasy sleep. When he opened his eyes, the chase was slowing outside his London home. The Mayfair house was a handsome one, with a fine white façade, neat railings, and large windows, which would have seemed inviting. It had been closed for numerous months, with only two elderly servants to keep an eye on things, so now the place looked almost gloomy.

Stepping down from the chase, Richard reviewed the London street. He had arrived in the late afternoon, almost evening. Were anyone beyond the servants working, he might have been noticed, but he hoped he could slip unnoticed into his home and await Mr. Clifton.

"My lord." It was the reedy voice of Mr. Wilson, the family butler. Unbidden, a smile formed on Richard's face. It was a sweet, familiar reminder of the past.

"Good to see you, Wilson." Striding up the steps, Richard made it inside the hallway and resisted the urge to question Wilson. The old man needed to proceed back inside.

"There is..." Wilson's voice trailed off, and he gestured over towards the main parlour, "a gentleman waiting for you."

Frowning, Richard moved forward. Woolwich would not be depraved enough to have had him followed. Swinging the parlour door open, Richard was surprised to see Verne sitting by the empty grate, a book of poetry resting on his knee and a reflective expression on his face.

"His Lordship will not be staying," Richard snapped. If Verne thought Richard could be chased out of London, then he had another thing coming.

"I hate to contradict you," Verne said. "But I do think you will wish to hear what I have to say. It concerns your Mr. Clifton. And the child."

"Please see that my bags are sent up." Richard closed the door and turned back to his guest. He had never been close to Verne per se. There was something almost too relaxed about the man; he gave the impression that he was easing one into a stupor before striking. But his reputation for intelligence, and his ability in the ring, proceeded him. Making his way forward, Richard chose the chair farthest from Verne and sank into it, before waving his hand. "You may proceed."

Drawing out a small snuff box, Verne took a sniff, stretched, and then began in a light manner. "I hope my reputation proceeds me."

"To what do you refer?"

This caused Verne to smile. He gave an almost Gallic shrug. "In that case, I shall simply say that I am said to be a good judge of character."

"If you say so."

Verne did not immediately voice a reply to the comment, but he did glance away from Richard. "I have never been one who has come under the sway of the stunning Lady Annabelle Bradley, as was. Our dear Duchess of Woolwich, as is."

"While the rest of us followed at her heels, you mean?"

"Quite." Verne smiled. He had an unnerving way of forming a grin which did not reach his eyes. "This luck, shall we say, meant that I never bought Woolwich's accusation against you."

Richard could recall the *dark day* still and did remember Verne calling out, reminding Woolwich... well, he had stopped the duke from killing him.

"Not enough to do anything about it," Richard bit out. The resentment he felt, the rejection and bitterness, had consumed him; how easily they had gone along with Woolwich's say. "Was it because he's a duke? You didn't want to offend someone so powerful?"

For the first time, a flash of emotion—was it anger or something else—passed over Verne's dark features. But then it vanished, smoothed away, and he resumed his easy, calm look.

"Don't you know that guilt can work in unusual ways?" Verne

asked. "It has worked its wiles on me." When Richard made no reply, Verne continued, "I noticed that you had your own reasons for keeping quiet too."

The night I spent with Annabelle was a mistake. She had already suffered enough. What was I supposed to say that would ever remedy it? Stuffing such delicate thoughts away, Richard stiffened his resolve. Just because he had been chased out of society, didn't mean he couldn't rescue his child.

"I prefer to work on evidence. And my knowledge of people's characters. They usually give me enough disappointing information to reveal themselves," Verne continued. "It is the most effective way of operating."

"What evidence did you find?" Richard asked. He could see the way Verne was going, and this could take all night. The man was impressed with himself.

"If I share this with you, I want your word on two things. The first, that there will be no reactionary gestures against the duke or the duchess. Two—"

"If I wanted to do that, I would have done so already."

"Two," Verne carried on as though he had not been interrupted, "I want you to release the services of the numerous Bow Street runners you had hired over the years. Their services could be put to better use than searching through foundling hospitals. It is at the request of the British government."

"Why do you care about that?" Richard had made his way over to the nearest bookshelf and started through a leather-bound book. He wasn't about to give up the good men he had hired unless Verne was going to give him something better in return. "The note I received mentioned that the child was a girl. That..." For some reason, Richard could not quite form the words. "There was drawing of her."

"I did that. It's not an exact likeness. I cannot say I am a gifted artist."

Richard was across the room in a flash, pulling Verne out of the armchair and to his feet, his hands tightening around the other man's neckcloth. "You know where she is. Give her to me."

"I don't," Verne said with maddening calm, "have her with me. But I saw her, and I am prepared to tell you all that I know, provided you agree to my stipulations."

"Yes, yes," Richard snapped, releasing his hold on Verne. He was in a vile mood; the idea that the child could be close by was eating him up. He could still recall Woolwich's taunt about brothels. Some places specialised in children. He shuddered at the idea. "Get on with it."

"I saw the girl. She is the tiny twin of Annabelle, unmistakably her daughter, in a small rural village in Sussex."

"Her wellbeing?" It was not at all what Richard would have imagined. His fears were confounded, and he found himself listening in confusion.

"From what I could see, the child seemed well. Happy too."

"What else?"

"I watched the pair of them, the child and who I assumed was…" Here, Verne paused. "Well, the child was accompanied by a very striking woman who was looking after her. I believe her to be Woolwich's mistress."

Here we go, Richard thought. *He is punishing me by raising my daughter with his jade.* "You have their names?"

"Indeed. I heard the woman call the child Harriet. I made a few discreet inquiries around the village and discovered she is a foundling known as Harriet Milton. A foundling who lives with the Pendletons."

It all sounded far too respectable. So unlike everything that Woolwich had threatened.

Glancing up, Richard met Verne's eyes. "If you are lying—"

"Then feel free to returning to using the runners and resume paying Mr. Clifton his huge fees."

"The name of the village?"

"Alfriston. Just five miles away from Lynde's family estate."

The idea that his old friend might have known Harriet's whereabouts wriggled its way around his brain, painful and gnawing. But then Richard squished that emotion back down; what good would it do him to dwell on that? He now had the best opportunity he'd had in years.

Her name, her location... Sussex, just a matter of a day's travel away.

"Richard?" It was Verne who called him back to himself.

Not bothering to turn around, Richard paused; he had been bent over his desk scribbling these scant details down.

"I suppose Lynde knows already."

"I thought it best and only fair for me to tell you first. But I will make a call on him tomorrow or the following day."

"Give me the whole of tomorrow. You owe me that." He locked eyes with Verne. "What did she do that convinced you?"

This earned him an amused look from Verne. "I thought the rest of us could burn in hell?"

With a careless shrug, Richard drummed his fingers on the wooden surface. It had been years, so why did they still have the power to hurt him? It was the lie; they were liars, holding him captive in such a way.

"She asked after you. Annabelle." Verne spoke into the silence. "It was a small question directed to me, just a passing remark, but when pressed, well, she confirmed my doubts."

"How good of you." A flare of bitterness had returned to his tone that Richard could not control.

The expression on Verne's face was neutral, that of a gentleman. "This means you won't have contact with Woolwich or Her Grace? No matter who Harriet has been raised with. I don't suppose either of them will wish to, Her Grace is in a delicate condition, and I thought—"

There was a break in Verne's speech, and Richard could imagine the rest. Verne believed that Woolwich, distracted with Annabelle's new pregnancy, would let the previous child go. How innocent Verne was in the true maliciousness that Woolwich had left Richard in.

Swallowing down any surprise at the news of Woolwich's impending fatherhood, Richard said, "Tell Lynde whatever you like when you run off to tattle to him. And I don't give a damn about the others. It's all for Harriet." He did not look back to Verne and waited for the man to leave the room, so when he repeated it to himself it was more of a benediction. "I don't give a damn about anyone else."

CHAPTER 2

Miss Prudence Pendleton gazed out over the summer-flecked fields of the Sussex countryside, her eyes following the movements of her little charge. Harriet Milton was playing in the small garden. The child was three years old, a bundle of happy innocence. She always seemed to have bright, flushed pink cheeks and curious hands that loved nothing more than to create great blooming bouquets or attempt to make daisy chains.

"Don't pick all the flowers," Prudence called out to Harriet.

"Yes, miss," Harriet called back.

Prudence sank farther back in her seat. She was the daughter of Alfriston's only vicar. It was a tiny Tudor village, a good twenty miles from Brighton. Very little of note occurred here, other than the occasional rusticating tourists returning from jolly Brighton.

Prudence had been motherless since she was six, a loss she still felt, even if the memories of her mother had faded now to a gentle sort of pain. Her only real keepsake from her mother was the small ruby cross she had at her throat. The faint memories were more a sensation that she was missing a crucial element from her life, rather than any real memories to cling to.

Prudence had been educated at home, first by their dear housekeeper, Mrs. Foley, then after the age of seven, by her father, Vicar Anthony Pendleton. Her father was a prematurely greyhaired vicar who liked nothing more than a good, slow walk and to talk through a well argued religious or theological debate. This bookish existence was the norm for most of Prudence's life. Things had changed when Vicar Pendleton had found a second wife, who brought the first real taste of London glamour with her to the quiet village of Alfriston.

Prudence's stepmother had married the vicar when Prudence was twelve. The three of them had rubbed along very well together until the unusual and unexpected arrival of Harriet, five years later. It had presented something of a mystery to Prudence and continued to do so.

The carriage had come late at night, past ten o'clock, after both the vicar and Prudence had gone to bed. Neither of them had been expecting Mrs. Pendleton's return from London until the following day.

The noise of the private coach-and-four had thundered down the small pathway of the sleeping village, the whinnying of the horses and the cry of the driver waking half the place and making the cottages shake in their timbers. If whoever had arranged this night-time trip had wanted to be subtle about it, they had failed. Carrying a candle, Prudence had emerged from the vicarage, blearily staring up and down the street until her eyes alighted on the private form of transportation.

"Who's there?" Prudence had called out. "Who's in there?"

Prudence looked up at the driver, who remained silent in his perch, his face in shadows. *How rude*, she thought, but her anger dissipated as the door of the carriage opened.

Mrs. Pendleton climbed down the steps, a bundle heavy in her arms. Prudence went to help, but the older woman pulled it closer to her as she turned to gaze into the carriage interior.

Then came a rough male voice emerging from the depths, "Keep her secret." Somehow it sounded like a threat.

Mrs. Pendleton hadn't uttered a reply. The speaker hadn't expected one because the carriage took off at once. Uttering a loud grumble, Mrs. Pendleton turned on her heel and went into the cottage without a backward glance, leaving Prudence staring after the carriage, her mind full of questions. None of which were answered.

It wasn't from a want of trying. The village had been informed that baby Harriet was a foundling. The vicar had christened the infant Harriet Mary Milton, and a majority of the Alfriston inhabitants had lost interest after that. But not Prudence. It seemed this strange little arrival, one which Mrs. Pendleton would tell Prudence nothing about, stirred her curiosity further. It was from Harriet's arrival in her life that Prudence marked a change in herself—a strong desire to leave Alfriston and explore beyond the narrow confines that her father gave her. It opened the wider world up to her in a way she hadn't expected. It was important for her to have an adventure of her own, no matter what her strict father ordered.

Every time there was a chance, she asked her father if she could go to London, where Mrs. Pendleton's family had a townhouse, but he insisted she stay put. So, Prudence poured all her rebellious and curious intentions and interests into Harriet, building up the most glamourous and exciting of backstories that would explain how the baby ended up in her tiny corner of Sussex.

The years had trickled by, and Prudence had come to adore Harriet, almost as much as Harriet loved Prudence. It mattered to her that, since she was as motherless as this child, Harriet would always stay with her. No one should go without a mother's love.

"Pru..." the child called out as she lifted her hand into the air, the chubby fist aimed at the highflying, orange butterfly. "Thith ith for you," Harriet lisped. She handed a squashed bunch of rose petals plucked from the vicar's flowerbed. Laughing, Prudence took the handful.

Kneeling in front of her, Prudence smoothed out the child's dark blonde curls with her free hand. She was the prettiest child Prudence had ever seen, with large eyes that were the colour of the sea after a storm, a happy blend of blue and melting turquoise. She was blessed with a small rosebud mouth that could pout in both annoyance and delight. Her pink cheeks were more prone to curve up with laughter than anything else.

"Thank you, Harriet." She pulled the child onto her lap, enjoying the warm, sweet scent of the girl's body against her own. It was all good practice for when she had her own children.

Whenever that would be.

"What will we have for supper?"

"Tonight, I think it will be lamb stew."

"And cake?"

"Not tonight."

"But it's my favourite." The little girl wriggled in Prudence's arms, somewhat annoyed at her request being denied. "It's my birthday."

"No," Prudence said, "it's not your birthday until October."

Harriet frowned, her pretty face creasing in confusion. "Can't it be my birthday today?"

"That is not how it works, I'm afraid." Prudence laughed. She was almost tempted to give in to the girl's demands. Leaning back amongst the cornflowers, the tips of the plants tickling her skin, Prudence let out a sigh as she pulled Harriet down next to her. It was one of those warm April days that had occurred over the last week. It made it a joy to be outside, and of course, it meant the occasional tourist here to rusticate. There had been several more visitors in recent days. One had shocked Prudence as he had watched her and Harriet shop during the market, his piercing dark eyes following her. He was the sort of interesting, gentleman-looking sort that Prudence and Clara Blackman often speculated about.

Summoned, it seemed, by the thought of his younger sister, Prudence heard Thomas Blackman calling her, "Miss Pendleton." His rather reedy voice made Prudence sit up. Prudence adjusted herself hurriedly. Crossing the garden, was Mr. Thomas Blackman, Clara's older brother. The Blackmans were a prosperous merchant family, with three daughters and one son. The older daughters, Agnes and Isabel, were married off with both of them now living in Eastbourne, only eighteen miles away. Not quite as fashionable or as fast-paced as Brighton, but at least it overlooked the sea. There was the promenade, a theatre, and a public dance hall which, sadly, Prudence had only ever walked past.

Hastily, Prudence made herself smile and got to her feet. "How nice to see you, Tom."

"Miss Pendleton. Yes, your mother—stepmother, I mean—said you'd be out here." Mr. Blackman had adopted a formal tone ever since he had gone to university, as though Prudence had not known him since she was born. He was slim and of middling height, with close-cut brown curls that clustered around his head, his expression tense as he viewed Prudence.

"You've bought me a book?" She looked down at the leather-bound item he held.

"It's from Clara. She wondered if you had finished with the Matthew Lewis yet?"

How like Clara to demand a favourite book back early. "I can run in and fetch it for you."

"No... no..." Thomas shoved the replacement book at her, and when their fingers touched, he turned crimson. "Just return it at some point."

Then he darted off, back towards the cottage. Glancing down at Harriet, Prudence could not help laughing. Thomas was a very strange fish.

"Before lunch, would you like to go for a walk?" Prudence

asked her charge. She knew that Clara wanted her book back. In walking to the Blackman house, they would need to walk out of town and past the Brookes' farm, where a Great Dane named Toby lived. He was one of

Harriet's favourite sights. "We might see the dog—"

The child let out a little cry of delight. "The big dog?"

"Yes, I should think so," Prudence said. She took Harriet's hand. The two of them started to make their way back through the garden towards the cottage.

As they walked, Prudence thought about the idea of Thomas Blackman. He was her chance for romance; at least that was what Alfriston village assumed. It was hard to imagine a great passion forming around him, and yet, what other options did Prudence have? It was better to marry well and go into a family she knew and liked. Although somewhere, at the back of her mind, there was a voice that cried for something more exciting.

Harriet pushed ahead, leading the way back inside the cottage, pulling Prudence after her.

"There you two are." It was Mrs. Pendleton, who was seated in her armchair, fanning herself frantically. She was a plump, handsome woman in her late forties, with a face that always reminded Prudence of a sunflower.

They entered the informal back chamber, which Mrs. Pendleton liked to claim as her own. It was rather messy, with an assortment of unwrapped sweetmeat wrappers, discarded novels, and fragments of pages dotted throughout the room. Both sets of windows were open, and there was a discarded tea set that had not been cleared away by Mrs. Foley. The front room, the more formal of the two, was visible through the open door, but no one liked to sit in there unless they were receiving guests.

"What did you say to Mr. Blackman?"

"Almost nothing," Prudence replied. "But I thought we might go up to see Miss Blackman."

"Well." Mrs. Pendleton lifted her pink, plump palm up to her face, dabbing at her mottled skin. "Don't you think it is too warm for a walk?"

"It would be good for us to get out," Prudence said.

"We're going to see the big dog," Harriet explained.

Mrs. Pendleton nodded along and pressed her head back amongst the pillows. "Do give Mrs. Blackman my kindest regards."

Prudence went upstairs and fetched down *The Monk*. She had read it once before, but it was just like Clara to demand it back, not giving Prudence enough time to finish it. Clara and Prudence shared a love of novels, always the gothic ones. Sometimes Prudence thought it was her only real chance at escape.

When she returned to the parlour, Harriet was on Mrs. Pendleton's lap, and the two of them were giggling together.

"What is so funny?"

"We were just saying what an exquisite bride you'd make," Mrs. Pendleton said.

"Wouldn't Harriet make the most adorable bridesmaid?"

"Would I get a new dress?" the little girl asked.

"Of course, and so would Prudence. It would be a wedding gown."

With as much dignity as she could manage, Prudence pulled down her own bonnet and shawl. The latter item seemed a touch too much on a warm day, but it was the dowdiest thing she owned, so if anyone saw her out, no one would accuse her of flirting. Not that she was. She didn't want Thomas to think of her like that; she didn't want anyone to think of her as a flirt. If she were to be perceived in any manner, it mattered to her that her mind, her imagination, her desires be considered.

Adjusting the bonnet, she returned to the backroom and called out to Harriet, "Come on, little one, let's go and find that dog for you."

The walk was not as refreshing as Prudence would have liked. She had to adjust her long-limbed frame to the slow, pausing pace of the child. Harriet would stop and point out sights every minute or so with a fresh pack of questions. Her favourite theme seemed to centre on Prudence getting married.

"Will you wear a big, lace veil?" she asked. Her voice was high enough to catch the attention of the couple ahead.

Prudence hung back, pulling Harriet to a stop so they could let the pair proceed past them. She forced a smile, although she suspected they had overheard the child's question. The cobbled village was surrounded by a series of stretching green hills flecked with trees. Being so encompassed made Alfriston feel small, and it was easy for rumours to feel like fact. "What would you like to see most in the world?" she asked Harriet.

"Toby the dog."

"I meant in the whole world."

"Ice cream. Mrs. Pendleton says I may have it. One day."

She squeezed the little girl's damp hand. At night, sometimes, she would hug little Harriet to her, when the child cried about her parents. That was something Prudence knew Harriet wanted more than either a dog or ice cream.

"I'm sure you will," she said. "I promise, today, you shall either have ice cream or see Toby."

It was just like children not to ask, so Prudence asked herself instead, *I would like to race in a carriage, to see a duel, or visit the theatre. Anything that isn't confined to this village.* They neared the edge of the village, and she forced herself to concentrate on Harriet.

"Yes, please, let's see Toby now." Harriet released Prudence's hand and bounced into the roadside.

The street curved around the corner, the thatched buildings dropping away to reveal the distant fall and rise of the hills that made up the South Downs. The hedgerows were peppered with small pink-and mustard-coloured flowers. The Blackmans' little estate was a mile up the pathway. They would bypass through the farmer's fields and away from the centre of the village. On those pathways, they were unlikely to see anyone. Walking back from the Blackmans when she was younger, Prudence used to yell, calling out to the skies far above. Sometimes it was fun to imagine still doing this, being as loud as she could, in no danger of being heard. Distantly, she heard the rumble of the four o'clock coach making its way towards Alfriston, where it would stop, and passengers would alight. Harriet broke away from her and dashed to the pathway towards where Toby lived. Laughing, Prudence chased after the girl.

The sound of the carriage was fast approaching, the beat of the horse's hooves pounding on the road. It occurred to Prudence that it was strange that the coach would take this side route into the village. Besides, it should not be arriving for another twenty minutes. A carriage did appear on the horizon, but it wasn't a public stagecoach. It was a gentlemen's phaeton, a smart little sprig of an open carriage, of the sort she'd seen in fashionable magazines, driven by the most magnificent set of black horses imaginable. On the front seat, sat a man dressed in black, with only a tiny flash of white at his throat. He wore a thick, dark hat pulled low over his eyes. The carriage was too far away to make out his appearance, but to Prudence's eyes, he seemed taller and broader than any man she had seen before. He looked like the very greatest devil, descending on the quiet quaint village.

"Harriet," she screamed out, scared that Harriet would somehow end up under the wheels.

The noise and the pace of the phaeton spooked Prudence. The girl stopped and looked around, pausing where she stood.

"Harriet," Prudence yelled again. She hurried to lift the girl up into her arms to hold her close.

As the phaeton drew nearer, she could make out the man's face. His shrewd eyes travelled from the child in her arms up to Prudence's face, and his look was one of fury, his green eyes flashing at her. The look of cold determination terrified Prudence, and she took an uneasy step back from the road.

With amazing skill, the man stopped the phaeton in front of the pair, all the galloping speed slowed in a moment, leaving a plume of dust in its wake. He glowered down at her. "Are you Pendleton?"

In one deft movement, the man jumped down onto the roadside. Once on the pathway, he pulled down his face covering whilst continuing to glare at Prudence. He had to be well over six feet tall. His colouring was dark, with well-formed curling hair that might be argued to be a touch too long. His face was all smooth planes that hardened down into lips that stayed in an aggressive thin line. His eyes dropped to Harriet and blazed with a strange light.

My word, he's handsome, Prudence thought, despite herself. He was staring doggedly at her.

"Yes," Prudence managed to say. "My father is—"

"Give me the child," he snapped, his hands twisting the reins around the thin rail of the phaeton.

Unable to form a response, Prudence tried to move away from him, but her limbs were stiff with fear at being spoken to in such a manner. His voice was rough, but each word was uttered with clipped precision, as if he were a member of the aristocracy, although no gentleman would bark at a woman in such a manner.

"Give Harriet to me. She's my daughter. Give her to me now." He took another step towards the pair of them.

In desperation, Prudence opened her mouth to scream, even though she knew there was no one nearby to hear her.

It was over in a second, as the man slammed his hand down over her lips, blotting out her attempt to shriek for help. With his free arm, the man yanked Prudence to his side by her slim waist and started dragging her towards the phaeton.

CHAPTER 3

The little hellcat fought against him with her free arm; she had a ferocious energy that impressed Richard, despite himself. "Do stop it," he told her. "I just want the child."

"Get away from us," she snapped back, her words muffled beneath his fingers.

The young woman, he thought her about twenty or so, gazed at him. She was blessed with bright, deep blue eyes the colour of the heavens, which were lit with a plain fury. Her hair was a dark brown mess of curls which bloomed from her head and tumbled down her back, no matter how many pins she tried to control the strands with. Her features, in particular her nose and chin, were neat and patrician, but it was her lips that were her crowning glory. They were a rich red and curved, so much so they might have been painted. A beauty like this had to be Woolwich's mistress. Her plain clothes must be a disguise.

It was unfortunate he had come upon them in the lane, but he could not give up the opportunity of rescuing Harriet now she was so close.

The female only had one free hand, but with it, she beat

against his chest, trying her best to get free. In one quick movement, he spun her around, so she was facing away from him. He thought her about five or six inches shorter than himself, which made her a good height for a woman. She seemed to have a wiry strength in her girlish figure. Her back was now arched into his side, and it rather surprised him to feel the girl's rounded bottom bump into his hip. If it were just a fraction to the right, she would have found herself accidentally rubbing against him. It was strange to be faced with, or rather to consider, such an erotic thought in that moment, but whoever this young woman was, she was a sight for sore eyes.

Richard wondered if he should explain it to the woman, but what explanation would suffice? Besides, what if Woolwich had got word of his arrival? Who knew what spies the duke employed about the place? He couldn't risk Harriet disappearing once again.

The girl was holding on to Harriet with a tight grip, but with her free hand, she scratched at him. Her legs kicked out, catching at his shins. He hated the idea of what a passer-by might think of the scene. But then again, the priority was Harriet, and everything else be damned.

With more speed than was necessary, he bent and scooped the young woman up in his arms, walked forward a couple of feet, and deposited the two of them into his carriage.

"Run, Harriet," the woman said to the child. But Harriet didn't move; she was watching Richard with a mixture of curiosity and fear.

She must be so scared, Richard thought, hating himself. He grinned encouragingly at the child, but she remained, looking between the two of them, her expression muted.

Richard's eyes met the strange woman's, and she turned on to her side and tried to escape out the other section of the carriage. She had looked so determined, if a little absurd, that he was tempted to laugh at the scene, but he was done underestimating women. He had suffered the consequences of that already.

Richard leapt into the carriage and grabbed the woman around the waist, pulling her up to sit beside him.

"Harriet stays with me," he said. Drawing in a breath, Richard repeated himself. "Harriet needs to stay with me."

"We don't have much money," she said. She reached to her neck and lifted a small piece of jewellery. "But there's my mother's ruby cross. You can have that if you let us go."

Richard frowned; this homely little response did not fit. If she had offered him pots of gold, it would have been more suitable. He shook his head and flicked the reins. Off the carriage set, and the woman wet her full lips and tried to start screaming again. Leaning to the side, closing the distance between them, he pressed just one finger to her lips. He watched her dark blue eyes widen, and then he whispered, hating himself as he did so, "Do that again, and I'll throw you out of the phaeton."

The young woman shifted back in her seat, pulling Harriet onto her lap. The child gazed between the pair of them.

He turned his focus back to the road. The carriage had set off with some speed, the horses restless. He didn't have time to waste in these backwaters. Now he needed to be gone. He had no doubt about the consequences of his actions and their potential repercussions for everyone. Woolwich would make his move soon but waiting for his enemies to act was not a course of action that Richard wished to adopt. Not in relation to his own flesh and blood.

The phaeton cut away from the village; he couldn't have her drawing any more attention to them. He shot a quick look at the woman beside him. He would not have put it past her to try to throw herself from the phaeton, which was one of the reasons he kept it moving at such a pace. The countryside blurred past them in a series of flowering hedgerows, tall, swaying trees, and pleasant farmyard fields. The occasional house or manor appeared amidst the green, blotting out for a moment the beautiful countryside.

The road curved up ahead, but he picked up the pace. Years

ago, he'd visited Lynde's home. He wanted to be at the manor within the next half hour. He'd borrow fresh horses from Lynde and then head up to Brayton. Anything to make sure Harriet was safe and away from Woolwich.

Turning down the driveway towards the Hurstbourne Manor, Richard dropped the pace a little and let the manor come into sight. It was on the grander side, but not as impressive as Brayton. However, he was not there to admire the architecture, but to make use of whatever carriages Lynde, or Lynde's father, might have available. The horses could not manage the journey back. It would be easier to move Harriet in a closed carriage than a phaeton.

He would have to hope he got away with tricking Lynde's staff and borrowing one of Lynde's carriage and horses. Richard reined in the horses next to the stables, hopped down, and called out to the servants. He kept close to the phaeton throughout, his hand resting on the woman's leg.

A boy emerged from the stables. Richard waved in greeting. "Lynde asked me to collect a carriage. It should all be arranged. Please see that it's ready," he called to the boy. The chap vanished, and on his turning away, Richard leant forward, pulled the woman out of her seat, and down onto the driveway. "I suggest you follow me," he told her.

A somewhat frail butler appeared, and Richard repeated the lie of Lynde telling him to make use of the estate, as well as handing the man his card. The butler glanced down at the paper, nodded, and appeared to go along with the ruse as he ushered all three of them inside, to a small private sitting room.

"No one in the family is at home at the present," the butler said only to Richard as he bowed himself out.

In his determination to get Harriet back, Richard had indeed become impulsive in his actions. He cursed himself now that Verne's words had motivated him to act so, with all speed and little consideration for his choices.

Richard glanced at the woman, but she didn't seem to have heard the exchange. He had to admit he had expected something to go wrong before now. It made him nervous, the sort of energy that pumped with his blood and made his mind buzz with different ideas and suspicions. They couldn't risk staying here for long. Woolwich would hear what had happened; that was inevitable, and he would want revenge. The sooner they could get to Brayton, the safer Harriet would be.

He did not want the woman to realise how appealing she was to him; it was an odd thought as this time. The drawing room wasn't vast, although it would have to be impressive to a female who was little more than a mistress or maid and one who lived so far away from sophistication. She hadn't spoken at great length, so he wasn't sure if she was educated. It would have been preferable, Richard thought. It always improved a beautiful woman if she happened to be clever.

She had taken several steps away from him to stand in the middle of the little room, looking from him to the door, and then to the windows, presumably wondering if she could risk escaping through one of them. But given that she held Harriet in her arms, she wouldn't have gotten very far. He would give her credit, though, she seemed devoted to Harriet, and therefore the woman couldn't be all bad.

He coughed, and the young woman turned her furious blue gaze on him with a look of undimmed hatred that he supposed had been warranted. If only she would listen, she might understand his actions.

"Take a seat," he said in a kinder tone than he had tried before, but it still came out as more of an order than a request. He sank into a chair, hoping to be less intimidating.

The woman stayed standing, although she did lower Harriet to the floor. The child wrapped her small plump arms around the legs of the woman. Harriet eyed Richard with nervous caution.

"You, sir," the woman bit out her words, her tone haughty and spoke of her being an aggrieved gentlewoman, and with as much dignity as she could manage, she continued, "you have made a mistake."

There was no mistaking Harriet. No mistaking that child as Annabelle's daughter. As Verne had said, she was the replica of Annabelle. This must be his daughter. A rush of emotion came to him as he looked at the little girl, and he realised how much he had missed of her life. He had missed her birth, her infancy, and the change that was morphing her into a little child. Bugger Woolwich to hell for trying to prevent him from protecting his daughter.

Leaning forward in his seat, comfortable given his security in his one-time friend's home, and far more knowledgeable than this woman, Richard said, "Is that so?"

"Yes, yes, it is," the woman said. "I am the daughter of Vicar Pendleton. You have no business at all kidnapping me. Give me one reason why I shouldn't scream the house down and have you arrested?"

"And how do you explain that I know the child's name? She is a foundling, isn't that correct? Has anyone else claimed her? No? I assert that she is my daughter," Richard asked, watching the woman, waiting for her to lie.

Richard looked away from the angry blue eyes of the inflamed woman and down to the little mite who had consumed his worries for over three years. The child deserved more than to be hidden away in the countryside with Woolwich's mistress. What was this supposed vicar's daughter going to be able to teach his innocent child?

Drawing from his pocket, Richard presented a small, china ballerina doll to Harriet. "I thought you might like this."

The child, who had been looking close to tears, edged nearer, her eyes alert. Richard bent his knees. He wanted to be cautious, and he had imagined seeing his child so many times that he didn't want to ruin it.

"What is her name?" Harriet asked. Her small hands stroked the doll's hair.

"You can name her, she's to be yours. You look after her, and I will look after you." Richard pressed the doll into her hands and spotted Harriet's dimple as she looked at the present. He resisted the temptation to hug her. As much as Harriet resembled Annabelle, Richard thought he could see something of the Cavendish line about his child. Perhaps around the firm set of her chin. He got to his feet and locked eyes with the woman. "Harriet will be cared for by her father from now on."

"I-I…" the woman started to say.

As she struggled to find the right words, Richard gazed at her. She was a very pleasant sight to behold, although he viewed this as a mixed blessing. Beauty cut both ways. If she were similar to Annabelle, then this woman would not hesitate to use her beauty as a means to an end, to lie and win whatever she wanted. In which case, Richard would not be tricked again.

"How do I know you are telling the truth?" She formed her sentence and continued, "You may have overheard my family using Harriet's name. As it happens, she is part of my family."

"Are you attempting to tell me that she is your child?" Richard asked with a disrespectful glance as he took in the beauty's slim body, his eyes raking the length of her form. "I assure you, given that I am claiming this child is mine, I would have remembered the experience of fathering her."

The girl flushed, the peachy skin of her cheeks blooming with colour at the implication. He wondered at how natural her embarrassment seemed and put it down to her being a very skilled actress.

"I do not care for the tone of your comment, sir." Miss Pendleton's voice was a little shriller than before, but otherwise, she continued to stare across the drawing room at him, as if daring Richard to say something else. "No, sir," the way she uttered the word sir, rather implied she didn't mean it with any degree of respect. "Harriet is not my child, but she has been raised a member of my family. No one has ever mentioned you in my life. Not as the child's father."

"I did not give you my name, miss. So, how would you know?" His question forced the woman to either lie or to admit that she had no clue what the truth was. Miss Pendleton looked down at the floor, uncertain of which answer she should pick.

Drawing from his pocket, Richard offered the child a sweetmeat. Harriet's eyes widened in delight, and she let go of the doll in order to move forward once again. In a quick movement, the woman grabbed the child up and pulled Harriet back to her side.

Surprised by himself, Richard found he was on his feet. "Let go of her."

"Sir," Miss Pendleton faltered, her voice startled, but Richard pushed past her response.

"No. Harriet is my daughter. I don't care whatever lies Woolwich has fed you. She can eat a sweet, for God's sake."

The woman took a step back. Then she turned and took his advice, sinking into a nearby chair. Her expression swung between confusion and nerves, but still, she did not release Harriet from her grip.

Harriet, whose great big eyes had filled with tears at the exchange, made Richard feel awful. He had not meant to lose his temper, but with the way his daughter was treated in the past, it was hard not to feel furious at anyone who stopped them from connecting.

"I will admit," the woman started to say, but then the door opened, and the butler returned to the sitting room.

The man looked between the two-seated figures, and then the child, before addressing the three of them. "Your carriage is now ready."

Richard got to his feet and nodded at the servant. The man vanished back from where he had come from. It was now or never. He needed to go. To leave. But something obvious had occurred to him. In his eagerness, he had brought nothing with him, save for the doll. All the items he had prepared for Harriet's collection had been left in his London home; they would need to go there first. He had nothing with him now for a child. He hadn't even arranged for a nurse. He had merely headed down to Sussex like a demon chased him, fearful he'd lose her trail again.

The terrible truth was, as much as he loved the idea of Harriet, wanted to protect her from the fate of being labelled a bastard, of being disowned and abandoned by Woolwich, Richard himself had no experience with children. He was the youngest child in his family. There were village children, laughing and sweet little rascals he would spot about the various estates he owned, but otherwise he had no more idea of what was involved in a child's upkeep than any other member of the aristocracy.

Looking at his daughter now, a lump formed in his throat at the idea of her suffering. He wouldn't allow it. He'd murder anyone who ever tried to hurt Harriet, who would be rude to her, or make her cry. Harriet was gazing up at Miss Pendleton, or whatever the woman was actually called. He doubted she was a vicar's daughter; Woolwich would not have picked a naïve type for such a game.

"I do not know who Woolwich is," the woman said, "nor do I like any negative implication that would tie myself to the man." She leant closer to Harriet, soothing out the uplifted curls on the child's head.

Richard watched Miss Pendleton move. He didn't know why she was lying about Woolwich; perhaps she thought it would spare her his anger. But why else would she be there, so willing to protect Harriet? No other explanation made sense. After all, Annabelle was not someone other women felt any loyalty to. He struggled to work out what else it could be. No, the simplest explanation was the best one. The easiest answer was that she was Woolwich's mistress, as Verne had suggested, and was therefore paid to feel loyal to the man.

Miss Pendleton coughed, and Harriet snuggled closer to the woman. The warmth between the pair of them was blatant. If it was what his daughter wanted, he would cross any boundary to make the scamp happy. Based on the look on Harriet's face, what she wanted was Miss Pendleton.

He was tired already and didn't relish the idea of a ride to Brayton, up near the Scottish border, with a crying child next to him the whole way. The priority was getting to his Brayton estate. Once there, he hoped there wasn't much Woolwich would try to do, but during the journey, they would be vulnerable.

"Miss Pendleton," Richard spoke with as much kindness as he could manage, "I am returning to my own estate. I will be taking Harriet with me. You are faced with a choice. Either you may return to the village where I found you and scamper back to Woolwich to tell him all about my plans, or you may remain with us. With Harriet."

The girl pulled her lumpy grey shawl to herself in a gesture of protection. It was not for the most obvious of reasons that Richard hoped she would pick the latter option. He told himself it was because she was gifted with the child, and that Harriet was fond of her. He had no desire to upset Harriet. That his reasoning had nothing to do with how her body had felt against his. Or that he was curious to know what her pink lips would taste like, if they were as delicious as they looked. He told himself he was better than that.

Crouching down to the ground to give Miss Pendleton room to decide on her next move, Richard edged nearer to Harriet. In an undertone, he said to the child, "I want you to meet your great grandmamma. She is looking forward to making your acquaintance."

"Pruedence will come too." The words were lisped out. For a moment, Richard did not understand what Harriet meant. Then it clicked. Prudence, it was her name. It suited her, if only in the way he wished to do *imprudent* things with her.

Richard got to his feet, shaking off that thought. Now he knew Miss Pendleton's first name. It was not the most obvious of mistresses' names. In fact, it did rather fit with the idea that she might have been a vicar's daughter, but he'd never been one to write off the lengths that women might go to, in order to better protect themselves.

"And what will Prudence think about that?" Richard asked.

The woman's eyes flashed at him, the blue darkening, and she looked ready to tackle him again. "I did not give you leave to use my Christian name."

"My deepest apologies," Richard said, in what he thought was a further teasing tone.

"Come, Harriet, we are leaving."

"I will come with you on two conditions." Prudence's voice wobbled for a fraction of a second, but when Richard turned back, she had on her most militant expression. Any inkling he had had that she might be a vicar's daughter was dismissed; an innocent young woman would not agree to go with an unknown gentleman, no matter what the inducement. No decent woman would be so foolish.

Richard forced a light smile onto his face. His heart sang at her agreement. He told himself it was because he had the welfare of his daughter at heart. But if he was honest, that was only part of the reason. It might be weeks before Woolwich would be able to get up to Brayton.

"For Harriet's wellbeing, I must insist that my knowledge of her directs when she should go to bed, should see a doctor, what she should eat must be followed."

This was, after all, the primary function he desired Prudence to fill, and Richard bowed his head. As long as she knew what these little things were, why would he try to stop her? This would be very useful.

"The second is, I will have your word as a gentleman, that there will be no more... no more..." Prudence wet her lips, having no idea how tempting this made them appear. "There will be no further comments on anything illicit. And you are not at liberty to manhandle me again."

"I understand," Richard said.

"Do we have an agreement then?" She reached over Harriet's head and offered Richard her hand.

He looked down at the elegant fingers that were before him. So delicate, they were used to playing the piano or painting watercolours. *Perhaps there was more truth than fiction to her story*, Richard thought. *No, do not let yourself be fooled again, be more ruthless than you were previously. You will not be hoodwinked by yet another pretty face.*

Richard took the proffered palm. He resisted the temptation to raise her fingers to his lips. "Agreed, Miss Pendleton." As he looked at her, he wondered how much she really knew and how much she had been held in ignorance. *I will keep my title a secret, and when she asks for my name, I shouldn't tell her that I am marquess. It will be a test. If she is his jade, then she will know my title... let us see how much she wants to play pretend.*

She was the first one to let go of his hand. She bent down and picked Harriet up before following him out of the sitting room.

The carriage that had drawn up was far more elegant and comfortable than the phaeton, especially for the journey to London. Miss Pendleton looked around herself, taking in the estate. She watched Richard as he handed a note to the butler intended for Lynde, explaining that he'd return the horses and carriage as soon as possible.

"Will you also deliver a note to my father?" Miss Pendleton asked.

For the first time, Richard felt a twinge of his conscience, but he didn't want to tip the scale too much in Woolwich's favour and have the man notified too soon.

Richard waited until the butler had moved away before he answered her, "We will send it once we reach our first stop. Would that be agreeable?"

Miss Pendleton paused, weighing her options before she nodded and got into the larger carriage.

Richard walked up to the driver, informing him of their exact route. Of course, he knew that once this driver returned to Lynde, Woolwich would know of their plans, but that couldn't be helped.

In haste, Richard made his way back to the carriage, climbing inside. Miss Pendleton raised her eyes to Richard's as he entered the carriage; her lips tightened, and she gave him a slight nod of acknowledgement.

"Harriet's gone to sleep," she said. Her hand ran up and down the little girl's back, soothing the child. The woman's lips curled in the most beautiful smile as she viewed his daughter. It spoke of a deep, heartfelt love for Harriet, which touched Richard more than he cared to admit to himself.

With real care, Richard reached over and passed the woman a blanket to wrap around Harriet. Once again, their eyes met. Prudence's smile slipped off her face, and Richard felt a stab of guilt for robbing the woman of her easy-going joy. He sat back in his seat and wished he could make her smile like that at him.

CHAPTER 4

The carriage should have been uncomfortable; at least, that was what Prudence kept telling herself, even though it wasn't. It was snug and lulled them back and forth between squishy pillows, the sway of the horses making the rocking sensation of the carriage rather enjoyable. Private transport was far nicer than any public coaches she'd ever been in.

The carriage cut through the countryside like a knife through butter, and it would have been far too easy to fall asleep, but Prudence wasn't that much of a fool. She tried to keep a tight hold of her initial fear at being grabbed so. But it wasn't possible to maintain that level of fright for a continued journey. She had watched the dratted man with Harriet and could see a sheer tenderness that hinted at his goodness. Her innate curiosity was edging itself forward.

She should have been more nervous, should, in fact, have been terrified of the man who sat opposite her. He was everything a woman like herself had been warned against. Far too good looking. Tall with broad shoulders, he had a rough, abrupt way of speaking, but more than all that, he was a man who had fathered a child out of wedlock. All these things were, to Prudence's mind, awful. That was what she'd been taught. If he had been plain and dull looking, perhaps she might have been more understanding, but the very fact he was so tempting, well, that just told her everything. Though, the worst thing was the fact that he saw nothing wrong with snatching women off the side of the road. But now she knew his reasons—the rescue of his daughter—it started to explain the situation, although it did not justify it.

Prudence looked down at the little girl huddled against her side. Harriet was sleeping, making soft little mewing noises like that of a cat. Prudence knew there were people within her father's parish who had judged little Harriet and would go further and say the innocent girl was a sin herself. What idiots they were, she decided. Harriet deserved only the best, no matter what society said. On that, at least, the two adults in the carriage were united.

The man's long legs were stretched out before him. His dark green eyes were hooded, but she did not think him asleep. Someone like him would snore if they were.

"Do you want to ask me a question?" he asked her, having caught her watching him.

An immediate question flashed into her mind. *Why do I not feel as nervous as I should around you?* No, that would be too revealing of how he made her feel. What about, *are you still in love with Harriet's mother?* No. No. No. She couldn't ask him either of those questions.

Prudence gave herself a little shake; she wasn't acting as a respectable young woman should. Still, she didn't want to employ her stepmother's choice of actions, which would have been to scream and scream and then most likely faint. That would have found her abandoned on the side of the road. Reputation saved, but without Harriet.

"Well," she said, "how should I address you?"

What she expected from him was just his name. That wasn't too much to ask. Then he would settle back in his seat and go to sleep. That would give her leave to continue examining him at her own leisure. She wanted to try to find a flaw in his handsome exterior. Perhaps, she thought with a frown, perhaps some would say his nose was too Roman, but to Prudence it gave him authority. The passing lights from outside the dark carriage revealed him only in flashes, but each time, Prudence thought she could understand why Harriet's mother had found him so irresistible.

"Mr. Richard Cavendish, miss, at your service."

She eyed his outstretched hand. He held it as if this were just an ordinary introduction and there wasn't anything unusual about it. Slowly, Prudence raised her arm and shook the proffered hand. Neither of them wore gloves, and the warmth of his palm rushed against her fingers before he clasped her hand. It should have meant nothing, have been nothing, but when they were hand clasped, the carriage jumped a little over a pothole.

Richard shot out his other arm to steady her as Prudence bounced forward and out of her seat. Harriet wriggled backwards into the pillows, unaware. And Prudence, much to her own horror, found herself back in his arms. This time they were face-to-face with each other, only a foot between them. The carriage was large enough for Richard to be almost standing upright. He would only have to bend his head forward a couple of inches for their lips to touch. This meant that she could feel his breath stir the loose strands of her hair and the top of her forehead. She gazed up at him, seeming to memorise his features. The generous mouth. The cynical eyes that gazed at her a bit too knowingly. The carriage continued on, rumbling as it went, giving the impression that nothing odd had happened, and it had not played a part in pushing the two of them together.

He was looking down at her, his expression visible in the still dying afternoon light. The brightness of his green eyes was noticeable in the confined space. Prudence looked away, her vision dropping down to his mouth. Now she could see the stubble that peppered the lower part of his firm jawline. She had thought his lips were too thin, but up close, Prudence decided that no—no, they were enticing. Thick enough to imply definition but mobile enough to make one think the man liked to laugh. Prudence froze in high, red-faced embarrassment. She tried to shift backwards in his hold.

Richard made no comment and went to place Prudence back in her seat. But Harriet had shifted, pushing out her little legs across where Prudence had sat and taking up the rear seat of the carriage. She lay in a pose that resembled a sprawled cat.

Prudence would have preferred to sit on the floor than next to him, but Mr. Cavendish didn't think this was a viable option and pushed her down into one of the two-seater cushions beside him.

The ladylike thing, Prudence thought, would have been to adopt a complete and utter silence. That would have been dignified, but the truth was Prudence was too stirred to remain quiet. Her blood pumped through her body, warming in preparation for an argument. "Do you go around kidnapping young women, Mr. Cavendish?" Her question was muttered in an undertone, but even in the fast-moving carriage, she knew he'd heard her.

The dratted man laughed. "No. It is not my style."

Prudence shifted and pressed herself against the side of the carriage, trying her best to sit as far away as she could from him.

"What is your style then?" She bit out her response in a rush, without really thinking it through. She did not want him to think her slow or unwilling to challenge him. The question surprised him with its bluntness.

"Do you refer to my clothes?"

Prudence flushed at the question and made no reply.

He laughed at her expression. "If not that, then what? With women, do you mean? Do you wish to compare styles? I will admit that Woolwich's whoring has been confined to his youth. At least, that is what one hears. Do you tell a different tale?"

The ease with which he uttered the sentence unnerved Prudence. He hadn't listened to her at all, it seemed. Not in the slightest. He was still convinced that she was some man's mistress. Although, Prudence admitted to herself, perhaps after she had got in this carriage, she wasn't too different from that sort of woman, really. At least, that would be the impression in Alfriston now that she was unchaperoned, in a carriage, with a man she wasn't related to. Prudence's mind panicked at the thought, trying her best to come up with an explanation her father and the small village society would understand. *So why did you do it?* she wondered to herself.

"I don't know who this Woolwich is," Prudence repeated. "I've never met anyone by that name."

"Don't tell me your loyalty is to the duchess then?" He folded his arms over his chest. It emphasised his frame and broad arms. He was seated so close to her, any movement of his seemed to close the gap between them. Prudence looked up at the padded carriage, admiring the soft cushions that lined the space. Yes, that was preferable, rather than gazing at the stern man next to her, who was far too good looking for his own good. Whenever she glanced at his expression, it seemed that he was aware of his own appeal, and she looked away. "No, I didn't think that was the case," he answered, his expression smug.

Prudence was beginning to lose patience. It was she who was going to suffer for this decision, not him. Turning in her seat, and therefore breaking her rule and having to move closer to him, Prudence said, "I am no man's mistress. I only feel loyalty to my family and that includes Harriet."

The horrible man yawned at this, turning to rest more at ease amongst the pillows. His soft brown hair fanned out at the edges, brushing the plushness of the squished cotton. It was unfortunate to admit, but he was exactly how she had imagined rogues to be. If Clara were here, she would have fluttered her eyelashes and tried her best to encourage him to steal a kiss, but that wasn't Prudence's way.

"Zounds," Prudence said, with a complete lack of Christian charity.

"Tut, tut," Richard replied, his green eyes bright mocking her,

"I thought you said your father was a vicar. Do try to keep your story straight."

"He is," Prudence said. She was trying not to think about his good looks too much. Instead, she turned her anger back on him. "If you are a gentleman, do not be surprised that my father will call you out."

He shifted in his seat a little but did not seem too worried about the potential threat to his life. He crossed and uncrossed his legs with a casual ease that further frustrated Prudence.

"I'm a crack shot. And..." Here, Richard paused. "How old are you, girl? Eighteen, nineteen? Well, this father of yours would need to be at least forty-five, shall we say. I'm not too worried about being beaten in the ring by an old man."

"Have you no dignity?"

"You have no need to worry," he said. He even leant forward and tapped her knee. "I no longer associate with liars unless it is strictly necessary."

Prudence swatted away his hand. He seemed to have an answer for everything. It was rather like arguing with an unsympathetic brick wall. With all her suppressed anger, she wondered if she could take up the pistol herself. She sniffed down her annoyance. "Perhaps I will shoot you myself."

"That seems a rather dramatic cause of action," Richard said. "Besides, do you have a pistol on you? No. I assume you would have used it already were that the case."

"Would you give me one honest answer?"

"Of course," he said, his humorous look dying as he viewed her with a serious expression.

"Where are we going?"

"To my home."

"You will not tell me where?"

"No, not as yet."

"And my reputation?" It was that word that Prudence stumbled over. Every time she thought about it, her stomach quivered with a sensation she could not quite name. She lifted her nervous eyes to his face and was surprised to see a flash of confusion pass over his features.

"You should have no fear of me, miss." She felt her stomach settle. "I would never..." He paused over his words, swaying between teasing her and reaching for something more sincere. "I shan't touch you."

"Blondes are more your type." Prudence said the words without really thinking them through, her mind on the bright curls that decorated Harriet's head.

He looked at her in surprise and then laughed. He threw his head back, exposing his fine, strong throat, and Prudence dropped her eyes once again, feeling like a fool. Sometimes her outspokenness really did get the better of her.

"So, you do know the Duchess of Woolwich then?" he asked.

"No, but... Harriet doesn't have your colouring."

"What else did you figure out?"

"Oh, lud..." Prudence tried to sound sophisticated, but it hardly flew off her tongue. For some reason, she didn't want to tell Mr. Cavendish about the night-time arrival of Harriet to Alfriston all those years ago, or the echoing command of, 'Keep her secret.' Did that moment make her as complicit? In the end, she said, "Most people know that Harriet is a foundling."

"That's all you know?" He again sounded as though he didn't believe her, but Prudence didn't care. Trust went both ways.

"That's all I know," she lied. "But if you're claiming to be her father, then that would tell me an awful lot about you."

"And Harriet's mother?"

Prudence nodded. She didn't like to speculate about a woman she didn't know. If she had been lulled by his tempting wiles or similar... she could easily imagine Mr. Cavendish in such a role.

"Annabelle was the most entertaining debutante on her come out. Made a right splash."

"Was she your fiancée?" Prudence asked, desperate to excuse whatever had created her dear little Harriet.

"So keen for some semblance of modesty to Harriet's birth?"

"It's none of my business," Prudence said, although, yet again, her curiosity was piqued.

She wondered if she had missed an opportunity in not pressing her father on letting her visit Mrs. Pendleton's family. If she had, she wouldn't be such a country bumpkin now, wondering who everyone was, how they were connected and what the rumours were. She would have had a better idea of what was going on. Perhaps she would even have met this Woolwich and his wife, or at least have some idea who they were. After all, wasn't Mrs. Pendleton's brother-in-law a knight? But as it was, she did not know any of their names or which families they belonged to.

"Don't sell yourself short, you're in this business now," he said. "So, you want the sordid details?"

"No, no, it wasn't my intention to—"

"Come, girl, either you want to hear about the affair, or you don't. About how the great beauty found herself with child by another man, and not her husband."

Prudence found herself too scared to answer and instead satisfied herself with shaking her head. Her eyes dropped to the floor of the carriage, and she refused to look up, despite the fact she could feel his eyes locked on her profile.

He waited for her to speak, but she didn't respond and finally, he let out a long, low sigh. "Another time, then."

"Your disgraceful behaviour isn't something that should be lightly discussed in a carriage," Prudence piped up, "and I may be far too naïve to know about what you refer to, but…"

Prudence stumbled through the words. She had a semblance of an idea of what he was alluding to, a slight one. One didn't grow up in the countryside without seeing animals rutting around together. But humans didn't do that. They would need to be confined to the bedroom, to a bed. That was what was referred to as the marriage bed. It involved kisses. She'd been warned about letting anyone kiss her without having an engagement ring first.

Thomas had once kissed her cheek, during a Christmas celebration last year, after the man had drunk at least three glasses of punch. It was a wet slap against her cheek, which had stung with the force of the boy's lips. It seemed strange to think of Thomas now; he seemed like such a child compared to the man who lounged in the seat beside her. Prudence still remembered her reaction after that kissed cheek. In her nervous excitement, Prudence had asked her stepmother if it meant that she might have a baby. Mrs. Pendleton had giggled and then said that, no, it involved a lot more than just one kiss.

"Naïve?" he asked.

His question, if it was a real one, was absorbed by the noise from outside the carriage, a rumble of a passing coach. A bright splash of colour flashed past them. Prudence had a wild idea of throwing herself from the carriage to attract fresh attention. But she dismissed the idea as a daft one. She was sensible enough, she assured herself, to be able to work out a solution.

Bravely, she looked back at the man. "You seem to think of both my choices as a disadvantage, so whichever I might pick, whether I say I am a fool or a whore, you will judge me."

"No, no... you may be whichever you prefer, whichever works better for you. I assumed that no one woman who looked like you would be..." For the first time, he seemed uncertain of his next words. "You are a confusing blend of confidence and innocence, Miss Pendleton."

"I assume you mean that as a compliment," she said.

"It was intended as one."

They lapsed into silence, and Prudence wondered if she had other questions. Her mind was buzzing with all the things she should know about Harriet since she had staked so much on her love for the child.

"So, what can you tell me about her education?" he asked.

"I have been in charge of it."

"What are your qualifications?" His tone was not respectful, but Prudence ignored that.

"I know Latin and Hebrew as well as French and Italian. My father has educated me in theology and—"

"Can she read?"

"Oh," Prudence fidgeted, "yes, at least some basic words, and we have been teaching her some conversational French."

"By all means, teach her the other languages too." His tone was jesting, throwing her somewhat. Didn't he think her a whore? Or was he coming to believe her at last?

"I hope I will be able to," she replied.

Whilst they were talking, the city edges had grown around them. Prudence had spotted the sights out the window, eyed the forming edges of the city, and realised she was about to make her first entrance to London. At least she assumed so. Now might be her only chance of an escape.

Richard seems scared of one thing, Prudence thought, *some man named Woolwich*. It wasn't much to go on, but it was better than waiting around and hoping he wasn't a villain. If she could find Woolwich and his duchess, would there be a way for Harriet to be safe?

The carriage stopped, and he got to his feet. By Prudence's calculation, they had been driving since midday, and it would now be at least five o'clock. Her stomach lurched; she had forgotten about her parents, so caught up in unwinding the mystery of Harriet's origins. Not to mention the man who supplanted all her previous thoughts on the topic. Prudence berated herself; she was a terrible daughter. The smell of the city, the unmistakable scents of sweat, pollution, gin, and decay had permeated the walls of the coach. It had to be London; they had been driving north.

"I hope you feel guilty," she said. "You will have terrified my parents."

There was a slight flush to his high cheeks, but when he

spoke, there was no semblance of culpability. "It was your choice to come with me. You could have stayed at Lynde's or walked home and warned them all about me."

She opened her mouth to snap a reply, but Mr. Cavendish cut her off. "Stay where you are." He climbed out of the carriage, and she heard the noise of low male voices discussing items, plans. He did not want her to know where they were going or their location.

Prudence wondered what would happen if she were to desert Harriet. She could not carry the child through the streets of London without being caught. Could she make it to wherever Woolwich was? The only problem with that plan was, of course, she had no idea where Woolwich would be. She had a vague idea that Mrs. Pendleton had mentioned Putney as the location of her sister's family. But she could not recall their name. Was it Bronson? No, Bailey? That wasn't it. But that might just have been somewhere they liked to visit on occasion. Mrs. Pendleton talked about a lot of different places in the city. But London was huge, stretching for miles and miles. Prudence had an image of herself, wandering the streets, getting more and more lost, unable to help. Having a roof over her head and remaining with Harriet was preferable to that fate, wasn't it?

As she weighed her options, none of which looked tempting, the carriage door opened, and Mr. Cavendish put his head back inside. "Come on, wake her up," he said. His eyes were looking to where Harriet was napping.

"What are we doing?"

Reaching out his hands, he eased Harriet from the seat. "Come on, poppet, time to see your London home."

Prudence followed in his wake, her mind still whirling through all the different options and possibilities. If only she could see a policeman, or a clergyman perhaps, then she could report Mr. Cavendish. Even in her own head, this sounded infantile.

The street was quiet. They stood in front of a handsome stretch of terraced buildings, all of them cream with contained black boxes around the windows and fencing that encircled them. The only people who were present, other than Mr. Cavendish and Harriet, were what looked like a housekeeper and a butler. They had to be part of Cavendish's household.

"Are you coming?" He looked back over his shoulder at Prudence. She followed him inside the house.

"Mrs. Wilson, have you set the room up?" Richard asked.

The housekeeper was busy staring at Prudence and the sleepy child. She seemed unable to form the correct response, so much so that the butler ended up answering for her.

"Of course, this way." He was an older man who seemed to have mastered a way of looking at people without passing any judgement on them, without any interest.

"Then that will be all," Richard said. "Thank you for waiting up. Go off to bed now. I'll ring for you in the morning. Please ensure that Clarence is ready for the journey and the fastest coach set up."

The two servants nodded, turned, and left them, moving down the passageway to the rear of the hall. Richard started up the stairs, leaving Prudence frozen near the door.

"Well? Do you want to stay down there?"

Prudence followed him up the stairs, watching him while he went, and all the while planning her strategy for escape.

"Whereabouts are we located?" she whispered.

"Don't you know London well enough for that?"

"I have never been to London."

They reached the landing, with him having given no sign of having heard her.

"Here we go, pet," he said to the resting child in his arms. He paused and pushed open a nearby door. Prudence was about to follow him in, stopping only when she saw it was a bedroom.

"Don't think so highly of yourself. I have been travelling for the last ten hours in total. And that's the last thing on my mind." He laid Harriet down on the bed and went to the door.

"Are you going to stay in here, then?"

"Yes," Prudence said.

"Very well," he replied, "here you go." He handed her a little silver key. "This can lock the door from the inside. So, you can be safe from me, for as long as you like."

Prudence snatched the key from him and slammed the door in his face. She felt sure she could hear his laughter from the other side.

She let out a shaky breath. Being so much in his presence, she realised he unnerved her in a way she couldn't quite describe. In a way that had far more to do with all her latent imaginings of dashing heroes. Ideas she had tried her best to ignore over the years, but now seemed embodied in that man. Prudence stepped away from the door. She was giving him too much credit, too much power when he already had so much.

Just because he was attractive, didn't mean he could get away with his despicable actions. As far as Prudence was concerned, it was absolutely clear that Mr. Cavendish was used to getting his own way.

She had read just as many fanciful gothic novels as Clara, in preparation for a situation just like this. Although, Prudence thought, she hadn't acted as the heroines in those novels did. She hadn't fainted. She hadn't had an opportunity to scream.

Prudence was now on out and about, with only her wits to guide her. Hadn't this been what she had always wanted? *An adventure. A real opportunity to get away from her father*, her mind whispered. Perhaps that was why she hadn't stayed at Hurstbourne Manor or run home. That was the problem with the gothic novels and romances. They involved pirates or witches or ghosts, and none of those were very likely to occur in Alfriston, but this *had*.

Prudence knew her father well enough to know that even if she had wanted to go to Brighton, he wouldn't have wanted her to leave. He'd never let her out of the vicarage now. With that in mind, Prudence couldn't help the little curl of excitement that gathered in her stomach. It was exciting to be caught up in something as dangerous as this was, where she could play her own part and have her own say. And if this was the only chance she was ever likely to have, well, why shouldn't she make the most of it?

She looked round the bedroom. There was a low fire in the grate. Harriet was asleep already, her little chest rising and falling. It was a pretty room, Prudence thought despite herself, with golden-patterned wallpaper, and neat, well-made furniture. Whoever Mr. Cavendish was, he had money. Prudence tried to run through her options—run, get to Woolwich, get to her stepmother's family home, or stay where she was.

Walking across to the child, Prudence stroked Harriet's hair. Wasn't this what she had always envisioned? That the fateful night when Harriet was dropped off in Alfriston was the start of some great crime?

Prudence returned to the fireside. She gazed down at the burning logs. The only answer was to raise the alarm because she wasn't going to be a passive victim; that was for certain.

CHAPTER 5

In all truth, Richard couldn't explain why he had stayed downstairs in the front room of his Mayfair house. He was tired. No, exhausted. And he would have liked nothing better than to crawl into bed and sleep for as long as possible. The problem was the anxiety that came with this stop in London. But if Verne kept his word, he had time.

Stretching out his feet before him, Richard surveyed the situation. He never bothered to stay at his Mayfair townhouse. It brought back too many memories of George. But he couldn't sell it, it was entailed, and so he may as well make use of it now. The Wilsons were getting on and should be retiring soon. Once that was done, well, he could rent it out to some nouveau riche family and be done with it.

His thoughts drifted away from that and up the stairs, to Miss Pendleton. It defied reason that Woolwich would leave his mistress in such a quiet little backwater. Perhaps there was more logic to Miss Pendleton's story than he had given her credit for. By God, she was beautiful. It had thrown him. Completely. He could not remember being that shaken and boyish for years. From the way she moved and talked, it felt that she would have to be unaware of the effect her presence must have on any male with a pulse. She didn't know that eyes must follow her and lust after her. If Richard had met her in any other circumstances, he would... well, he wasn't sure what he would have said. It was an adjustment for him to come to terms with his title, and before he'd realised all his obligations, the whole Annabelle incident had begun, and the dark day had descended on him. The end result being that whilst he had money and a powerful title, he did not have time for pursuing a wife. Harriet was his sole priority.

If Miss Pendleton was who she said she was, well, then he should ask Mrs. Wilson to accompany them up north. Make the poor girl feel a little less like he was some murderous Viking, and she...

That make-believe image played out in Richard's mind, and he had to blink several times to try to clear the appealing idea away. But the thought of kissing her in that scenario was a difficult one to shake. He imagined thrusting his hands into her rippling hair. He would kiss his way from the tip of her chin down to her collarbone and rip away the high-necked material that covered her breasts. He would tear it away and ease his fingers over each of her breasts, slowly and teasingly, until she moaned and wriggled beneath him. Then he would...

God, he hadn't had sexual congress in a while. He had forgotten the last woman he had bedded; it hadn't seemed important. But now, in the presence of such a creature as Prudence, it seemed to be a pressing issue.

All this would be resolved once they were returned to Brayton. He would go to Carlisle and find himself a woman.

Feeling a touch more resolved on embracing his better nature, Richard leant back in his seat, ready to have some sleep. These chairs were a lot harder than the ones at Brayton. But nevertheless, he would try to rest. Richard focused on clearing out of his mind the image of Miss Pendleton writhing beneath him on the floor. It was not one of the most soothing in nature, but needs must when he was worried that Woolwich would somehow arrive unannounced at his front door.

Above him, there was a creak of the staircase as someone started to descend the steps, and Richard jerked upright, alert. Someone was trying to get out of the house. It wouldn't be either of the Wilsons or Clarence, his groom, since they all slept next to the kitchen, below the sitting room. He doubted Harriet would wander around a house she didn't know, which only left one person. Despite being as drained as he was, a little coil of tension in Richard's stomach twisted with the idea of seeing Miss Pendleton again. He eased the chair round, so he could see the end of the staircase and watch her descend.

She was still dressed in the same old gown with her shawl about her shoulders. The drabness of her clothing did nothing to diminish her overall looks, and for a second or two, Richard was reminded of his childhood stories, hearing about Cinderella and her rags. But this fairy-tale girl had a letter clasped in her hands, and her pretty face was cautious as she glanced around the hallway before looking his way.

"Looking for something in particular?" Richard asked. He got to his feet before strolling forward and reaching the hallway.

Miss Pendleton's eyes widened, and she rather obviously stuffed the letter behind her back. Richard leant back against the doorframe, still giving her space. He gazed across at her and waited. All his good-natured intentions towards the girl had vanished with the sight of that letter, but he still didn't want to spook her. To his mind, that letter could only be intended for one individual—Woolwich. The man who seemed to take a cruel delight in keeping Harriet and him separated. Why Miss Pendleton want to aid in that particular action, he couldn't fathom.

"Struggling to sleep in such a new place, miss?"

"Yes, I thought I would find some milk," Miss Pendleton mumbled.

"I'm afraid I can't offer you that, but perhaps a splash of something stronger?"

Richard reached out and took her by her elbow, leading her out of the hallway and into the sitting room. "Do take a seat." With a gentle push, he guided Prudence towards the sofa, which was opposite the chair he'd been sitting in, before making his way across to the alcohol cabinet.

"Brandy or whiskey? Or something a little more feminine, like ratafia?"

"I don't know," Prudence said.

He sloshed some liquid into two glasses and brought them back, handing one to her. He watched as she brought the glass to her lips and took a sip. Her eyes blinked several times, but then she downed it in one gulp, and placed it on the side table.

"It tastes adequate," she told him.

"Excellent," he said, continuing to sip his.

Miss Pendleton gazed back, unmoved. Her back did not relax, nor did she look mollified. "I am sure, sir, that you felt justified in your actions. You do not appear to be out of your wits."

"But?"

"That only makes your choices far worse. If you were so afflicted, then there might be some justification for your choices."

"Does not a father's love, a parent's love, justify almost any action? I'm sure your parents, if they are living, would wish you only the very best."

"It does not justify kidnapping."

"Now... I did give you a choice. You could have left."

"And left a child behind, with a man I didn't know. And she didn't know you, either."

"That is no fault of mine."

"But why," here, Prudence leant forward as she tried to pin him down with her firm blue eyes, "is that my fault?"

"No, miss, I never said it was."

In frustration, she leant back again and raised her eyes to the ceiling, revealing the long, elegant column of her neck. At the base, was the small, red-stoned necklace; it shone against her skin. His mind filled once more with images of nuzzling her exposed skin, Richard decided he may as well test his first assumption out. If there was just a little truth to her being a kept woman, well, he would be prepared to offer her, twice, no, three times what she was paid previously. He could easily set her up in the village close to Brayton, or... "Another glass?"

"No, thank you." She eased herself forward once again and let out a sigh.

Richard got to his feet and stoked the fire, the flames jumping a little higher in the grate. "I wouldn't be offended, on any level, were you to tell me about your past," he said.

"My past?"

"If it were about Woolwich or any other gentlemen... I would not prevent you from seeing Harriet, once we are in Cumbria. At least, not until she was old enough to make her own decisions on the company she kept."

"How generous of you."

"I just meant—"

"I take your meaning, sir."

"Everyone must earn their trade somehow."

"I do not like the allusions you make about my reputation, sir."

"You came with me, so..." Here, Richard took a tentative step forward. Whatever her reputation might have been would be gone in a puff of smoke, now. If any of her acquaintances were to learn that she had spent a night under his roof... "It may be illogical, as nothing has occurred between us, but no one will believe that."

"Then wouldn't it be best if no one were to find out?" she shot back, her cheeks a little pink.

"There is another alternative," Richard said. He would have liked to make his way over to the sofa and sit next to her. It was always easier to conduct a seduction at closer quarters, but he did not want her to feel pressured into a situation. If she could see the merits of the position, then perhaps he could convince her.

"You will let us go home now?"

"Harriet is home. And my solution didn't concern her, it was about you."

"Me?" Miss Pendleton got to her feet and moved across to join him by the fire. She was taller than a majority of the women he knew, although she still only came up to his chin. She poked him hard in the chest. "Me? I am of no concern to you."

Richard caught her hand, imprisoning it in his own. She was cool to the touch, and her skin felt like satin beneath his palm. Hand clasped, he looked down at her. "Surely," he said, his voice low, "you must have been asked before?"

"Asked what?"

He couldn't quite decide if Miss Pendleton was confused, or slower than he'd believed her to be. "You are a delight," he said, almost without meaning to. A look of shock appeared on her face as she looked up at him. "If you desired to continue as a mistress..." he looked at her meaningfully, his desire clear.

"You are making me an improper offer?" There was something a little pained on her face when she heard his intentions. Then it was gone, before Richard could quite place it. She stood up on her tiptoes and pushed once more against his chest.

Using his free hand, Richard stroked one dark curl off her face. "Whatever he offered you, I'll double it." He thought it was working until, in one swift movement, Miss Pendleton prised her hand free and slapped his face. It stung, although not as much as the barrage of words she aimed in his direction.

"How dare you? You are the lowest of men; never have I been spoken to in such a–a– a manner."

Sinking back into his chair, Richard admired the sight of her raging and rubbed his sore cheek before he spoke, "Do you want to give me that letter now or later?"

This stopped the virago in her tracks, and the spark of anger disappeared.

"I assume it's for Woolwich." He stretched out his hand in the most commanding of manners. "Give it to me. Don't make me pull it out of your hands, my dear."

Miss Pendleton lifted her left hand out and proffered the letter. He was right. The letter read, *Duke of Woolwich, London.* A small wave of disappointment rose in him. He had wanted to be wrong about her. That, if it had been addressed to that supposed vicar, would he have felt differently? He walked to the fire and tossed the envelope in amongst the flames.

She made a small noise and then watched the fire lick its way around her letter. "I have only tried to do the right thing," Miss Pendleton said in a low, defeated sort of voice.

"I have found that doesn't make a person happy."

"Do you think you have found what makes you happy?"

"I am beginning to at least give it a try, I believe. Now that my daughter is returned to me and not made to be hiked between different peoples, I believe I shall be more contented."

"You have gone about it in the most ruthless of manners. Without any consideration for how this may affect others."

"I tried that the first time," he snapped at her, conscious that he was being unfair to poor Miss Pendleton, levelling the blame of the last four years all on her. "I tried to behave as well as I could, and where did that get me? No daughter. Friends who believed the worst possible version of me. No, Miss Pendleton, I am afraid I will not go along with everyone else's demands of me. Sometimes, I have found I must be as selfish as everyone else is."

"Well, what would you suggest I do?"

"I've already made my suggestion. It is not my fault you did not care to take me up on my offer."

"I have more ambition than that."

"What is it, then?"

This seemed to silence Miss Pendleton because she froze

where she was, and her gaze dropped, although her lips continued to move. She was debating the whole situation under her breath. It was quite fascinating to watch, Richard decided.

"Sir," she said, "you have no rights to know what my ambitions are."

"Is that the conclusion you've come to, after all this?"

"No, I've just decided that whatever my ambition might be, I am not under any obligation to let you know."

"No doubt it is rather mundane," Richard said in a bored tone. "Marry a wealthy gentleman, become the belle of the ball... etc."

"For all you know," spluttered out Miss Pendleton, "I could want to be a pirate or a witch."

"How much have you had of that stuff?" He pointed towards the cordial cabinet.

Prudence frowned at him and resumed her seat on the sofa. "Not enough."

"So then, you're the audacious sort? What entertained you in such a quiet little place?" He offered her the bottle, and much to his surprise, Miss Pendleton lifted her glass and allowed him to pour her a generous helping.

"Again, I am under no obligation to tell you that."

"Then, you must leave me to speculate."

"It won't be any more absurd than your previous assumptions."

"Well, I remain unconvinced that a girl like you really could be a vicar's daughter. It's that, or I've underestimated the amount of time I should have been spending with the clergy's offspring."

This, at least, brought a smile to her lips as she sipped the wine. "No," she said, after swallowing the liquor, "I am just far better versed in all the genre."

"Genre?"

"Yes, I have been schooled in all manner of what one is to expect."

"To what do you refer?" Richard wondered if she was about to launch into a detailed account of her previous lovers, and the idea bothered him more than he cared to admit.

"I have read a great many novels that Clara said I should, even the ones I shouldn't have, and so I am as prepared as I can be."

"Novels?" The question popped out of him, and Richard struggled not to laugh.

Of course, Miss Pendleton looked outraged. "How else am I supposed to know what to do when faced with someone like you?"

"May I suggest doing some living?" At this question, his companion reddened, and she tried to straighten in her chair. Then she started to fiddle with one of her loose curls, a nervous, childish habit. Her hands twisted the thick strand, which seemed to have been designed to grab and hold Richard's attention.

"I intend to," she said, her voice angry. "But, well, you wouldn't believe me."

"Go on, try me," he said.

She gave a little shake of her head, as if she couldn't quite believe what she was about to say, before fixing him with a level stare. "I have always wanted to leave home."

"Why can't you?"

"If you'd let me speak, I would tell you."

"Go on."

"Well, my options are somewhat limited. I could always marry someone," she said. Richard wondered how many men were left crumbled to bits at her feet. "Or I could try to be a governess. Or..."

"What are your other thoughts?"

"I have a great many."

"I have no doubt," he soothed.

"I want to read a great deal more."

"Of course."

"And I would like to study and visit Rome and Dublin and the pyramids."

"That's quite a diverse list."

"It would have been boring to just say Paris. Aside from it being currently rather risky." "Very true. Horrible to be clichéd."

"Have you been?"

"Yes."

"Oh." She let out such a sigh, and her expression was so wistful and keen, that it was moving. "I wish I could see Versailles."

"Could you not convince one of your many conquests to take you?"

"I suspect we would not get any farther than the Isle of White." She sounded so morose that Richard laughed.

In response, Miss Pendleton smiled. "No, it's true. Sometimes, I think men are given so many options on what they would like in the world, and we are given so few. But then, men never make the most of their choices."

"You sound rather political."

"I'm sorry. My stepmother says it isn't done for women to talk on the matter."

"My grandmother does at great length, but then again, she is a…" Richard stopped himself. He had almost let slip his grandmother's title, but if she was telling the truth and had no idea who he was, he had no desire to tell her. He still wasn't sure he trusted her. "A character."

"I should like to be described as such when I am older," she said and downed her glass.

Instinctively, Richard refilled her glass and then his, the drink warming them both. He sat down opposite her once more. She was such a sight, and it was an age since he'd been in such company. He watched her blue eyes and rich, full red mouth and wondered if she had kissed Woolwich with those lips.

"How do you know Woolwich?"

"I don't," she said in annoyance.

"You were writing to him."

"Just to ask for his help."

"Why do you think he wishes to help his wife's bastard?"

"No one should use that language for such a child. Harriet is well cared for in Sussex."

"For years, that man has kept me from my daughter as an act of petty revenge."

"You must have done something unforgiveable."

Richard sat back. "What do you think would be such an unforgiveable act?"

"Did you steal something?"

"In a manner of speaking. But that is not what Woolwich has accused me of."

"Then what?"

"He thinks I tricked his wife." Richard said it flatly and to the sitting room, rather than to her. "That I persuaded her with lies and said that I would wed her after their divorce."

"I don't know the woman of whom you speak."

"Do you think I'm lying?" It mattered a great deal that she believed him. That she did not think him a complete villain.

"You did kidnap me," she said. "That does not tip the scales in your favour."

Richard would have liked nothing more than to reach for Miss Pendleton's hand, but he knew that would be too much. He couldn't tell if it was a gesture of solace or something else. "Do you take me for a liar?"

"I do not know you well enough to judge that."

"But would you believe me if I said that going to Woolwich may be unsafe?" He said the warning lightly, but he knew it would draw her back to him. She did stop and linger close, her tempting little figure caught between the sofa and the door. If only, he thought, it was not this particular conversation which had rooted her to the spot. Perhaps seduction on lighter subjects were now beyond him, and Richard was trapped with serious, heavy matters to entertain women. It was a sorry state of affairs, and his younger self would have judged him for such an action.

"Sir." She had walked a little nearer to him. "A sinner is never above repentance. If you have done a wrong, then confess, admit it, and you might well feel relief."

Her hand touched his shoulder in a gentle, soothing manner, and for a moment, Richard caught a whiff of her rose-scented soap, hidden amongst the folds of her dress. It was so sweet and alluring that it surprised him.

"Theology now, Miss Pendleton?"

"Perhaps one cannot escape what one's parents have taught one." She sounded almost a little sad at the idea.

But it rang true to Richard. He was trapped with his father's inheritance, even when it should have gone to a better man than him. George. He was tempted to tell Miss Pendleton all about his older brother, George Walter Wendel Cavendish. Briefly Marquess of Heatherbroke, holding the title for two and a half years, when it should have been for twenty times as long as that. He wondered if Miss Pendleton would sympathise at all.

"One's family is indeed a curious blend of joys and curses," she continued.

Richard laughed at the turn of phrase. "Where's that from?"

"I made it up."

It was on the tip of his tongue to call her back to him and tell her all about the incident. All about his night with Annabelle. But to reveal all of it, before a woman he did not know?

Richard swallowed down the tale.

"Are you prepared to go back upstairs, then?"

I do not feel soothed, do I?" she countered. "It isn't much comfort being told you won't be believed, whatever you say. Although I assume that is how you feel? No one believing your side of things?"

The question made Richard feel uncomfortable. She was right, he realised; she was suffering by his hand the same sort of cruel accusations he had gone through after his affair with Annabelle.

"Very smart, Miss Pendleton," he said. "How about we both agree to trust each other a little more?"

"What would that involve?"

"I promise to believe you," he said. Although he still doubted someone who was as alluring as she was, or as sharp, could be as innocent as she claimed. "And you—"

"And you promise to leave off making any inappropriate remarks to me."

"None at all?"

"None of your droll little comments, or anything which might be considered lewd," she said.

"I should be able to manage that," Richard said.

"Good. I will need your assurances that my father will be written to. He will be fit to burst with worry." She waited for him to reply.

"I shall send the letter tomorrow."

Miss Pendleton offered him her hand. "Then we can perhaps work together, assuming only the best about each other."

Their palms touched, and a warm shot of sensation went straight up Richard's arm, tightening his muscles as if he couldn't quite control himself. She was looking down at him expectantly. Richard released her hand and got to his feet.

"So, we are in agreement about working together for the benefit of Harriet," she said.

"That is all I want," he said. It had been true for the last few years, had become an obsession, a drumbeat by which he marched. It was because he couldn't fix the mistake of his brother's death, but he would be able to at least help mend things for one member of his family. He could at least save Harriet. Now, of course, she was back with him, and soon they would be in Brayton. But then what would he do? Would that be enough to sort things out for himself?

Would this make him finally happy?

Miss Pendleton was watching him, still adjusting herself to the deal she had struck.

"Of course," Richard said, part in jest, "you might miss my jokes."

"I don't know about that. Although it has at least prepared me a little better."

I have been preparation? Richard thought as he gazed at the enchanting creature before him. How best to reason that out in his mind's eye?

"Oh, yes," she continued, "the novels did not prepare me. I was expecting far worse from you."

"Worse?"

"For certain." She lifted her glass up and returned it to the cabinet. "You see, I have decided to behave much as I would at home. If we are to bounce along together, almost like we were siblings, then..."

Her tone was firm and mature, and Richard felt his eyes widen. Never in his life, had a beautiful woman been so keen to dismiss him. "I take it you know that is far from a compliment?"

"It was meant as such." She laughed. "As I said, I've very little knowledge of men that wasn't gained from my father or his parishioners."

"I thought you were to marry one of them. Isn't that what you said you could do?"

"Oh, well, there's really only Thomas. Mr. Blackman. But, no, I couldn't."

"You call him by his first name?"

"I've known his family all my life."

"Childhood sweethearts?" Richard asked.

"It isn't like that. I doubt Mr. Blackman thinks he could offer for me for years. He won't have the money. And," Prudence fidgeted with her hands, "it would be quite a long wait for me."

"But were he to ask?"

Miss Pendleton shook her head. "It is little more than a fairy-tale, like the ones Harriet reads."

"She likes fairy-tales?" Richard asked, planning to contact his bookseller as soon as they were in Brayton and order every single title in English that could be described as featuring a fairy, a princess, or something fantastical. "Would she let me read to her?"

"She would adore that. And it would give me a rest."

"I would imagine you have quite a pleasant reading voice."

"Not when I play the giants."

Richard found himself getting to his feet and walking with Miss Pendleton to the staircase. "We are agreed, then. We shall try our best to get along as well as we can, for Harriet's sake?"

"Yes, sir." She turned and went up the stairs, and Richard hoped that their little treaty would last. He would like to be able to trust a woman again.

CHAPTER 6

When the knock came at the locked door, Prudence was awake. She had lain in the neat bed and luxurious sheets, dwelling on the deal she had struck.

She slipped from the bed and opened the door. Mrs. Wilson nodded her head at Prudence and then handed over a hamper as well. "Good morning, my dear." Mrs. Wilson's tone and her expression were a lot softer and less suspicious than yesterday. "There's fruit in there for the little one." Then she turned and hurried down the stairs and out of sight.

It did not take long to wake Harriet. "Where are we going now?" she asked as Prudence tugged on the child's coat and did up her shoes.

The question made Prudence pause. It had not occurred to her to ask him last night. How could she forget something as crucial as that, or think it unimportant? That was ridiculous of her. But it was pushed out of her mind by the deal Mr. Cavendish and she had struck. She had agreed to trust him. Had she been a fool to go along with this? Her madcap scheme of finding Woolwich had lost its appeal. Prudence had come to think that if Mr. Cavendish was telling the truth, this was the right place for

Harriet. Hadn't the child always wanted her family? Hadn't Prudence always hoped that Harriet's parents would find her?

She thought back to Clara and her abandoned vicarage. She was sure Clara would have followed Prudence's choice.

"God. I can't read another word." Clara had thrown the novel onto the sofa and gazed across at Prudence. "Why don't you let me paint you?"

"No," Prudence had replied, "you're terrible at it, dear. I will end up with a frightful double chin."

"To think, the amount of money my parents wasted on all three of us Blackman girls, myself included. We will only ever marry men in trade."

"You don't know that. You could marry a prince. Or an earl."

Clara had rolled her eyes. "Phah. I can't see that's going to happen. The earl is as old as anything, and his son never visits Sussex. There aren't many other options, in terms of titled gentlemen in our society."

It had struck Prudence then, how few options she had in comparison to Clara. Her friend at least could go and visit her sisters. She could convince her father, Mr. Blackman, to take her to London for a season. There she could go to the theatre, eat ices at Gunter's, walk through Hyde Park, try to secure tickets to Almack's.

"What sort of thing did you have in mind, to find something suitable?"

Leaning forward, Clara had plucked up her book from the sofa. "A pirate or a spy, perhaps. Why can't that sort of thing happen to us?"

"Both at the same time?"

"Yes, you must read it."

"My father—"

"Oh, of course!" Clara had flopped back down and rolled her eyes. "He wouldn't approve."

THIS WAS TRUE; VICAR PENDLETON WAS LIKE THAT. It wasn't malicious, and it wasn't cruel, but he did not want Prudence to leave Alfriston. But that was then, and this was now. The choice over her mother's life had been taken away from him, and so he tried his best to control hers. At the back of her mind, Prudence hoped her father would see that it was not acceptable to always keep her in the dark, away from society.

Here Prudence was, miles and miles away from Clara or her father. She was in London, and despite herself, despite all the possible risks to her reputation, Prudence was excited. She would protect Harriet. If she had to, she would pawn her mother's necklace and go home, but at the moment, why should she?

Looking down at Harriet, Prudence smiled at the child. "We're going on a journey, but whatever happens, I will look after you."

They climbed into the carriage and waited for a few minutes before they were joined by Mr. Cavendish, who carried with him a neat stack of books.

"Well, hello, Miss Harriet," he said after he had taken his seat. "I find I must apologise for my treatment of you gentle ladies yesterday. But today is going to be better. First, allow me to introduce myself. I am Richard, but you, my dear, can call me Father."

Harriet took the proffered hand as the carriage took off. Out of the window, Prudence spotted parts of London flash past. Great, grand buildings, far larger and more impressive than anything she'd seen before. As she watched the view, she listened in on the conversation between Mr. Cavendish and Harriet.

"Father?" Harriet asked.

"Yes, that is what I'd prefer. But if you like, you can call me

Richard." The little girl shot a nervous look at Prudence before she nodded.

"What's that?" Harriet asked, her chubby hand pointing to the stack of books he had placed down next to him.

"Well, a fairy told me that you were rather fond of stories."

"I am." Harriet squirmed on her seat, and Prudence lifted her up and placed her on her lap.

"Perhaps you can read to both of us," she said, gazing over Harriet's head.

"What an excellent idea."

"With the voices," Harriet added. "You have to have the right voices."

Prudence leant back against the carriage squab and watched the sights of London drift past, whilst Mr. Cavendish started reading his way through the books. On occasion, he would glance up and catch her eye, and Prudence would feel an unfamiliar flutter in her stomach and chest. It was both inclusive and confidential, and it gave the impression that he was pleased that she was with them. In the end, she had to look away; it was bringing back too many memories of the previous night and his inappropriate offer.

Was it wrong that she had been tempted? If only for selfish reasons, and if only for a brief second. There was something about his frank appraisal and appreciation that warmed her heart. It was nice, she thought, to be praised, admired, and—although she would never admit it to another living soul—desired. If Vicar Pendleton had his way, Prudence would grow into a spinster.

"How do you like the story of the beanstalk?" he asked.

"Well enough," Prudence replied.

"It's not romantic enough," Harriet piped up. "They're Prudence's favourite." "Hush, that's not true," Prudence said.

"Yes, it is. You said Rapunzel was the best," Harriet persisted. She wriggled her way off Prudence's lap and wobbled across the short distance to land next to Mr. Cavendish. "Does it have any pictures?"

Able to mask his surprise well, Mr. Cavendish reached down and scooped Harriet up to sit next to him. She reached for the book and started flicking through the pages. "It's the same one. Look." She held the pages open to Prudence to show her the bookplate with the picture of Rapunzel on it.

Very nice," Prudence said.

Harriet quieted, pleased with herself, and sat back in her seat. Mr. Cavendish resumed reading. The two of them listened, with Harriet leaning back amongst the pillows, until her eyes grew heavy, and she fell asleep.

"She naps a lot."

"Yes, we often have to work around it," Prudence remarked.

"You'll have to tell me how you manage it all, what I should learn. Once we are in Brayton." It jolted her. At some point, she would need to return home. They had not discussed it, but it would happen. Her mind had been focused on the journey, nothing beyond the journey, their own odyssey that would last and last. It was odd how upset the idea was to her that it would eventually end. Mr. Cavendish was looking at Harriet with the sort of naked affection that Prudence had read about. Yes, her own father was kind, well-meaning, loving in his way, but Richard seemed to have a type of intense devotion that seemed missing in almost everyone she'd ever met. Then again, Prudence reminded herself, she hadn't met that many people, so what did she know?

"It is the sort of thing that comes naturally to some," Prudence said.

"I wish I had your gifts for it."

"Well, perhaps it is all just a willingness for affection on my part."

"Hmm..." His handsome face twisted. "I think you will have to write me out some instructions. Before you leave."

There it was again, the idea of her leaving. "Just a list, will that be enough?" Prudence asked.

Mr. Cavendish shook his head. "Probably not. But I wish to be as prepared as I can be. She will have a difficult life. As much as I would like to have never lost my mother, the knowledge of that loss has formed who I am now. I would not be able to change it."

"Desiring to stop the pain is understandable. But unhelpful."

"Is that what your father told you?"

"No, it is what I believe myself."

"Wishing it away can't change it, either," he said, and Prudence wondered if he had lost anyone else, and that was what made him look so lonely and sad. She was almost tempted to ask him when he sighed and gazed out of the window.

"We're leaving London now. Should you like to go back one day?"

"Very much, when I am more at my leisure."

"Well, it's within my power to help with that."

"How much power do you have?" Prudence hadn't meant to say the question aloud, but it had slipped out. Having watched him for the last few minutes, it was too easy to picture his hands commanding servants or building boats or working in a factory. She shook her head. Oh dear, she was being like Clara and imagining too much.

"What an impertinent question." Mr. Cavendish laughed, although he didn't seem offended by her query.

It was true; Prudence could never have imagined asking any other man of her acquaintance such a question. How did he make her feel more confident and bolder, yet also conscious of every move she made? She could not tear her eyes away from him. From the solid, impressive shape of his shoulders, to how he sat with the breeches outlining his legs, to the jacket that hugged his frame. He seemed to have been designed to have all eyes on him, to drink in the adoration. If only Prudence had gone out a little more, she would know if this was because she was not used to masculine company and this was her reaction to it, or if it was just him.

"Penny for your thoughts."

"I beg your pardon?"

"You were gazing so intently. You must have been thinking about something very important. Since we now have our truce, perhaps I can help?"

"I was just thinking." Prudence rummaged through her mind, trying to think of something she could tell him that wouldn't be too illuminating. Something that was silly and light, so he wouldn't think her too serious. "When I return to London, I would like to go to at least one public ball."

"Will it have to be Almack's and nothing else?"

"I don't care about that." Prudence folded her hands on her lap. "As long as it was enjoyable, and I could dance."

"Were we to meet there, would you dance with me?" He leant forward in his seat, and she could see his features in the early daylight. It wasn't fair; why couldn't he be as ugly as sin? That would make this whole experience a lot easier."

"We would have to be introduced."

"How proper you are," he said. "Would I be made to bow over your hand?"

"Of course. I would prefer if you restricted your remarks to the weather."

"And all the while, you would know I had far more interesting things to discuss with you."

"You do?" Drat her curious tongue, darting out with yet another forward question.

"Indeed," he went on, "I need to find out how best to do a giant voice."

Without thinking, Prudence laughed; it slipped out of her mouth without any warning and warmed the carriage. She slapped her hand to her mouth. "You shouldn't make me laugh," she warned him.

"Why ever not?"

"It will make you believe we are onto an understanding."

"We do have a treaty. Negotiated with great care."

"Only in terms of Harriet's wellbeing. Other than that..." Prudence trailed off. She had locked eyes with him and was amazed to discover that he looked a little disappointed. "Between you and I—"

"Yes?"

"I cannot pretend that your actions against my person are forgivable." Prudence tried to make it sound as severe as she could.

"No, of course not," he said, but he continued to gaze at her with the same sort of frank appraisal.

"It would take some—"

"Manners on my part?"

That hadn't been what Prudence was thinking. In fact, her mind was more rooted in what she would change in herself. If she *were* Woolwich's mistress, then perhaps she would, in fact, be better suited for dealing with this situation.

"Just a little more trust," she said.

"What would you like to know?" He gave her a pleasant smile, encouraging her to relax a little more. It was disconcerting how it worked on her; Prudence could feel her muscles unwind beneath her gown in his warm presence.

"Where we're going next?"

"My home, an estate called Brayton. It is in the north of the country, close to Carlisle."

"My," Prudence said. Her geography was not as good as it could be, but even so, she knew that Carlisle was right on the border with Scotland. "We will be near Gretna Green."

"Are you trying to suggest something, Miss Pendleton?"

"No, sir. I swear." Prudence dropped her eyes in embarrassment. "Sometimes I just say a thing, without thinking things through."

"It is only thirty miles from Gretna," he said.

And where do we stop before that point?" Prudence asked.

"We will be stopping after Leicester," he said. "If you would like, I can arrange for a separate carriage to take you home, or to whichever destination in the country you would most like to go to."

"Thank you," said Prudence.

"I would not recommend London," he said, after she made no further comment.

Prudence glanced at him, but he did not elaborate. "What do you mean?"

"That if there was an association with Woolwich—meaning no slight to your character—that now would not be the best time to intrude on him."

She fidgeted in annoyance; her father could not afford a season in London. "I do not know Woolwich, and I am happy to avoid London for the time being."

"Brighton, then?"

"What?"

"Have you ever attended the assembly rooms in Brighton? Or Bath, say?"

"No," Prudence answered. She had been to Brighton often but only to walk along the seaside, or with her stepmother to see the shops and take tea. Never to dance. She wondered if he would believe her if she told him that. The frisson of nervous excitement had dwindled down, and they now spoke as distant acquaintances might at a party. He seemed to be playing along with believing her story. Perhaps she could use this to her advantage. "Will you let me stay as Harriet's governess? That could be a solution—"

"No," he cut her off, "but I would be prepared to give you sufficient funds to hire a maid, so you had the semblance of propriety."

To that, Prudence made no reply. She was too busy trying to

calculate the best course of action to take next. She had been considering the idea of a governess as a good solution, but it had been shut down. With ruthless force, Prudence said, "I need to make sure Harriet is safe."

"I take it you do not trust me," he said.

"You have done nothing to warrant it as yet. We have only agreed to a semblance of trust, not the realities of it."

"That is perhaps true enough, but please do not doubt my sincerity of feeling for Harriet," Mr. Cavendish said.

"For all I know," Prudence said, deciding to test the man; after all, it could be an act, so she needed to be sure, "you could fully intend to sell Harriet off to—"

"I have no intention of further harming my daughter. She does not deserve to suffer for the errors in my judgement."

"If I go along with your version of events, take it on trust," Prudence started to say, "will you—"

But her question was interrupted by a noise outside the carriage. The light of day had given way to the darkness of a coming storm, but neither of them had noticed that they had entered a small town. There was a constant level of noise from shouted voices varied in volume, the beat of other transports on the road, and the mingled neighing of horses. The carriage drew to a stop.

Prudence leant forward in her seat out of curiosity, but Richard pulled her back by her elbow. In an undertone, he said, "If you were to ask me to protect your reputation, then I would suggest hiding your face." With that, he climbed out of the carriage and started talking to the driver.

Across from her, Harriet woke up. "Where are we?"

Having no desire to lie to the child, and yet having no clue where they might be, Prudence went and sat next to her and muttered calming phrases into the little girl's hair. "I know you're not supposed to tell me," Prudence said, choosing her words with care, "but Harriet, do you remember anyone telling you about your father? Or anything you were told?" In the dimness of the carriage, it was difficult to make out the child's expression, but Prudence could feel Harriet tense.

"You need not worry," Prudence said. "I will look after you, whatever you tell me."

Harriet said, "Mrs. Pendleton said he was bad."

"Did they ever tell you his name or what he did?"

Harriet was already shaking her head; she buried herself closer to Prudence's chest, cuddling her way beneath the thin grey shawl.

"What did she warn you about?" Prudence pressed.

"She just said he wasn't good."

"I see." Prudence nestled closer into Harriet's side. Her mind was abuzz with what her stepmother might have told the child. "Don't be scared. I'll keep you safe."

She looked up and saw that Mr. Cavendish was poised in the door's window. In the distance, she could see his groom, Clarence, house the horses. Mr. Cavendish nodded at her before he spoke. "My wife and I are staying here tonight. With our little daughter." With that, he pulled open the door and offered his hand out for Prudence to take.

Shifting Harriet forward, encouraging the child out of the carriage, Prudence made eye contact with him. Silently, they communicated that this façade would need to be maintained. Prudence would be able to manage that; she just hoped that little Harriet would have the sense to keep quiet.

"I have to let them know that your belongings and those of the child were stolen," he continued to speak. "But also, that we have sent the maids ahead. I have asked for some fresh clothes to be bought for you both."

Once outside the carriage, Prudence looked around. They stood in the courtyard at the rear of a grand building that seemed to be a handsome hotel. People milled around, many of them servants who weren't watching the newly arrived couple, but one man lingered close to the "Cavendishes." Prudence adjusted her shawl and hid her left hand, which did not carry a wedding ring. The podgy hotel proprietor, however, was too busy fussing and cooing over Harriet to notice.

"Most welcome, most welcome." The man had a strong accent and his knees cracked as he bent over to speak to Harriet, who gazed back with frank curiosity at him.

He sidestepped the man and drew closer to Prudence, so his whispered sentence would only reach her. "This is Derby, not the place I mentioned, I'm afraid. The man believes I am a land clerk. Dobson is our name."

"Is that a colleague of yours?" Prudence muttered. She had no idea what Mr. Cavendish might be, really. He could be a barrister, she thought, or perhaps a banker.

He had smiled at her remark but made no response. Instead, he directed his comment towards the hotel owner. "If you please, Mr. Harrison, might we be shown to our suite now?"

The plump man cranked himself up and beamed at them. "Yes, yes. This way." He waddled off towards the building, and Mr. Cavendish took hold of Prudence's arm, pulling her after him. His breath stirred the curls near her ear and sent a shock of awareness over her skin, warming the hair that ran down her neck before disappearing beneath her gown. Prudence was shocked to discover she liked having him so close to her. It was invigorating and made her feel as if she had gulped down all the sweet treats, drank all the festive wines, and danced until her shoes fell apart. None of which she'd ever done, although she would be tempted in Mr. Cavendish's presence.

High above them, the heavens opened, drenching the courtyard with a heavy downpour. "Aren't we lucky to be stopping?" he murmured, his lips brushing her hair.

Prudence shivered against him and glanced around, catching the widening of his eyes.

He had noticed her reaction to him. Hastily, he dropped his gaze.

They entered the hotel. The walls were decorated in soft mauve, with small wooden picture frames dotted across it. Through the walls, Prudence could hear occasional conversation. It seemed that it was a busy afternoon, especially with the sudden bad weather.

Smiling and following after Harrison, Prudence tugged herself free from Mr. Cavendish's grip and went towards the stairs. The door of one room opened wide, and Harrison led the three of them inside, Harriet following close behind the plump man, nodding along to whatever he was saying. A small part of Prudence wondered if Harrison would be the best person to ask for help if she wanted to leave. He seemed kind, but then again, would that kindness last when confronted with the truth? How on earth would she explain it all to a stranger?

"Is this comfortable enough for you, Mrs. Dobson?" It was Mr. Cavendish who asked her. Prudence flushed; she hadn't been responding to her "married name." She nodded, and Harrison disappeared, keeping his head low. Turning, Prudence looked across the small parlour at him.

Mr. Cavendish stepped forward, closing the distance between them. "I am asking you to believe me," he whispered. "In exchange, I have ordered Clarence to find us a maid who will accompany us the entire way to my estate."

Prudence looked up into his face. Their eyes met. He smelt delicious, of cut grass and wood smoke, a combination of scents that she had always thought enticing. That made her mouth twitch and her body treacherous. It wanted to wriggle back close to him, to feel his breath stir her hair, for his lips to move closer still. Her mind jumped to how it would feel if he were to have his hands on her waist. In most of the novels she had read, that was where it had always stopped. This always left Prudence curious over what came next. "Then this will be the last time we are together, sir. Alone," she said, almost more to herself, and offered him her hand to shake. He took it and looked down at her palm, considering it. His knuckles rested against the back of hers, neither cold nor clammy, they might have been designed to enfold hers.

"Would you have preferred if I had turned in a more rakish performance?" Mr. Cavendish asked her, still keeping hold of her hand.

"What do you mean?" She was reluctant to break away. With great care, she raised her eyes to his and held his look.

At once, she wondered if it was a mistake. It was too easy to be sucked into those deep green eyes, to imagine him pulling her closer, to ask him to. With what Prudence hoped was a dismissive look, she yanked her hand free and stepped back. "As I said, it would only ever be at your command."

"I can't imagine that ever being the case," lied Prudence. She worried he would know it was a falsehood. He seemed able to read her thoughts.

Sometimes, she feared, before they had even formed in her mind.

CHAPTER 7

Richard had asked the question as more of a joke than anything else. He had thought, or perhaps hoped, she might see the humorous side or, if not, might adopt some of her earlier outrage. What he hadn't expected to see nestled in her eyes, was a jot of piqued interest. Perhaps the performance Miss Pendleton had put on was just that, and she had grown weary of it. That was one consideration. Or perhaps, Richard still had some of his old appeal, and she was rather charmed by it. He viewed her through his eyelashes, wondering if that could be the case. Four years ago, he was noted for his wit, charisma, and appeal. That was the case with Annabelle. Now, older and wiser, he was a lot less willing to jump to conclusions or believe what had seemed obvious. But drinking in the sight of Miss Pendleton before him, perhaps she would not mind a touch of seduction.

"Apologies, if my joke caused offence," he said. If it were the case, lording it over the woman wasn't the way to go. He shook himself. He shouldn't have behaved in the same manner. It was a matter of self-defence. But he was frightening the girl off when he needed her help.

With careful eyes, Richard watched Prudence. She was beautiful in a way he could not describe, and he was keen to put it down to her mysterious connection to the child, although he knew it was more than that. She wasn't his normal type. He preferred the small, fey-looking, blonde creatures, which seemed like a terrible mistake now, in contrast to the woman before him. Deftly, he gave her what he hoped was his most winning smile. "I couldn't resist; old habits die hard, but please think nothing of it."

Prudence sank into the armchair by the fireplace. She looked around the room, taking in the parlour's contents and the half-open door that led into the bedroom. Her eyes darted back to his for a fraction of a second before they moved on to the grandfather clock in the corner of the room.

"Harriet will be requiring her supper soon," she told him.

"It has already been arranged." Richard stepped forward and then sat in the opposite chair. It was rather comfy, which was just as well; he knew he'd be sleeping in it tonight.

"It might also be wise," she paused here as she considered her next words, "if I could know what you said to my father in your letter."

"The vicar?"

"That's right," she said. "He will be frightened half to death. You did promise." Only here, did her voice dip low, and she sounded miserable. With tearful eyes, she gazed up at him, forcing Richard to look away.

He'd sent the man only the briefest of notes, and to be so confronted with his selfishness did cause him some guilt. In haste, Richard looked away from her. "What would you write to him?"

"I-I," she looked down and a single tear rolled down her face, "I would tell him I was safe. And that Harriet was too. I might mention that her father had collected her, and I was travelling with them all to London. I would say there were maids and that you had a great aunt… a wife?"

"Woolwich would see through all of this," Richard snapped.

He couldn't help himself. He had acted without much thought, he knew this. But the idea that Woolwich might somehow locate them—he had made his decision. Now he had to follow it through. "How soon would your father follow after you?"

"As soon as he had found the magistrate."

"Do you not have a young lover you might have run off with?" Richard asked her. In a small village like Alfriston, a girl of her looks would have all the local gentry with their heads in a tizzy.

Prudence folded her arms across her chest. "I have no beau, no. And no fiancé."

A childish giggle sounded behind them, making both Richard and Prudence look around. Harriet was framed in the doorway between the parlour and the bedroom. With a small smile on her rounded cherub face, she pushed the door wider. "Prudence is going to marry Thomas. That's what Mrs. Pendleton said." Harriet followed these words up by hurrying forward and throwing herself into Prudence's arms.

"Harriet misunderstood the situation," Prudence blurted out.

"Mrs. Pendleton said you'd have a great big veil," Harriet insisted.

"Francesca said no such thing," Prudence said to the child.

"It's going to be a magnificent wedding," Richard said.

Prudence was too busy hushing Harriet, but one of the words Prudence mentioned drew Richard closer to the armchair. Franny. No, wasn't it Francesca? Or Frances? He remembered that name, that particular female name in connection with Annabelle. Was she a cousin or something else closer to Annabelle?

"Who is this Franny, child?" he asked.

Harriet turned and gazed at him. The firelight and the soft candles in the room made her seem like even more of a dream child, and Richard would have loved to kiss the little girl's face. *She doesn't know me yet. Give it time.*

"I meant Mrs. Pendleton. My stepmother," Prudence said.

It stayed in his mind, a link he would need to press upon

tomorrow. He smiled and turned away; there was a connection there, but he couldn't place it. There had been some reason why Woolwich had chosen that village, and if it wasn't Miss Pendleton, then there was someone else.

The meal passed pleasantly enough, the food decent and wholesome, and the conversation focused on keeping Harriet entertained. Richard tried to keep his answers brief and to the point, but the child was curious about him. Miss Pendleton, likewise, had a gift of prizing more information than he was willing to give them. Between the two of them, they had already managed to find out that he was an able horseman, had travelled as far as Turkey and as far north as Iceland, and had met the Prince Regent. He found himself with no desire to lie to his daughter or, by extension, to Miss Pendleton.

"Does that mean you are a member of His Majesty's army?" Miss Pendleton asked.

He reflected on her question whilst looking over at Harriet. The child was caught between wanting to cram as much as she could into her mouth and yawning, and Richard found himself with no need to answer when the cream from the bun squirted down Harriet's dress.

"Do be careful," Prudence said, getting to her feet and ushering the girl out of the room.

Richard bowed his head low and backed out of the room, closing the sliding door behind him. It clicked shut and Richard walked back to the armchair, folding himself into the seat. With a great sigh, Richard sank into the plush velvet chair, stretching his legs out before him. The thick stockings were removed, and his legs were bare from his breeches down. Then he took off his jacket, placed it on the armrest, and twitched it over his legs in one fluid movement. Finally, he closed his eyes and hoped that sleep would come.

It did not seem like a long time to his mind. The warmth of the food, the heat from the fireplace, and the satisfaction in obtaining Harriet helped. Soon he found his mind relaxing, lulling him off towards darkness. He did not even mind the occasional sounds of the hotel and their inhabitants.

He must have slept. There came a noise that was not confined to the normal rumble of the hotel or to Richard's dreams.

Keeping still, Richard peeked out through one of his eyes, taking in the whole sweep of the room. The cleared table, the dead embers of the fire, the half-light from beneath the curtains and, in the corner of the room, ignoring him, was Prudence. She was crouched on the floor, leaning over his case and picking through his belongings. For one mad moment, Richard panicked, wondering where he'd put the pistol. Then he remembered that he had wedged it in the pocket of his great coat, which hung over by the doorway.

Prudence was tearing through his things, eager to pick through the stacks of shirts and a few discarded toiletries. His watch, a snuff box, a couple of novels, none of these were of much good to her. She had on her own large white shift, which hung long and loose on her body, now that her stays were removed. In this semi-light, Richard realised it was a little more see-through than he'd imagined. His eyes traced down her back, all the way to her bottom, to her toes that peeked out from beneath the hem.

Richard moved in his chair, positioning himself to better view her—in an attempt to see what she was looking for, he told himself. The woman's hand moved as she lifted a shaving razor out from the case, one that Richard had forgotten he had packed. For a moment, Prudence was poised with the knife in her right hand, angled away from her. But she was about to turn...

Without thinking, Richard was on his feet and across to Prudence in seconds. He tried to snatch the razor from her hand. The dratted woman had the open knife in her left hand and, with the jerked movement, had twisted around to defend herself. In a tumble of limbs, Richard, whose eyes never left the knife, rolled the pair of them over, landing on top of her and wrestling the item from her hand.

"What are you trying to do? Murder me?" He found that she was wrapped about him. Her arm was beneath his left side, his right hand having caught the handle of the knife and thrown it to the other side of the room. Their faces were close to each other's once again. Her breathing was coming in short, sharp intakes, and she gazed up into his face. The ground beneath them was hard, not the normal place for rolling around with a woman. Richard tried to sit up. Their legs were tangled up together, and as he tried to extract himself, he found that his hand came to rest on her thigh.

Prudence let out a strange little gasp.

She had moved. Her long, brown hair was in complete disarray around her shoulders. Her cream shift had fallen open. He could see the outline of her breasts beneath the material, and the faint circles of her pink nipples, which had hardened to points. She gave him an almighty shove. The force of the push surprised Richard, and he found himself sliding backwards. As he fell, his left hand caught one of her loose dark curls and pulled her into closer contact with him.

"That hurts." She grabbed at her hair, trying to pull it free.

"You, madam," Richard said as he released her hair and repositioned himself into a better stance, "should stop."

But she wasn't listening to him. She wriggled off him, her body pressing against his in a manner that seemed aimed at seducing him. Her hips nestled close to his. But when Richard looked up into her face, he could see that Prudence was more focused on trying to free her curl.

"Will you keep still?" he asked, his voice pained, given how aroused her wriggling had made him.

She frowned at him in mild curiosity, her face lit by moonlight. "Did you land on the knife?" The tone of her voice implied that she was concerned for him.

Richard shifted again, desperate to get her to move. If she were to shift her weight lower, she could find out first-hand, so to speak, why he was so unmanned.

"Just get yourself loose," he muttered.

Prudence shifted, adjusted herself, then she scrambled upright, and away from him.

Richard sat up, trying his best to think of the least erotic thoughts available to him. The good old fat Prince Regent. Any member of The House of Lords. Church services. All plump grey things, masculine, lacking in humour, lacking in sweet, beguiling looks, scented hair, and large, long-lashed eyes. "Can you explain why you were going through my belongings?" Richard asked in his most haughty tone.

"I wanted to see if you were a liar," she said. "I tried to trust you, but you're a thief."

"Me, a thief?" Richard was still a little befuddled. He would have preferred to have gotten to his feet, but the sight of her was still having an effect on his body, so it was better to stay sitting rather than shock her with his amorous reaction.

"I found a seal, a book, letters addressed..." she said. "They all belong to the Marquess of Heatherbroke, and you've stolen his things."

"Is that the most logical of conclusions?"

"What would be the other one?" she snapped back. Her eyes had gone to the razor. She did not seem angry enough to try to use it on him, but then again, people could behave in some very strange ways if provoked.

Easing himself forward, Richard had straightened so that he was perched on his knees, giving Prudence at least a good five feet with which to play with. He would not be foolish enough to tackle her again. Most women of his acquaintance tended to have very little training with a knife, but so far, Miss Pendleton had proven to be as unlike other women as Richard could imagine. When he thought she would be quiet, she had tried to fight.

When presented with a likeable host and a chance to make an escape into the labyrinth of the hotel, she had taken advantage of neither, choosing instead to dig through his belongings, trying to unearth the truth.

"Did you ever read about any of the old families in the United Kingdom? Any of their surnames, and who was who?"

"No," she said in indignation.

"If you had, you would know that Cavendish is my surname, but my title... I am Heatherbroke. I assumed you already knew this, and if not... well, what was the harm is being just a normal mister for a few days?"

The girl giggled. "No, you're not." She stared up at the ceiling, shaking her head in disbelief. "You can't be. It's too farfetched."

Again, this was not the reaction that Richard had expected. He got to his feet. "Why not?" It bothered him that there was something so lacking in him that prevented him from being considered a marquess. It had been his title for four years; surely, he was done adjusting to the role.

"You just don't seem the right fit..." the girl trailed off. She appeared to have righted herself in her seat and turned to look at him, to really gaze at him through the dim lit room. "No. I don't believe you." She said it to rectify the error. "There must be some mistake."

"Cecil will be thrilled," Richard said, more to himself than anything else. His bored, difficult, fifty-year-old cousin would have been delighted to inherit the title.

"What?"

"It doesn't matter," he said. "What makes me so wrong for the title?"

"You don't look like any member of the aristocracy I've ever seen."

"Have you seen a great many of them?"

"Well, no, but Earl of Hurstbourne came to Eastbourne, and I saw him from the promenade, and you're nothing like him."

The reference to Lynde's father made Richard shift in his seat. "Are you acquainted with the family at all?"

"Only through my father. He does the service for one of his parishes," she said. "The earl wouldn't remember me."

"Perhaps from a public ball? Would you know his son?"

"Not at all," she said. "I've never been to a ball."

"I am sure you would be the belle of one if you were to go."

"Flattery doesn't become this situation. You may desist."

"Even my own daughter sees how lovely you are." Richard pressed his hands into his legs, digging his fingernails into the flesh of his thighs. He couldn't understand why Miss Pendleton was so resistant to compliments.

"No," Prudence said. "Harriet is just wedding-obsessed and wants to see a ceremony, that is all."

"I thought all women were wedding-obsessed," Richard said. No one had regarded him as much of a catch until his older brother George was thrown from his horse four years ago, breaking his neck. There had been a little speculation in the gossip sheets, but since he never went to London, Richard had avoided the season for years.

"We are not given many other options, other than weddings," Prudence said.

"Some women would choose a different calling," Richard replied. "Those women think they have more choice."

"That might be true for them, but I could never do that to my father," Prudence said. She had brought her hands to rest on her lap, and for a second, Richard believed her. Believed that she was the vicar's daughter she claimed to be. Believed that he had unknowingly ruined another young woman. The idea ran through his mind, cartwheeling and climbing in ever larger circles that scared him. Then he looked at her again. No, he told himself, no, it defied logic that a well-born, middle-class girl, a religious girl, would have stayed with him.

Richard went over to stand before Prudence. He reached

down and took hold of her elbows, easing her to her feet. He did not take the obligatory step back, so yet again they found themselves close together. He did not release her arms, but instead gazed down into her face, drinking in all her delicate features, from the upturned nose to the long eyelashes, to the sheer volume of her haywire of spiralling curls, and then to the fullness of her lips.

Again, he found himself wondering how they might taste. There was a faint smell to the air, which Richard realised must come from her. She smelt of fragrant, crushed, wet roses, the sort one found in the summer, hidden behind overgrown trees. Unable to resist any longer, Richard closed the distance between them, lowering his head and brushing his lips against her own.

Tentative at first, he began the kiss with his mouth closed. To give Prudence time, he told himself, all the time she might need to step back and away from him. He stepped back after that one soft brush of his lips against hers. Richard opened his eyes and saw that she was watching him, her face still turned up to his, her expression curious but undaunted. She did not move away. In fact, she swayed a little closer to him. Her tongue darted out to wet her lips, and Richard raised his fingertip to touch the dampened bottom lip, to press his finger against the petal softness of her mouth.

"Do you want me to do that again?" he asked.

He expected her to laugh or to push him away with one of her normal barbs. But she didn't. Her face flexed with a bundle of emotions that Richard couldn't place, and then she looked up into his eyes. Now would come the rejection.

But she didn't give him time to act. Instead, she placed her own hands against his chest, one above his heart and the other on his left shoulder. Then she moved her right one to cup his cheek and pull his face down to her own. She pressed her mouth against his, keenly peppering dozens of little kisses on his lips, one after the other, again and again, with amazement that he was letting her do so. Her gesture took Richard by surprise, the sheer vehemence with which she started to kiss him.

She continued, pressing herself against him, while her hands reached up and wedged themselves in his hair. Her fingers dug into his scalp as she held on to him. The sheer abandonment of her movements rather jolted Richard. He was so close to believing her innocent façade. He pressed himself closer to her body, bringing his arms around her. His left hand lifted to try to capture her neck, and his right to press the small of her back flush against him. For a moment she stilled, and he realised his mistake. Her body froze, and he stepped back, realising that while her enthusiasm was genuine, it was built on sheer curiosity and a total lack of experience.

Her hand came up and held on to her cross necklace as a source of reassurance. She was an innocent. It had not been the way he intended to discover it, but he believed her now. There had been too much genuine curiosity in the way her lips had moved against his. The slight start when he'd touched his tongue against the seam of her mouth, pressing her to open her lips. Guilt rolled through him at the realisation, and the memory of what he'd accused her of, that he'd acted wrongly once again, the same way he had with Annabelle.

Richard opened his mouth to try to tell Prudence this, to find the right words to apologise, to offer some kind of comfort, desperate to tell her something—anything—that might be reassuring, but she didn't give him time. When he looked into her face, she emitted an odd sort of startled cry and darted past him, out of the room, and into the bedroom.

"Damn it," Richard said under his breath. He could follow her to explain his error. That would be disturbing, and he would not blame the poor girl for screaming the hotel down. No, he would have to wait until the morning.

CHAPTER 8

It had not been the easiest night's sleep for Prudence. She had tossed and turned this way and that. Unable to stop thinking about those stolen moments she had indulged in. Unable to stop berating herself for doing so. What would he think of her? What did she think of herself?

This was what her father had always warned his flock about.

Temptation.

That just means, Prudence told herself, *you are very bad at this. You have fallen at the first hurdle*. Ever since she had learned that Harriet's mother had had an affair, she had judged the woman. Oh, she had tried not to. Her father always encouraged Prudence to be as generous and as kind as she could be, but part of Prudence wondered how anyone could take such a risk? *But I have been just as guilty as she was*, Prudence thought. *I was so tempted to stay with Richard and continue kissing him. To continue as we were.* No, if she were honest, to go further. It was so comforting, but also wondrous and exciting to have him so close.

"Well," Prudence said aloud to herself, "that will teach you. Don't you go judging anyone again for something you'd like to do yourself."

She rolled over onto her side and brought her knees up close to her chest. She told herself not to think about him. But, of course, it didn't work. His hands were in her hair. The smell of him, a blend of woodsmoke and after-dinner coffee, was stronger when he'd been closer to her, dazzlingly so. His stubble had rubbed against her cheeks and neck. So, it was still sensitive now. His breath had nuzzled her collarbone before he'd bent his head and started kissing her exposed skin. It had made her tingle and itch within her core, as if she were desperate to wriggle free of herself, rather than away from him. It was, she realised, the temptation to nestle closer still that bothered her.

Unable to stay in bed any longer, Prudence got to her feet and started to pace backwards and forwards. She moved with careful steps, so as not to disturb him or the sleeping Harriet. She berated herself, *oh what would my father think of me?* But the admonition didn't hold her as it once had.

Try, she told herself, *to think back to the village, to Alfriston and all the people I know there.* How would they judge her? These were the people who had known Prudence all her life, and she could not think of a single way to explain any of her actions. *He just looked so handsome*, she said to herself, *so lost and so lovely*. It sounded mad even to her own ears.

Besides which, he wasn't any of those things, she reminded herself. This was the man who had kidnapped her and Harriet. He had seduced a married lady. Again, and again, he suggested she was little better than a liar, and if she wasn't that, then she might be a jade.

"Gah," muttered Prudence, her thoughts spiralling. She was prepared to forgive him, because if she'd been told she couldn't see her own daughter, she would have acted in a similar manner. There was warmth and humour there, at least, for Harriet. He was choosing to hide these better characteristics, but they still lingered, visible, despite himself.

"What am I going to do now?" she asked the empty, quiet

room, not expecting any kind of answer from it. Slowly, she returned to her bed and a restless slumber.

***

Bright sunshine poured through the window of the Derby hotel. Prudence rolled over and looked across the little bedroom to see Harriet in the window seat. The girl was peering out the window down to the street below. Harriet turned and looked back at Prudence, grinning, before tearing back to the bed and throwing herself down on top of her. Sleepily, Prudence tickled the little girl, and Harriet started to squeal with laughter.

"You'll wake the whole place," Prudence told her, cuddling Harriet close.

"What's going on in there?" Richard called from outside the bedroom.

It stilled Prudence, making her feel self-conscious and nervous. Last night… it didn't bear repeating, but the consequences of her actions were still haunting her. What if Mr. Cavendish, or rather Lord Heatherbroke, thought she had attempted a seduction just because he was a marquess? She suppressed a shudder. He wouldn't understand if she told him why she had acted in such a manner. If she explained that, since her reputation was crumbling, well, shouldn't she at least get something out of the situation?

One kiss had seemed innocent enough. At least, in the books, they had been. Except it hadn't been innocent at all. Even now, she could feel her cheeks flame in delightful remembrance.

"Just a second," she called, climbing out of the bed and pulling Harriet out too. "We're just getting dressed."

A thought hit her as she made her way across the carpet. Prudence lifted her faded calico day dress. It was a little splattered and stained from everything that had happened in the last few days, but it was all she had with her, unless she wanted to emerge in her shift. No, that wouldn't do at all. In a hurry, she started to dress herself as Harriet copied her, both of them pulling on their own gowns. With a couple of shakes, Prudence attempted to remove the grime, but she would try to look her best. All the while, she could hear him moving around in the next chamber. A door opened in the other room, and a low rumble of voices could be heard. Harriet, alight with curiosity and now dressed, set off to explore. With utmost care, Prudence finished her toilette, brushing her hair with the hotel-provided brush and splashing her face in the water.

Following at a discreet distance, Prudence emerged and saw that breakfast had been laid out on the table. When they entered, Heatherbroke turned to them and smiled. "I have been fortunate enough to secure the services of a lady's maid, who will travel with us for the remainder of the journey. I also took the liberty of sending my man to the nearest shop." He stepped away from the table and motioned towards the nearby armchair. "They might not be of the best taste, but they will at least provide you with a change of clothes. I am sure Clarence did his best."

In great excitement, Harriet ran towards the bundle and grabbed up the stack of folded dresses, unearthing a red-wine-coloured shawl and pansy-coloured day dress, to reach her own clothing. There was also what appeared to be about a hundred ribbons.

"Thank you, thank you," Harriet squealed, holding up her own small blue dress before running off, leaving the two adults alone together.

"Miss Armstrong will come with us all the way to my estate," he said, "or accompany you home. As you prefer."

Prudence didn't move. He was giving her a way out if she chose to take it, but it meant leaving Harriet behind. "That's very kind of you, Your Lordship," Prudence said.

"Think nothing of it." He took a seat. "Would you care for some tea, or would you prefer chocolate?"

"I..." Prudence stopped and looked about the room. She couldn't see the maid that he'd mentioned, but Miss Armstrong couldn't be too far away. "I fear," she said, "I must apologise." When she looked at him, he was staring at her with a confused expression on his face.

"Please, miss." He smiled. "Do take a seat." He gestured to the chair opposite him.

Prudence took a careful step forward and sank into it.

"There now," he said. He leant forward and poured some tea into the little delicate cup. "I always find that tea helps me in the morning."

In gratitude, Prudence nodded. He was right, she thought, as she sipped her tea and watched him drink his. It was soothing.

"Miss Pendleton, if anyone should have to apologise for last night, it would be myself. I misspoke." She could see he seemed a little lost with his words. "It is I who mistook you for Woolwich's mistress, and for that... all I can say is, well, I've known the man for years and do not hold a good opinion of him. But I shouldn't have let that affect my opinion of you."

"I do not know the man. I hope you believe me?" Prudence asked.

"He and I were at university together. A great many of us were. A rather useless set of boys, I suppose you would say. All far too privileged and used to getting our own way. Then there was Annabelle. Or Lady Bradley as she had been to the *ton* then. She was the belle of the season. We all fancied ourselves in love with her, but it was Woolwich she wanted. He had a grander title than all of us, being a duke and all."

Prudence had leant forward in her seat, eager to hear more. The mention of Annabelle's maiden name lingered in her mind, but she was not certain why. "Please," she told him, "please continue, it would be so helpful to know a little more of Harriet's background."

He stared at her. She couldn't quite read his face, but she

thought he looked angry. "I won't have Harriet judged for the mistake of her parents."

"No, of course not," Prudence said. "That's not what I meant. I-I've known Harriet all her life, and yet I also know almost nothing about her. She is the dearest, sweetest little girl who doesn't deserve... well, no, I should say who deserves the very best."

"Yes, yes, that's right." He pressed his fingers together. Prudence tried to avoid looking at his hands. It was too easy to imagine them rubbing their way along her shoulder blades and then dropping down to hold her waist.

"I knew Lady Annabelle, as she was then," he began. "I met her during her first season. We were down from Oxford for Lynde's sister's come-out ball. It was a rowdy evening. Have you ever heard of Graton's?"

"No," Prudence answered.

"Well," he said, "please don't judge me too harshly."

"I'll try not to, but I cannot promise anything."

"You are a vicar's daughter, then?"

"Yes," Prudence said.

"Perhaps," his lips formed into a playful smile, "perhaps I should treat this like a chance at redemption. Might you offer me that, miss?"

"I doubt even I could do that, my lord. Your sins are your own."

"So, I won't receive any absolution from you?"

"I didn't say that," Prudence replied, "but I will try not to condemn you too much."

"Because you have never committed a sin?" he asked.

"I didn't say that. Everyone alive has committed a sin."

"What terrible sins have you committed then?"

"None that..." Prudence fiddled in her seat. He had such a way of turning the conversation back towards her, when all she wanted to know was what actions he had committed in London all those years ago. But he was watching her, an expectant look on his face. "I'm sure I've made a lot of mistakes," Prudence said, "but none that have resulted in the birth of an illegitimate child."

"No, that will be the stick that beats me until I'm dead, I suppose. You want to know how it happened then?"

Prudence resisted the temptation to say, "Yes, rather." She straightened in her chair and shook her head.

"No, it is probably for the best that I don't go shocking you right next to the porridge. I do not think this the fit place for tales of debauchery."

"I agree," Prudence told him, without thinking through her words, "it would probably be best to wait until a more opportune moment occurs."

"A more opportune moment for debauchery?"

"For the discussion of it, sir."

"Of course," he added, "I wouldn't want to sin, or to commit an act of debauchery, without the proper permission."

In her haste to hide a small laugh, Prudence coughed. She was not sure she was successful.

"Please believe," he continued, "that I do not find it possible to say I regret my actions."

"Why not?" Prudence asked. Was it because the sin was too enjoyable? No, she shook her head. Oh no, she would never be able to ask him that. But there must be another more logical reason. She asked, "If you could take something back that was wrong, wouldn't you?"

"Not if it meant losing my daughter. Surely, Miss Pendleton, there are mistakes you've made that you would not take back?"

It was here that Prudence noticed he was watching her rather intently. She realised that he had worked the conversation back around to an allusion of the previous night.

Prudence sat forward in her seat, having put the teacup down on the table. "I don't know what you mean," she lied.

"It's not a very noble story. Nor does it paint me in an honourable light."

"No," Prudence said. "I didn't think it would."

"You want to hear it all? As in, you would like to know all the details?"

"Well…" Prudence thought back to the conversation she had had with her stepmother about how many kisses would lead to a baby. Perhaps she should have pressed a little more, to know what took place between two people. "No, you don't need to tell me everything, but I do need to know a little more about the Duchess of Woolwich."

There was a noise from next door and out came Harriet. She had managed to dress herself in a yellow taffeta gown, the ribbons dangling at her sides. She hurried across the room towards the pair of them.

"This is my favourite dress," Harriet said.

"It's very fine," Prudence replied.

"Like a fairy?" Harriet asked.

"Like a fairy princess," Prudence told her.

"Why don't you go and get dressed too?" Harriet asked.

Prudence gave the two of them a rather awkward smile before leaving the room. Once inside the bedroom, she looked down at the garments that Harriet had left strewn on the floor. Oh, to have the innocence of youth that thought nothing of wearing a new dress. She could hear the two of them talking through the walls. He was asking Harriet what she would like for breakfast, whether she preferred bacon and eggs, or perhaps porridge?

In haste, Prudence removed her old worn gown and picked up one of the others, one of the new ones. The material was pleasant between her fingers, softer to the touch than her normal cotton gowns. Perhaps they were made of silk. She lifted the turquoise dress up to her face and pressed it to her cheek. It wouldn't do, to be seduced by a mere dress. There were smaller, puffed sleeves on the sheer pink, and it was tied with the loveliest of buttercup yellow ribbons. There was a navy-blue pelisse and a dozen silk stockings.

As she dressed, Prudence mulled over what Heatherbroke had said, attempting to piece together the tale. What was it that she was missing? She was good at guessing the twists in the gothic novels far before Clara could.

Pulling on the new stocking, smooth and seductive in its own right, Prudence dwelt on the people. Lady Annabelle, beautiful and a fool… no, there was no reason for her to pick Alfriston. The duke? She wondered if he had been the man in the carriage all those years ago?

"Why didn't my stepmother tell me such things?" There was a growing list, Prudence realised, of things she wished she had been told before.

But that was it, her mind clicked. Her stepmother was key. She knew she'd heard the name Bradley before. Her stepmother's sister's name. It had been years since the wedding, but she had a vague recollection of a Lady Bradley attending the wedding service.

It had been obvious, she realised now, why hadn't she seen it before? That was why Harriet had been hidden with them. It slotted into place, and Prudence smiled at the subterfuge. It was clever of the duke. Her smile dropped from her face as she realised that Heatherbroke would consider them all culpable. Would she be damned by association?

"I must remain calm," she told herself. The first and most important priority was to get a note from her to Vicar Pendleton. It would be more reassuring for him to read. She knew that her father would be beside himself and not comforted by the marquess's correspondence. She wondered, of course, how much her stepmother might say about Harriet and Prudence's disappearance. Would Mrs. Pendleton let her husband know who wanted Harriet and why?

"Stop being a coward." Prudence had paused, unable to step

outside, nervous now she knew part of the story of how Harriet had ended up in Alfriston.

Heatherbroke got to his feet when Prudence entered the room. "I'm planning to leave in the next half hour. Does that suit you? If not, as I said, Miss Armstrong will accompany you home?"

"Sir, you promised that I would be able to write to my father. Do I have your permission now to send him a note and assure him of our well-being?" Prudence asked. She knew she should have said she would go home, but her curiosity was getting the better of her.

"Why would he care about Harriet?"

"The child has been living with us for years, and we are all very fond of her. Including my father and my stepmother."

"Have they been long wed?"

"I beg your pardon?" Prudence replied.

"Your father and stepmother," he pressed again.

"I believe it would be eight years."

There was a break in the conversation as the anxious butterflies in Prudence grew and swelled until they were the size of birds. *Tell him.* She battled against the fear of what his reaction would be once he realised that she was culpable, if only in a small way.

Heatherbroke moved around the chamber, passing the occasional comment about Cumbria now and then, letting either Harriet or Prudence reply, until the latter felt sure he'd dropped the topic. Then she found him by her shoulder.

"May I ask your stepmother's maiden name?"

"I..." Prudence considered lying, but his gaze was pressing into her forehead and when she looked up, she knew she couldn't. "My stepmother is related to Lady Bradley and I... and she is the duchess's aunt."

"Ah," he said as he stepped away from her, "the truth will out."

"What are you talking about?" Harriet asked.

"How you came to live with us," Prudence replied.

"Oh, that's because," Harriet said, "I am a foundling."

He looked across the room at Prudence, before bending his knee before Harriet. "You were always wanted by me. I have been looking for you for years. You are my lost jewel."

In that moment, as Harriet viewed him, Prudence felt a sudden rush of fear that she too would lose Harriet, a child she had nurtured and cared for. Tears welled in her eyes, and she forced herself to look away at the prospect. Should she have continued to lie?

"No, ma'am," Heatherbroke said almost like he was answering her unspoken question. His tone was abrupt and clipped, the earlier friendliness and teasing gone now as he moved towards Prudence. "I see you must have colluded with the Bradleys to keep this child secret, all to protect the duchess's great match. Now excuse me. I must make arrangements for our departure."

He made his way towards the door.

Prudence hurried after him. "I need to write that note to my father. I know he will have gone to the local magistrate." The truth was Prudence had no idea the lengths Vicar Pendleton would go to if Mrs. Pendleton had let slip all she knew about the situation. "My lord." Prudence put her hand out and grabbed his arm to hold him back. Their fingers brushed each other's. His hands were warm to the touch. His back was turned away from her with his profile visible.

"Yes, ma'am?"

"You did promise," she said.

"Write whatever you like. You can help yourself to the paper. There's some in the trunk." He indicated his travelling case. Still, his expression did not change, and he viewed her with distaste.

"I-I..." Prudence wished there were better words to try to frame what she wanted to tell him. He was too grand, too important to understand the way of a small village. To understand how this momentous happening would be the talk of the parish by now. No matter how well her father had acted, or her stepmother.

She did wonder how far her father could push the matter. What would his authority be? Would he have the power to insist that the marquess apologise publicly? Or swear on a bible that nothing had ever happened between them? Now that, of course, would be a lie. She'd thrown herself at him.

He left the room. Prudence made her way back to sit next to Harriet and begin her rather cold breakfast.

"It is like one of those stories," Harriet said. "I have been rescued."

"Indeed," Prudence forced herself to say.

"I don't think he's very bad. Mrs. Pendleton must have been wrong." To that, Prudence made no reply.

"How much longer do you think we'll go travelling today?" Harriet asked, cutting into Prudence's confused thoughts.

"I don't know, but I'm sure it will be very pleasant, and I will tell you a great many fairy stories if you like."

"Will you tell me the one about Cinderella? And all the princesses with broken shoes and the one with the golden ball?"

"Yes, but only once each. This time, I'm not going to tell them again and again."

"What's your favourite one?" Harriet asked

"Do you mean fairy story or a myth?"

"What's a myth?"

"King Arthur and his Knights of the Round Table. And Queen Guinevere."

"Yes, I like the queen." Harriet had gotten bored with her food and climbed out of her chair, coming over and standing next to Prudence. "One day, I want to see a play with King Arthur, Queen Guinevere, and Lancelot and the Green Knight. All of them."

"I'm afraid I don't know all the stories as well as you do."

"I don't mind telling you them."

"Why not go and gather your things together? I need to write a note." Prudence shooed Harriet towards the bedroom.

The child ran from the room; the noises she made as she gathered her shoes and clothes together were quite loud. While Harriet did that, Prudence went to the case and drew out a piece of paper. She needed to inform her father where she was. What had happened. Who had taken the pair of them. But if she put too much down or gave too much away, would Heatherbroke read it and stop it from being sent?

Prudence took a window seat that overlooked the rear of the hotel. She brought her feet up onto the cushion and rested her head on her knees. Then she raised the pencil and wrote.

Dear Father,

Please do not worry. I am unhurt. As is Harriet. We were given very little choice but to leave the neighbourhood. I apologise for the hurt and fear this must have caused for both of you. You see, Harriet's father found us. I do not know how much my dear stepmother has told you about this man. But I found I could not leave Harriet on her own. She needed me. She needs me still.

Here, Prudence paused, her pencil resting against the page. She bit her full lip, pondering what to say next. It felt wrong to lie to her father.

We are both safe. We are journeying with Harriet's father to one of his northern estates. As soon as the child is ensconced there, I will be escorted home. It is all very proper. We have a great many attendants, and we are being well looked after. Please, Father, do not tell all and sundry about what has happened. I cannot stop fearing what everyone will say when I return.

. . .

Again, Prudence paused. She dwelt on what she had written. It felt abrupt and cold, rather like an acquaintance than her own dear father. But she had no idea how the strict, well-meaning man would react. He seemed so calm and so rational, but then again, Prudence had never done anything to cause him any worry. She returned the pencil to the page and wrote the final sentence:

I am thinking of you both and hoping to be home soon.
  Your daughter,
  Prudence

There. She folded the page in half. That would have to do. She couldn't think of anything else to write. She hadn't given anything specific away that would anger or upset Heatherbroke.

Prudence got to her feet and made her way to the table. She laid down the note, then turned back and called to Harriet. She needed to be practical. "Are you all packed in there?"

"Nearly," the child replied.

"Excellent, I need to come in now." Prudence went into the bedroom and helped Harriet pack their remaining items. Halfway through doing this, she heard the arrival of the servants. They were quieter and more discreet than that man. When she peered out into the room, she spotted a woman she assumed was Miss Armstrong. She was squat and had a round face, a little like a toad, with a sagging jaw line and faded blue eyes. Prudence was about to go out and introduce herself when *he* entered the room.

"We should be on the road already," he said to the room. "I trust you will help her finish in here and bring everything down?" He looked across to Harrison, who stood by the door.

From where she stood, Prudence couldn't hear the reply, but

the next second, he was across the room and pulling open the bedroom door, catching her in the act of spying on him.

"There you are, wife," he said. "Come along, come along, we need to be out of here."

"My note to my father." Prudence pressed it to him as they went past the table.

He accepted the piece of paper and slipped it into his waistcoat, then he brought his hand down, clasping her elbow and propelling her forwards through the room, down the stairs, and into the salon. He didn't speak as they walked through the hotel but kept staring ahead. They were out in the sunshine.

The busy, bustling street was filled with workmen, servants, tradesman, and the occasional lady moving along the walkway. In front of the hotel, where they had spent the night, was the carriage. Prudence found herself pausing to suck in a breath. She had thought that whilst she might have embarrassed herself the night before, at least in the morning they had found a little more in common with each other than they had understood. But he had returned a different man, and he thought her complicit.

With an ill-favoured, bad temper, knowing they would spend hours cooped up together in the confined space, Prudence wrenched her arm free of his grip and climbed up into the carriage. Moments passed, long drawn-out moments, where she could hear the bustle of the town move past. Then the carriage door was once more opened, and Harriet hopped inside, followed by Miss Armstrong. She nodded at the maid, who dolefully bobbed her head back and settled into her corner. Then the carriage took off, and Prudence realised that they were not to be joined by him. There would be no chance for her to make amends. Or for him to.

CHAPTER 9

It had seemed like a good idea to ride on horseback, rather than to sit inside the carriage. All the better, to keep the distance between them. If he were honest with himself, which Richard was not inclined to do, he would recognise he was more scared that he would forgive her. He needed to cling to the protection of his anger. *She is a liar. She deliberately misled you*, he told himself, but it didn't stick. He was already more than willing to forgive her, which only made it worse after his years of resentment. She was part of a system that had kept him from his daughter, despite the whirring voice of his conscience that said she was just as much a pawn in the machine as he had been.

With sheer stubbornness on his part, he had climbed up on the hired horse and set them all off. Their number had grown now that they had a driver as well as Miss Armstrong. As they had left Derby, his stubbornness had dissipated, and his irritation over Miss Pendleton, for want of a better word, had shifted. It must also be acknowledged, Richard thought, that the length of the journey was having an impact on him.

It was all her fault, he thought. But he knew that was a lie. She had been almost entirely honest in the time they had spent together. She would be terrible at playing cards, her face displaying deep emotion from sheer delight to outrage. But she could also be evasive, and there was something she was keeping back. He was sure of it. That was part of the problem, he realised. How did he know if he could trust her? Being too *laissez-faire* with one's trust had laid him here, friendless and cut off. That, and his own stupid lust.

In annoyance, Richard turned his thoughts back to last night. It was thrilling to see that she had wanted him. A boost to his ego, a stroking gesture that had made him feel far better about himself. Yet would that not be giving in to his baser instincts again? That was a real problem, since he had made a promise to his grandmother, his family name, his one-time friends, and himself, to behave with absolute honour. That did not include seducing innocents. Of course, it was easy to promise because that was before he had seen Prudence. Any kind of feelings of lust for her would need to be packed away, buried, in fact.

She smelt like roses.

The day was a miserable one, and having ridden through the bad weather, Richard was in a foul mood. He had had a lot of ideas about how rescuing his daughter was going to play out. None of these plans had involved bringing a bossy, opinionated, beautiful young woman along for the ride. He had avoided the polite company of women since Annabelle, really after the death of his older brother George. He had become very good at hiding the softer, more vulnerable parts of his emotions, which Prudence Pendleton appeared to have a gift for drawing out.

He thought back to the first evening he had ever seen Annabelle, in an effort to rile himself up, to remember his justifiable anger. She was a diamond of the first water. Everyone had said so. It was undeniable. She seemed to glitter in a ballroom that was lit by candlelight, and yet she had shone the brightest there. Perhaps it was her blonde hair, or perhaps it was the slow and graceful manner with which she moved, or even the shimmery golden dress she had worn. Richard didn't care much for women's fashion, but he remembered that dress. He remembered, too, the expression on Annabelle's face when she realised everyone in the room, every man in the room, was watching her. It seemed to dawn on her that she held a sort of power over them.

Richard put himself back into those shoes, back into his old self, who he'd been then: the younger son, belonging to a set of friends he had only managed to get into because his older brother was their ringleader. He had tagged along with them; that was how he'd always felt. Thinking of Annabelle again in that first light, he knew she was little more than a fantasy for him, one which was never meant to be a reality. It had never surprised him that she had picked Woolwich from their ranks. It made perfect sense. A diamond of the first water, as Annabelle was, had picked the attractive, domineering, highborn Duke of Woolwich. The only other person she might have considered would have been George. It fitted, in the world that they all belonged to, that she had married the most important member of their society.

Richard attended their wedding as a groomsman and watched in mild envy as the Duke of Woolwich married Annabelle. It had been a brilliant match for Annabelle, her father having only been knighted in the last ten years.

The wedding where he had watched the bride and groom kiss, and the Set had teased the pair of them, had seemed all part of that social whirl that was his world. The truth was that no matter what came afterwards, he had never intended anything beyond a mild flirtation with Annabelle. But intentions and actions were two very different things.

The journey had drifted past in grey, sloping hills as they worked their way up to the north. The driver had insisted this was the quickest route, leading them through the moors that surrounded Derby. Crisscrossing the various counties had become a habit in the last few years, giving him an idea of the lay of the land and insight into the differences and anxieties that existed throughout the kingdom.

Richard had picked Brayton because it was his family's oldest and most prestigious estate and where he felt safest. Brayton, where his grandmother was housed, was the only property that created a sense of security. It was home. He didn't want that to end. In fact, he wanted his little daughter to feel like Brayton was hers too. She deserved that, after Woolwich's treatment of her, packing her off to the countryside, parcel-like, to be ignored now that Woolwich had his own child. It was not as bad as Woolwich had threatened, however. Harriet had been raised well. Perhaps Woolwich wasn't—Richard cut himself off. He was justified to be furious. He was.

Richard shook his head, and his horse shifted underneath him and let out a snort. It was hours before they would reach the next stop in their journey. Looking at the driver, Richard judged the man's knowledge of the road better than his. He had been secured in Derby, and it allowed his groom a rest. It was useful to have a local guide cutting them through the moors and off the busier roads. There lingered the idea that Woolwich might hear of Harriet's rescue and stage some attempt to steal her back.

Making a clicking noise to the horse, Richard pivoted and moved behind the carriage, allowing the animal to ride at a slower pace. This should be enjoyable, he told himself. Just as that sentence was uttered internally, there came a shout from the driver. It took a moment for the realisation to set in. He was being called for, by both the driver and his groom.

"My lord." The carriage had stopped and his groom's pink, anxious face was poking around the side of the vehicle.

Making an encouraging noise, Richard urged his horse past the carriage, forcing himself not to look inside.

How had Woolwich managed to overtake them? Find them? He had moved as fast as possible, admittedly weighed down by a girl and woman.

Up ahead, across the woodland road, stretched a felled tree. It was the spring; no recent storm would have brought it down. It was large enough to make their progress along the road impossible. Richard's eyes moved to the trees, to the hedgerows, and to the mass of leaves that effectively blocked any view into the woods.

Descending from his horse, Richard took the reins and hurried back to the carriage. His groom was already off his seat and had drawn his pistol. It felt close to tempting fate, but Richard pulled his own from his coat and cocked it.

"Deliberate, like?" Clarence asked, as he came to stand next to him. They had played their roles of master and employee for years. If anything, his groom knew the lengths to which Richard had gone to find Harriet better than many. He had been with him, on those reckless journeys across towns and cities, searching through charity homes, all for a whisper of the child. To get so close, and then to find themselves trapped...

The man's remark now sounded to Richard's ears less like a question, and more of a confirmation of his fears.

Still up on his seat, the driver's sallow skin was nearing ashen, and he appeared to be close to twitching. He eyed the forest, clutching the reins tight enough to turn his knuckles white.

"Sir," Richard called up to him, and the man glanced down, gulping as he did.

"My wife says it's common enough. But I never did believe her. I say, in all my thirty years of this, I ain't never seen," he lowered his tone and muttered with a dramatic flair, "highwaymen."

Breaking into the uneasy sentence came a snort, and all three men turned and looked back at the carriage window from where the sound had come from. Miss Pendleton had stuck her head out of it and was surveying the scene. Her refined brow puckered.

"No," she replied, rather like she was an authority on roadside robberies, "all the books say they strike at night. Why would anyone..."

She leant forward as she spoke, giving the distinction impression that she meant to exit the carriage.

"Bloody hell," Richard roared, "stay in the carriage."

"We can help you move it," she said back, her calm tone at odds with how on edge he was.

In response, Richard marched forward and leant against the carriage doorframe. "Stay in that vehicle, you hear me?"

"I—"

"You came all this way to look after Harriet. This is the best way." His fury swelled within him. He wanted to direct it against her, and yet as he looked up into her face, he knew he was being a fool. But there was a difference; he found that whilst realising his own foolishness, he could not bring himself to stop. "Stay put."

She sank into the darkness of the carriage interior.

"Stay with them," Richard said to the driver. He moved back towards the tree trunk, crossing the twenty feet in quick strides. He did not wish to continue listening to her; it was a petty gesture, he knew, but still, it was a balm he clung to in these moments. *Keep that distance between the two of you, if only literally.* The irrational annoyance at finding she had kept something so crucial about Harriet back from him still existed, confirming his initial suspicions that she was a liar. *What else are you keeping hidden, Prudence?*

But it was not just out of rage, he had snapped. She might be a target, too, for a licentious highwayman.

Upon closer inspection, Richard judged that the tree had been rolled by at least three to four men. Its placement in the road seemed too convenient to be anything else. But if that was the case, why hadn't they been set upon? Minutes had ticked by, and no one had emerged.

"Worthwhile turning the carriage round and heading back the way we came?" Clarence asked. "I wouldn't want to wait for nightfall."

"You're right. I don't like the idea of waiting around for them.

Besides, I doubt either of us—" Richard started to say, when a tremendous scream wrenched the air and forced both of them to turn on their heels and sprint back towards the carriage.

It appeared to be swarming with men, two surrounding it, one making for the driver, another two running towards Richard and Clarence right now. He counted five, no, six of them, one of whom was still inside the carriage.

Time slowed down as Richard watched men pry open the carriage doors, the driver dragged from his seat, and first Miss Armstrong, then Prudence, and finally Harriet flung to the roadside. The china doll he had given to Harriet smashed beside her as she landed next to it.

God, in his first test as a father, he had failed once again.

He couldn't fight, not with Harriet so close. He couldn't shoot someone in front of his child. Yet all too soon, the robbers would see that whilst the carriage was an expensive type, they had travelled lightly with nothing of value. Then what would they do?

There was a blast from next to him. His groom had opened fire, and one of the men hit the mud path with a thwack.

"By God," Richard said.

The approaching robber didn't stop. In his hand, was a wickedly sharp blade, the afternoon sun glinting off its curved edged.

The pistol in his hand was loose, and his skin was sweaty, but Clarence was empty. He would need to reload.

Focus. You aren't any good to them dead.

"Be a good man and step aside, I have no objection to shooting another one of you." Richard circled the man with the knife; he made his voice steady with a sheer force of will.

"We've got guns too. And there's more of us." The robber, who was perhaps around Richard's own age, was too focused on the pistol, his eyes straining to follow the silver gleam of the barrel. As the rogue turned more fully towards him, both Clarence and he struck. He went for the knife, whilst Clarence went for the back of the young robber's head. The man crashed to the floor between them.

"Go to the driver, I'll take the others," Richard said, putting the knife into his pocket. His voice was commanding. He was the marquess, the one in charge, despite Clarence's age and experience. He glanced back towards the carriage, and four more of the robbers, that he could see. Of all the times to be set upon if it wasn't so dangerous... One of them was dead if Clarence's shot had been true. One of them was unconscious. A glance down at the man at his feet told him as much. Distantly, he could recall his training, lazy days spent at Kingston's boxing gymnasium, a golden glow that spread over his memories of his time with the Set. He could recall the laughter; he wasn't the best fighter, but needs must... *Focus.* Those old hazy recollections weren't much good to him now.

Focus. They still had work to do, and the odds weren't in their favour.

Another shriek echoed out, this one more mumbled than the first. Clarence had darted to the right and out of sight, making a strategic move towards the fallen driver, as Richard cut a broad path back towards the carriage.

"Get back!" His voice was not his own. It was etched with fear, driving high and he feared, almost hysterical. *Calm yourself, you have a right to defend what is yours.* Harriet was his, by blood. Miss Armstrong was in his employ and deserved his protection. He took in the shape of Prudence. Lord, what was she to him? Were the situations reversed, wouldn't she leave him?

Did he care if she would? No, he realised, he owed her the same protection as the others, but there was a twist of guilt at the idea something might happen to her.

He levelled the pistol in his hand at the man nearest to the pair of them. The other two were rooting through the luggage they had grabbed from the cases. "Step away from them," Richard called out to the huddled men.

"Ooh, Guv'nor." There was an unpleasant laugh from the man closest to the women. He seemed to have been left to guard them. The final one was liberally laying into the driver; the beaten man's noise was a frightening one. Clarence would deal with that. Richard needed to concentrate on extracting the cluster of women from harm's way. They could leave all the belongings, he cared not a jot for that.

"We don't have anything of value. No one travels like that now. Your reputation precedes you." Richard modulated his voice, driving out the seam of refined culture and trying to sound like the character of Dobson he had played so recently. *I'm a land clerk, I have very little money on me, but by God I have the most precious cargo in the world in my care.* He hoped to high heaven they didn't realise how much he valued the child's life.

"Ain't no one travelling like this, in this carriage, without money."

There was a clang as the small case was dropped to the pathway. "It's just clothes," one of the two men said, a real sense of injustice to his voice. "Might sell for a bit."

The crunching sound of the driver being beaten had stopped, and Richard prayed that Clarence had saved the man. The three others were looking at him expectantly.

"I've some notes with me. You just have to let us go. You may have the money, if—"

"There ain't no ifs and buts here," one of them shouted back, his jagged teeth resembling those of a wolf.

"Give us the money; we won't be asking twice," said the largest brute of the lot.

"What about her?" asked the jagged toothed one. He was nearest to Prudence, and he levelled his knife at her. The look on his face was unpleasantly calculating; he seemed to be weighing up the mercenary value of Prudence's person. "You're a right pretty piece, aren't you? Got anything about you? Women like you like to travel fancy."

Prudence leant back farther, cushioning herself against the ground. As she moved, she loosened the hold Harriet had on her, pushing the child towards the silently rocking and terrified Miss Armstrong.

In hopeless horror, Richard watched one of the robbers reach down and grab Prudence's arm, hoisting her upright.

"Don't women like you always travel..." His hands went out to start feeling their way over her body.

In one quick movement, Prudence slapped him, and the man rocketed back on his feet, surprised by the sheer force of the contact. Richard pointed his pistol at the nearest man to him and shot. He watched in a blend of disgust and satisfaction as one of the attackers crumpled to the floor, close to where Miss Armstrong was whimpering. The poor woman had wrapped her arms around herself and looked close to fainting.

The remaining uninjured man looked at Richard and charged. He was a large brute of a figure, far taller than Richard's six feet. He didn't have time to reload the pistol. Bracing himself, Richard prepared to fight. He doubted he would last long, but as he squared up, he felt the weight of the knife he had stolen.

The brute swung a fist and Richard ducked, lowering his head as he struggled to free the knife from his pocket. An almighty weight crashed into his back as the other man beat against his shoulders. Richard turned as he staggered back, only just maintaining his balance. The knife was in his hand, steady whilst his innards quaked.

Don't think about them. About Harriet. Or Prudence. The brute charged again, not seeing the knife. In one swift gesture, more skilful than he had imagined himself capable of, Richard flicked the blade up and lodged it in his attacker's throat.

Shock rocketed through him at the impact as he watched the larger man wobble and stagger. His eyes rolled back in his head, and he landed in a heap on the mud track.

Looking back to the scene, Richard could see what had happened, although he still felt close to casting up his accounts.

Miss Armstrong was holding Harriet's hands, and there was a splayed figure—the robber Richard had shot—lying close by. Clarence had emerged, along with the bloody and limping driver, to comfort the sobbing Miss Armstrong and Harriet.

Richard's feet carried him forward to snatch up his daughter. God, he'd never let her leave Brayton. He'd lock the door and bar her, anything to keep her safe. She was small, weighing less than he imagined as he crushed her to him. Her blonde strands lifted and caught in his nose as he let out his breath.

"Jesus," he said. There was a crucial person missing. No, there were two. The last robber, the one with jagged teeth and vile eyes, and Miss Prudence Pendleton.

"The man," Harriet tried to say, tears spilling out of her bright blue eyes, "he took her with him." Her chubby hand reached out and pointed towards the overgrown thicket, and the nerves he had felt earlier rushed back to dance painfully through Richard's skull.

He looked around at their carriage, at the dead men who surrounded him. He had never killed anyone in his life, and now there were two lives he had taken. His gaze found Clarence. The groom was looking a little worse for wear but considerably better than the driver.

No carriages had passed by in the last thirty minutes, so they had little chance of a rescue any time soon from fellow travellers. He was a fool for trying the quicker road.

Damn it. He couldn't leave Prudence in there.

"Right," Richard said as he lowered Harriet to the ground, who immediately clung tightly to his leg. He bent to offer his hand to Miss Armstrong and gave her an encouraging nod. "Right, this is the plan. Gather all that isn't broken. All of you get into the carriage now. You hear me? Clarence, I need you to drive everyone to the *Boars Head Inn* at Halifax. Once there, find the magistrate, tell him what happened. If I'm not there by tomorrow morning, then take Miss Harriet to Brayton. Leave my horse here."

"And you, my lord?"

"I'm going to get the girl." As he spoke, the other three started to gather up the dropped and discarded items, hauling them into the carriage. Richard made his way back to his abandoned pistol, silently accepting a bullet from Clarence. In a rather grisly show, Clarence leant down and pulled the stained knife out of the robber's throat, wiped it on his trouser leg, and passed it to Richard.

"Doesn't it bother you?" he asked as he pocketed the knife.

"Not since I fought the frogs," Clarence remarked. "Just remember it was a choice, either you or them."

I can't think about that now.

"You needn't worry about the girl." Clarence cut into Richard's thoughts.

"I trust you with Harriet."

"I meant the other girl. She's a good one, she's got gumption." Clarence backed up, and Richard looked towards the woods. He couldn't linger, he needed to be after her. He nodded at Clarence and then marched forward into the thick woods, praying this slight delay wouldn't be too much, for Prudence's sake.

CHAPTER 10

Plunging into the woods dimmed Prudence's uncertain vision, and she had to lift her free hand to protect her head from the low-hanging branches. Her other hand was clasped in the tight grip of the remaining thief. He was not like any of the robbers or highwaymen she'd read about, not in the least. There was nothing romantic or attractive about him, as the books had stated there would be. His breath was vile, his teeth crooked, and when she'd slapped him, he had returned the favour with no hesitation. He had then moved as if to attack Heatherbroke, stopping only when he saw his two remaining friends felled. She thought he'd go for Harriet, and in one swift movement, she'd tried to block him. That had been her mistake, because yet again, he'd backhanded her away, before lifting her up by the waist and making for the woods. Her cheek still stung where he'd caught her between cheekbone and eye, but at least the blurred burst of stars that had glittered in front of her eyes had now gone.

"Walk on yer own."

He was pulling her forwards roughly, through the catching trees and branches and with great alacrity; although with

Prudence tripping every foot or so, they did not make much progress. She was determined to be the worst possible detainee imaginable, although she was blearily aware that this did not seem to deter the man.

"I'll make a terrible hostage," Prudence said as they slowed for a moment. The man was looking at the forest, his vision moving about the trees, searching for a sign. Prudence saw that the trees were marked with small nicks in their bark at about shoulder height. It was a way of almost having a map of their route. "How clever," Prudence said. Perhaps complimenting the man might work, might soften the perception he had of her.

"Shut it." With his free hand, he raked his fingers through his hair, his movements aggravated and wild. He moved closer to the tree, feeling the shape of the marking before muttering something to himself.

Should I tell him everything? That I am not what he thinks me? But then again, Prudence wasn't sure what he thought her to be. Someone's wife, or a mistress, or just a servant?

You fool, he doesn't want you for what you are, he wants you for your body. Fear gripped her, an unpleasant mix that affected her hands, making them shake as well as her voice. She had always imagined being strong in frightening moments, but not now…

"This way," the robber declared, his apparent uncertainty gone. He dragged them deeper into the winding trees, slamming them into the wood as they darted along over knots of twisted brambles. Minutes and metres elapsed as they worked their way farther from the roadside.

He must be looking for their hide out. A secluded and secure point of rest. It was not a comforting thought.

The attack had all happened so quickly, from the conversation between the driver, Clarence, and Heatherbroke, to the sounds of the men setting upon the carriage. Nothing like the poetry or the romance Prudence had envisioned. Time had sped up, so that all decisions were abrupt that were not fully considered. She had no time to prepare, she told herself now, which was not reassuring. She wished she had at least grabbed a pistol, but there wasn't one to hand, so in the end, she had settled for Heatherbroke's razor, which was nestled in the top line of her bodice. She had no pockets in this dress. It was meant to be a last resort back in the carriage, but now it didn't feel like that.

Don't be afraid to use it.

Although, when that opportunity might be, was beyond her imagination. He would have to be in a state of befuddlement. Would he try something similar to a kiss like Heatherbroke?

Her body tensed at that thought, and the taste of bile filled her mouth.

Don't think about it.

High above them, the trees stretched, their leaves masking much of the light. Would Clarence follow after them? He had been injured, she thought, her mind casting back to the attack. Would Heatherbroke came after her? He hated her, that was obvious. She was as much to blame for the situation as the duchess, or so he believed. But still, would he leave her out here, on her own? What loyalty did he have to her or she to him? Had all her featherlike daydreams, any lingering softness she felt she had seen in him, been false?

The robber paused, causing Prudence to stop too. He crouched low to the ground and pulled her down to hunch beside him. The mud was pickled with broken grasses and mismatched footprints. His fingers moved over it in an almost affectionate manner. *He has abandoned his friends, most of whom were dead.* Would he want revenge against her for those crimes? Or was the expression "no honour among thieves" an accurate one?

With his free hand, he felt the mud. It was visibly imprinted with footprints; he fingered the shape of one footfall in particular before laughing oddly, a gleam flashing in his eyes.

He's not right in the head.

He was leading them back the way the robbers had come, of

that Prudence was certain. Sweeping her eyes over him, Prudence judged that he wasn't too muscled or too tall. If they were to fight, he would still have the advantage over her, even if she surprised him. As he was broader... it would have to be something sizeable that slowed him down, not just a quick shove and then her running off. After all, her dress would slow her down.

"You won't get a ransom for me," Prudence tried again. They were so close, only a few inches apart. She had the necklace about her throat, that might work, but if she suggested it too soon, then he would just take it, and she would be in no better a position. It was all about leverage. "But if you let me go now, I won't testify against you. I won't say anything. I can send you money or..."

Her words were abruptly cut off when the man slammed his callused hand against her mouth, the sudden movement juddering through Prudence. His nails gripped into the soft flesh of her face. Tears filled her eyes at the pain as she looked at him. There was no sympathy visible in the man's expression, no lightening in his eyes; they seemed almost bottomless with their stare. Again, the earlier tentacle of anxious fear of what he was capable of doing reared its head within Prudence's chest. If she wasn't careful, it would consume the whole of her.

"Will yeh shut the fuck up?" the man said. "I won't say it again. I'll gag yer." Hopping to his feet, he pulled her back up. His right hand was tight on her wrist, encircling it so it resembled more of a shackle than anything else. "Not another peep, yeh got it?"

Nodding, Prudence let herself be dragged deeper into the woods, her dress catching now and then on the outstretched branches. The greenery was becoming a blur.

It's no good, no one is following you. No one is going to rescue you. Even if one of the men had followed you, they wouldn't be able to find you now. The voice in her head taunted her, the fear manifesting itself into the popular girls she'd never liked in Alfriston.

Pain shot through Prudence as a root caught her foot and

yanked her back. She landed heavily on her knees and elbows, and the tears spilled over and down her face. This felt like rock bottom, but she was afraid it was going to get considerably worse. Bits of twigs and branches were digging into her legs as she shifted.

"Get up." He had turned, and she could hear him approaching.

Rolling onto her side, Prudence took her time, exaggerating each movement as she prepared herself. This was her moment. There was a series of broken tree branches to her right, within her grasp, and she used one to bring herself upright. It had a steady weight to it. A good inch in width and six or seven in length, it would do. It would be suitable as a weapon.

The robber was only a foot away; he had moved closer, waiting for Prudence to get up. She glanced up at him. His face was turned away from her, watching the horizon. He could not see her movements, his attention focused on surveying the darkening wood. He didn't view her as a threat. Prudence sniffed and let out a whimper. She saw the robber shake his head, letting out a sigh.

Now is your chance. It doesn't make sense to use the knife. You must use the branch in your hand, you will not get another chance.

Still exaggerating her movements, she staggered to her feet, which gave the impression she was injured and sore. The man glanced to his side, took in her "weakened" pose, and started to move away.

With one almighty swing, Prudence grasped the thick branch between her hands and brought it around, thwacking it hard into the back of the robber's head. It made a strangely dull noise as it collided on his skull. He let out a scream, both of surprise and hurt, and crashed to the woodland floor just as Prudence had moments ago. Hurrying closer, Prudence lifted the branch up to her shoulder height and braced herself to deliver another blow against the back of his head. Once more, the sound reverberated out.

She stepped back. In the dimness, she wasn't sure if it had

worked. With her toe, she poked the edge of his torso. Taking one hand off the branch, she withdrew the razor. If he awoke now, she had to use it. But there was no movement. With one quick jerk of her leg, she kicked him, and he didn't stir.

Run, the voice told her, *right back the way you came. You were smart to remember the changes in the trees, the breaks in the shrubs and the clearings, you know the way.*

Turning on her heel, the knife slotted back into her dress, and lifting the long skirts of her dress in the right hand, Prudence took off through the woods. There was a burst of pain in her ankle. Maybe the fall had twisted it, but she didn't care. She was away from the thief, and that was something. She had kept an eye on the route, with eternal optimism that told her to ignore the fear. Over a rounded hillock and mossy embarkment. She was going to get out of these woods. Soon she would be back on the roadside, and the carriage would be waiting. There might even be a constable. They would look after her. She was going to ensure that Harriet was safe. She was going to—

"What the hell?" Heatherbroke was striding towards her. He looked ruffled, muddy, and his lip was split, but otherwise he was unharmed. "My God. I thought..." He kept moving as he spoke, coming to stand before her, and then his arms reached out and pulled her to him. The embrace stretched, and Prudence realised she was shaking. Her body had been so poised for a fight, so now she was accurately aware that it was relaxing, the muscles in her shoulders dropping, her arms coming to rest on his strong back. She released the breath she hadn't even realised she'd been holding. It came out as more of a shudder.

To be held by him, felt safe. *Wasn't that an absurd thought?* But it was a true one. He was who she hoped would appear, more than anything else in these strange groves.

"Thank God, you've no idea. Or you might. I never... I just hoped..." His mouth was close to her left ear, so she caught most of his mumbled sentences which tumbled over each other, his nervous energy pouring forth. "I could murder him."

He shuddered at the thought and leant back a little, so that they were looking into each other's eyes. There was such a wealth of pain there that Prudence found herself transfixed. He had been terrified for her. He had left Harriet to search and save her. Even in her nervous state, she spotted a tiny freckle by his right eye, which made his lashes look even longer. That thought, as well as the others, made her smile, and she saw a similar one tug on his lips. With one tentative hand, Heatherbroke stroked a piece of muddied hair off her face, his touch lingering on the sore cheek and chin. The gesture was so soothing that Prudence felt the urge to close her eyes and lean in closer. She sighed, the noise in the woodland seemed to echo, and hurriedly, the marquess stepped back, putting a good foot between them, and looked over her mangled dress.

"You came after me. You followed me," she replied.

His hand, which had been such a comfort, dropped from her face, and his face paled. "You think so little of me, that I wouldn't—"

"No." The nervousness and fear that had eked out of Prudence had left bravery in its wake, and Prudence found herself pulling him back close to her. He was the solace she sought. "We had fought. I did not think that you would leave your daughter."

"You may think me the worst of men, but I would not leave a young woman to such a fate."

"It is precisely because of who I am that I thought you would send Clarence. You think I am a liar who tried to trick you. But I swear I had no idea about the connection between my family and Woolwich. I only realised..." She was clinging to him as she spoke urgently and only stopped when he pressed his forehead against hers. It stopped her words in their tracks.

"I was a fool." His breath warmed her face. "I believe you. I think I always did, but

God, I am stubborn. Can you forgive me?"

Prudence found herself nodding. "Not that you deserve it."

Heatherbroke laughed. "You are a better person than I."

"Oh, I know that," Prudence said. She leant back and viewed him. "You do believe me?"

"Of course." His lips brushed the skin of her brow. "I was so frightened when you had gone. I keep losing people who matter to me."

The admission surprised Prudence, but she did not wish to press him further for clarification. He seemed to include her into the count of people he valued. "I did not wish to be so cruel, so sudden. I reacted wrongly again and again because I fear... Each one of my family were stolen by disease, by accident... by vindictiveness."

"She is not lost to you."

Heatherbroke let out a breath, an uneasy sigh, and they stayed close together, allowing themselves time to luxuriate in the comfort of each other's presence.

"Blast it. I should have been the one to... Did he?" His eyes were wreathed in concern as he stepped back. "Are you hurt?"

"I managed to knock him out before he could." Prudence felt it was a lifetime ago. "He's unconscious back there." Prudence pointed behind her. "I took your razor." She fumbled it out of the top line of her dress and gave it to him. "I couldn't think of what else to do. But I didn't need to use it." She did feel relieved to be away from the robber, but she would prefer if they made their way back to the roadside. He had appeared to be in a deep stupor but then again, she wasn't a doctor. "I don't know how long he will remain so."

"You're extraordinary," Heatherbroke said, more to himself than to her. "Bloody extraordinary. And you're right, we shouldn't linger. I don't fancy riding during the dark."

"Did the others not wait?"

"I sent them on to Halifax. The driver needed to see a doctor."

Prudence nodded as she followed alongside him. The shrubs, brambles, and tree roots continued before them; on occasion, the sky's colour flashed through the leaves, and it was visibly growing darker.

"What about us?" she asked. "How will we get there?"

"We?"

She glanced at him, frowning. "Of course."

"You sincerely wish to continue with me?" His tone was teasing, and she saw that he was trying to cheer her out of their recent revelations or the fear she had experienced.

She grinned back at him. "Of course, I need to check on Harriet's welcoming. Ensure that she is safe and sound."

"It is... I like that you care for her so much."

"She is," Prudence started to say, but she stopped herself. She had been about to admit that Harriet was one of her key reasons for living. "She is very dear to me."

Heatherbroke lifted a branch out of her way, and they moved on, cutting through the reaching twigs and scratching leaves. It was a pleasant thought that Harriet was such a darling to her, but then what would she do when they needed to separate? Was that why she had clung so tightly to the child, a fear that such lightness, such joy and curiosity would leave her? It was Heatherbroke's fault, and yet, she could not blame him. He moved through the woods with a hard grace, lingering close to her protectively.

Her stepmother had been wrong; he had risked his life entering the forest to save her... not out of obligation, she fancied, but something else.

"How will we get to Halifax?"

"We'll have to ride," he replied and pointed through the trees. Prudence saw the distant sight of the road. "Are you a good horsewoman?"

"I've never ridden."

"I suppose we shall find out."

Prudence was about to reply when his hand shot out and clasped hers, their fingers interlinking. His grip strong, he looked back at her. "Stay close to me while we go back out there."

She nodded and followed him out of the woods. At first, she assumed it was because he wasn't certain if any of the robbers remained alive, then as they walked, she realised that, no, he wanted to shield her from the sight of their bodies. In a greedy excitement at having him close, Prudence clung to his hand, keeping her body pressed close to his. She could feel the heat of his body through his clothes as they moved forward, edging along the pathway, until they reached the secured horse.

"We're lucky he's still here," she said, looking at Heatherbroke. Now they were out of the woods, away from the sight of the attack, she could step back away from him. She really should, but Prudence didn't move.

"There we are." With his free hand, Richard stroked the side of the horse and then untied the reins, looping one around his left forearm in a secure manner.

"Here." He lowered himself and cupped his hands before her. "To put you up in the saddle."

"You'll go behind me?"

His lips jerked at something in that statement, but his eyes remained calm as he gazed up at her. "That's right. Don't be nervous. Put your weight on me when you climb up."

Stepping up, Prudence placed her left foot into his hands, gripped the mane and saddle, and pulled herself up on the horse, twisting to face him. It was not an elegant climb up, and she could not quite manage to hold herself steady as she perched sideways. Thankfully, the horse only snorted at the movement. In one quick movement, Heatherbroke hopped up behind her, lifting her so that Prudence sat more squarely on his lap.

She stared at him. There was nothing for her to hold on to, both legs dangling on the same side of the saddle.

"Put your arms around me."

"I will not."

"There's no one around to see."

"But..." Prudence bit her lip; he was right. *Curses.* With a great show of reluctance, she placed her hands on his shoulders. His hand came around her waist and yanked her closer. Now to all extents and purposes, they were simply hugging on top of a horse. The reserve she should have felt earlier reared its head now.

"I must look ridiculous."

"Close your eyes if it is easier." He clicked his tongue and moved his free hand on the reins to turn the horse towards the overturned wood. The horse nimbly stepped around, and they started off up the road.

I will get used to this. To being held so. So flush against his chest. Do not get too comfortable, my girl.

The pace he set was brisk and kept her holding on to him with a tight grip. "You were very brave," he said.

"Is that so?"

"Indeed, it is one of your many admirable qualities."

"Thank you." She lowered her lashes. "I have many flaws."

"Not that I have seen. You seem a jewel of a woman."

"A diamond?"

"No, something far better."

"I thought diamonds were the best."

"I'm growing partial to rubies," he told her. "They are clearly worth a great deal more. Your little cross, you weren't tempted to offer him that in order to escape?"

"I suspect that if I had suggested it, he would have stolen it anyway, and I would still be in the same position. I doubt he had any honour."

"Did you think the same of me?" The horse slowed down to a walk, and Heatherbroke moved his face to stare down at her.

Prudence could feel his eyes studying her. She glanced up, meeting his contemplation.

"I understand the desire too well to have Harriet close to judge you."

His mouth curved; the smile was one of disdain, directed more at himself than anything else. He made the clicking noise again, and the horse sped up, rendering a response too difficult. Prudence found herself pressing against him for both balance and for warmth. The feel of him, his thighs under her bottom, his stomach against her side, created a growing wave of awareness that pinpricked her skin, far below her dress. *It's a sin.*

His arm tightened about her waist, pulling her closer as the horse jumped the small, overturned, broken fence. Her head wedged itself against his collarbone, and even in the frowning darkness of the dying afternoon, she could see the featherlike curl of his chest hair.

It's worth all the sins to be held so.

She let out a sigh. She was too far gone to regret even the robbery; she was too won over on the entire adventure. The entire experience of being with Heatherbroke.

"Not much longer," he said reassuringly. "We'll be in Halifax soon."

She nodded against him, a part of her dreading the coming of the new town. She wanted more time with this Heatherbroke, this Richard. The man who confessed to his fears, the man who complimented her, who cared and who held her like she had dreamt of being enfolded in the arms of this man.

But all too soon, the lights and sounds of a coming town came upon them.

CHAPTER 11

Richard had stopped at *The Boar's Head* on previous trips through Halifax, and he knew the route there well, which didn't explain why he took the longer way to the Inn; it wasn't simply to keep hold of Prudence. At least that was what he kept telling himself.

She was clinging to him, secure in his lap, and it made his heart soar every time she shifted and snuggled closer. But the town wasn't that large, so eventually he reined in the horse and stopped in the Inn's courtyard.

"We're here," he said.

Her eyes lifted, her face in the shadows from the candlelight.

A stable lad was approaching, and as Prudence recalled where they were, and what position they were in, she started to wriggle. In haste, Richard eased her off his lap and down to the ground, before following her down. After a brief exchange with the boy, they went inside to a private parlour. Richard left Prudence by the fireside and went to talk to the landlord. He secured rooms for the party, as well as requesting a magistrate and a doctor to be sent for. It took longer than expected, and several hours passed before Richard could return to the private parlour. When he did, she was curled up in an armchair, fast asleep. He watched her, with her hand tucked under her chin, thinking back to the relief he felt on finding her safe.

Prudence had not been part of his plans or anything he could have foreseen. Richard gave a wry smile. He doubted anyone could have predicted anything quite like her. To his eyes, she was unique. It was a damn shame, he told himself. It would have been fetching to have met someone like her years ago.

His naivety had been dashed away with George's death and the affair with Annabelle. These two events moulded him into something very cynical and different from the young man he had once been. What he could have offered Prudence then would have been a lot more promising than now. Someone who was little better than his disgraced name. He imagined what would have happened had he met Prudence the way he would have liked to.

"How splendid to see you again, Miss Pendleton."

He would bow then, and she would curtsy, perhaps even blush.

"Would you care for the next dance?"

"My lord," she would say, *"now, you must arrive sooner when you wish to claim a dance with me."*

And he would laugh at that, because he would know that *his* Prudence had saved a dance for him, their favourite dance. He wouldn't have had to fight off any competitors; at least, in this little fantasy that played out in his mind, she would only have eyes for him.

The image faded, and Richard tried to slot in something he knew better. He had danced countless times with Annabelle. He had watched Annabelle dance with all the men of his acquaintance without ever feeling jealous. Yet the thought of having Prudence dance with one of the Set... But no, he didn't like that image at all.

There was a noise outside, and then the door was opened and in flooded Miss Armstrong, Harriet, and Clarence, who was supporting the injured driver. The noise, the talk, and the excitement spread, and in the kerfuffle, all his one-time dreams faded, but he kept hold of the sensation it created, one of security and warmth. He clung to that feeling for the next few hours in which matters with the magistrate were arranged, Harriet put to bed, and the driver treated by the doctor.

The following morning, a new driver had been hired, the women secured in the carriage, and Clarence had planned their route back to Brayton with the precision of an army general.

Richard lingered back. He could ride and continue to keep his distance. Or he could allow himself some more of that sweet, invigorating company that Prudence brought into his life.

"My lady," he said and waited for Prudence to lean forward and return his salutation.

"Sir?" It was not the same laughing tone he'd imagined in his played-out fantasy. Then again, he was not the same man who would have light-heartedly danced with her.

"Would you or your companions object if I were to join you in the carriage for the remainder of the journey?"

"No, sir." She shifted forward so that more of herself was visible in the window.

He made no reply and climbed up into the carriage. It was snug, and it smelt of ginger biscuits. Miss Armstrong and Harriet had taken one side of the carriage with one of the books he had brought, and on the other was sat Miss Pendleton, so she and he would need to sit next to each other. The seat did appear rather small now he was inside the carriage. After a minute, the carriage rumbled forward and then moved off through the town. He glanced to his left, surveying her in profile, waiting for her to speak.

She had nestled into him. She had kissed him just a day ago. She had been relieved he had come to find her.

It's what I deserve, Richard thought to himself; a form of sweet torture to sit beside a woman he felt certain desired him, and yet he could not act on it. Still, he took some comfort in knowing he had provided a chaperone, though a rather sleepy one, it must be admitted, in the form of the distracted Miss Armstrong.

Miss Pendleton seemed to be in no mood to make conversation; instead, she gazed out of the window, only looking back at the reading pair opposite whenever Richard moved.

Minutes drifted by, and Richard wondered if perhaps he had been rash in this choice, too, and if he wouldn't have been happier sitting outside on the horse, contemplating his fate. He was bound to be read some sort of riot act, first by his grandmother, and then by Vicar Pendleton, and lastly by whoever else fancied a shot at him. It was what he deserved.

"Miss Pendleton, how do you find the weather?"

She let out a rather undignified little snort of laughter which made Richard smirk, although he doubted that she saw it.

"A little overcast," she said but made no other remarks.

"Have you ever been to the north before, Miss Pendleton?"

"No, my lord, I have not."

"Have you ever read about it?"

"Geography was never a particular interest of mine."

"Have you ever wished to visit it?"

On his last question, Miss Pendleton shifted in her seat and looked across at him. Her bright, beautiful eyes a little confused, she lowered her voice when she replied, "My lord, what do you mean? No, it is the most ridiculous set of... I cannot go on acting as if we were having tea somewhere. We are not to speak of yesterday's ordeal?" Her hands twisted in her lap.

"Do you suffer from the memory of it?"

"No, I am relieved."

Unable to resist, Richard leant in closer, his voice for her ears only. "I feel the same."

"And the others? Shall we speak of it to them?"

"If you wish to." He wasn't sure who she might feel the need to tell, but if she wanted to tell her father, then the vicar would be justified in running Richard through. The niceties of a duel would not be required. "Please rest assured that I will do all that is honourable in making certain you are returned to your family in safety. I apologise for the loss of my temper and for blaming you in any way. I see my error in judgment. The mistakes of your extended family are not necessarily yours."

"Thank you." She nodded.

"You wish to add something else?" he pressed her.

"How on earth do you expect me to explain this to everyone? The kidnapping, this drive, all that has happened?"

He wondered if she was including their kiss in her list of grievances. "I did believe you to be Woolwich's mistress, or at least in his pay," he said.

"I have never met that man in all my life. If you had been allowed to marry Lady Bradley, that would have been the salvageable course of action?"

Richard leant forward a little in his seat, moving closer to Prudence so that he could whisper to her, rather than continue a conversation that could be heard from the other side of the carriage. "I'm afraid the said situation could not be rendered appropriate, given that Annabelle was already married to Woolwich when she conceived Harriet. She was a duchess at that point."

"In exceptional circumstances, divorces have been known to be granted."

"One was never sought."

"Did you wish to seek one?" Prudence hadn't moved away from him.

"It wasn't my place."

"I don't feel sorry for you," Prudence said.

"No, few people did."

"If you had been in love," Prudence said, "perhaps then it would have been more understandable. But if you didn't seek a divorce, then…" Her words trailed off as she tried to understand it all.

"How perceptive you are, Miss Pendleton," he said. She still hadn't moved away from him. Richard noticed that despite all her feigned haughtiness and her refusal to meet his eye, she was leaning into the cushions and closer to him.

"So, you weren't in love with her?"

"No, I don't believe I was."

"Do you make a habit of running through all your friend's wives?"

"Only one of my so-called friends is married."

The light was not very bright in the carriage, but it was an unmistakable sight, the look of confusion on Prudence's face. "So..." She bit her lip. "So, am I to understand that you forced yourself on her?"

"Good God, no," Richard said. "No, I would never do that to any woman." *Do you believe that of me?* was the question he wanted to ask her. But it was absurd to ask her.

"What I don't understand," Prudence said, "was how it happened, in that case? If you weren't in love."

"Do you believe two people could only be intimate if they were in love?"

"I assume, Your Lordship, that you allude to my actions... when I... when I kissed you?"

In fact, that hadn't been the reason Richard had asked, although now that Prudence mentioned it, he saw no reason why he couldn't at least tease her on the subject. "Surely, miss, you would not go so far as to say you were in love with me?"

"No. Definitely not, I-I was just, I was just curious."

"Curious?"

"In an academic manner," Prudence added. "Yes, an academic manner, that's correct. I suppose if one were to follow it through..." She was speaking fast, and it was possible to see that she was reddening. "I had never experienced a kiss," she struggled over the word, "but since you seem so very lacking in your judgement in general and have such a low opinion of me... I thought it would be worthwhile to—"

"Experiment?"

"Yes," she said. "No, I meant no."

Richard laughed. "How did you find your experiment? What were your academic

results if I may ask?"

"Stop teasing me, please."

"Very well if you insist. But I will just add, since I had such a very low opinion of you when we first met, what do you think altered my viewpoint?"

"I don't grasp your meaning, sir."

"Merely that my initial opinion of you was that you were someone's mistress. Perhaps I even hoped you were. That is no longer the case. I now believe that you are, as you say you are, a vicar's daughter. I can only apologise again for my earlier error. What do you think made me change my mind?"

His question lingered in the air between them, and Prudence fidgeted. "I-I do not quite understand. What do you mean?"

"Oh, perhaps that it was obvious after you kissed me that you never had kissed anyone before."

"So, you mean to say that I was bad at it?"

Her face, he decided, was adorable, and he would have liked nothing better than to kiss her again. But that could not be achieved when he was trying harder than ever to rebuild his reputation as someone honourable.

"I would not want to hurt a gentlewoman's feelings by saying so," Richard said. "Merely that more experimentation might help you."

She gasped at his meaning but said no more.

They settled back into a sort of quiet, false silence, although Richard was well aware that Prudence was pondering and overthinking their entire exchange. It would have been nice, or rather easier, if he had believed her to be just another one of the inane members of society who were keen to gossip and believe the worst of him. But he thought better of her than that. It mattered to him, despite what he had done, that she not hate him. In fact, he would prefer if she were to have warmer feelings towards him. Although he doubted that would be possible.

Hours ticked past. Their silence lapsed, and they resumed talking, touching on the attempted robbery, before moving on to brighter topics. The journey stretched, pausing only to change the horses and allow the travellers to relieve themselves. All the while, Richard waited for the companionship to fade, but he found it growing stronger.

They reached the edge of the Brayton estate as the sun settled low in the valley. Richard watched his family home coming into view through the left side of the carriage. He'd always known that one day he'd have to leave the place since it would be George's. He would visit and see George's family grow up there, but it would be George's responsibility to manage the fifty or so farmers and labourers who worked in the surrounding villages. It would be George's responsibility to make sure that they were protected and looked after. He'd never resented his brother very much, Richard thought, of that he could be truthful. He had never wanted the title or the pressures of it. But deep down inside, he had always wanted Brayton to be his. Had always thought of it as his. To his eyes, it was beautiful.

It was a vast building with over three hundred rooms, but that wasn't what made it special. It was the way the light hit the water at the front of the house, which made the windows shine. It was the handsome staircases throughout the building that he had bumped and rushed his way down as a child. But more than any of that, it was where his mother was. She had died when he was twelve and been buried in the local family church.

Memories of her were what filled Brayton. Sneaking down to the library and finding her there, with book after book piled beside her. Lady Heatherbroke's image had faded now in his mind's eye, and the portraits that remained of her looked stiff and nothing like the warm, loving woman he remembered.

No, in those portraits she looked just like other women. There wasn't anything special about her. He had forgotten some of the more important things in the intervening years about his mother, but he still remembered her reading voice. And her love of peppermints, so that whenever he smelt that peppery sweet scent, he thought of his mother.

"We're here," he said to his daughter, leaning forward and away from Prudence. "Wake up, pet." He tapped Harriet's knee, and the child opened her eyes. She yawned and stretched her little fat arms above her head.

Richard watched her to see any element of her mother peek out. It was strange and almost painful to see so much of Annabelle in the child. It would always be undeniable who her mother was. Still, Richard comforted himself with the knowledge that if he were to raise her, she would start to behave more like his side of the family.

"Here." He leant farther forward in his seat, picked Harriet up, and put her on his lap. He pointed out the window as they drove past the large wrought-iron gates. "Look," he said, "you can see all of Brayton out this window."

"Brayton?"

"It's where we're going to live," he said.

"Will I like it?"

"You'll love it."

The child was so close to him, she was ever so trusting and sweet, that Richard rested his head on top of hers. Her hair tickled his chin. He could smell the scent of soap and the sugar plums that Harriet had eaten. "Once you're settled here, we'll need to get you a tutor," he told her, "and you shall have friends in the village too."

"Friends my own age?" Harriet asked.

"That's correct," Richard said. He didn't think any of his

tenants would dare cause a fuss or would be likely to make any sort of comment on his child. He hoped that his grandmother, the Dowager Marchioness, would have prepared them, or at least made ready some of the more important servants.

"Do you see it?" he asked.

The carriage rounded the corner then, coming out of the woodland that surrounded the outer lawns of the estate and pulling into view of the house.

Beside him, Richard realised that Prudence had looked up. "That's Brayton," he said, unable to keep the pride out of his voice, as it really did look magnificent in the dying sunlight.

Prudence let out a strange sort of gurgle that he assumed was surprise, which was rather gratifying. It was pleasing that she could be impressed by the estate. A little part of him wondered if she might even quite like it.

"What do you think, Miss Pendleton?"

The maid, Miss Armstrong, had woken up, and she took a quick glance out the window before resuming her seat. She looked rather impressed too.

"It's superb," Prudence said.

"Yes, I agree." Their eyes met.

"I've never seen a more beautiful estate…" Her voice trailed off, and then her eyes dropped away from his and returned to looking out of the window.

The carriage pulled up in front of the house, and several of the servants emerged from inside the building. There came with them a sort of hush, and then they parted to make way for the Dowager Marchioness. Richard watched his grandmother approach. She wasn't typical of other elderly ladies who were prominent members of society, he thought. No, his grandmother moved too quickly, did not stick to the fashions, adored painting, and all too frequently, one was likely to discover that she had wedged a paint brush into her hair. In fact, Richard realised when she came to stop in front of the carriage, while she might not have a paint brush placed amongst the grey strands, there was a rather distinct blue smudge on her left cheek. When the carriage door opened, Richard and Harriet were the first to climb out.

"Let me present your granddaughter to you, ma'am. This is Miss Harriet."

The little girl dropped into a curtsy. "How do you do?" she said to her great grandmother.

There was a pause, in which the dowager looked down at the little girl with consideration, and then she smiled. "Why, she looks just like your mother, Lady Heatherbroke. Look at that chin. One couldn't doubt that she was a Cavendish for a moment."

Behind him, still in the carriage, Richard thought he heard Prudence let out a small sigh of relief. Turning, Richard put out his hand and offered it to Prudence to help her out.

"May I also present to you, Miss Pendleton, ma'am?"

The smile that was on the dowager's face fell, and she looked shocked and appalled. The dowager leant forward by just adjusting her hips and tilting herself at an angle. She said in a voice that carried, "Have you gone mad? And brought your mistress here?"

Richard, who had his back to Prudence, couldn't see her initial response, but he felt her push past him. He was rather impressed with Prudence. She squared up to his grandmother, and then said in a loud voice, "Madam. I'm not his mistress, but he did kidnap me."

CHAPTER 12

Her ladyship gasped, her eyes widened, and she turned an angry look on Heatherbroke. It was not a surprise to Prudence to see the response that her statement generated. She was not someone who ever sought out drama or too much excitement, but then again, drama had not occurred much or in any huge amount of frequency in her life—that is, before the arrival of Harriet and, by extension, Heatherbroke. It was the reckless part of her, the dangerous part; if she was honest, the part that had kissed him. She was discovering just how much fun it could be to be a little reckless sometimes.

She looked around now at the flustered older woman, whose shrewd eyes had smiled down at Harriet, but now seemed utterly bewildered.

"Come, Grandmother," Heatherbroke put his hand on the dowager's arm. "Let us go inside. All of us." He motioned his head to include both Harriet and Prudence. "I will endeavour to explain it all in there."

But the dowager was having none of this as she shook off his restraining arm and offered out her hand to Prudence. "I think," she said in a very firm and dignified voice, "I would prefer to hear it all from this young lady. Come, dear."

Feeling she couldn't refuse at this point in time, Prudence took the older woman's hand and allowed herself to be led indoors.

It really was, although she hated to admit it, the most beautiful house she had ever been in. Brayton. Once inside the place, it was even lovelier than it looked from the outside. It wasn't the high ceilings that domed over her head, or the beautiful, large glass windows that sparkled in the sunlight, or the marbled floors, or the paintings that dotted each room. No, despite its size, there was a sense within the house that was the sort of place a family would feel happy in.

"This way." The dowager tugged Prudence along the hallway and then into a parlour.

It was a smart, formal room, one that would have been used as a space to greet guests rather than sit with the family. "You have an honest face," the dowager said, having viewed Prudence for a good minute. Then the older woman took a seat on one of the rather severe looking sofas. She nodded her head to the one opposite for Prudence to sit too.

Prudence took a step forward and then sank down into the opposite sofa. "Thank you, ma'am."

"I am a little defensive of my grandson. But I'm not unaware of his faults. He is the only remaining family I have."

Prudence nodded and bowed her head.

"I have found," Lady Heatherbroke continued, "that my grandson has been judged by his friends for the last few years for his one indiscretion. Judged and condemned. So, you must understand my reaction when you mention or allude to the idea of you being kidnapped."

"I am sorry to disappoint you, but I did not lie," Prudence said, keeping her voice level and maintaining her dignity. "My father, Vicar Pendleton, was caring for Harriet, who I understand is Lord Heatherbroke's child. She and I were out walking and—"

"And you got in the way?"

"I did, yes."

The older woman's eyes dropped, and she raised her hands to her face and let out a sigh. "Oh Richard, Richard," she said. "He is prone to act first and think later."

A tiny part of Prudence was very tempted to tell the dowager that whilst she was furious and frightened in the initial moments of meeting Heatherbroke, his later actions were better. He had seemed high-handed, but not rude, driven by desperation. How he had treated her after she had made a fool of herself, came to mind. His kindness to her and Harriet did speak to a desire to avoid his baser instincts. But how on earth she could describe all this went beyond Prudence's abilities.

Thankfully, she had no need to answer, because it was then that the door opened and in walked Heatherbroke. He nodded at both women and crossed to the fireplace, where he placed his hands on the mantle, before turning back to look between the pair of them. "So, what's my punishment to be?"

"Do not be so flippant," his grandmother snapped. "Perhaps we should say that I was with you the entire time and acted as a chaperone to Miss Pendleton here?"

"That seems like a good idea to me," Prudence said.

"I do not wish for you to lie for me."

"Then what is your solution?"

Heatherbroke turned to look at Prudence, his expression was warm, and for a second, he looked almost boyish. He straightened himself and then said in a clear voice, "Miss Pendleton, would you do me the honour of accepting my hand in marriage?"

Prudence watched him, eager to see some affection on his face, but she couldn't perceive it. She balked at the idea of being forced into matrimony with anyone, despite the potential wisdom of it.

"No, sir," she answered. She couldn't quite explain the little flip her stomach made after she had said no, and how surprised she was to say that. Prudence hadn't been looking at Richard, just through her eyelashes. She could not read his expression, but she was a little shocked to see his eyes dropping to the floor for a fraction of a second. He seemed saddened by her reaction. She wondered if perhaps she had upset him with the speed of her answer. When he spoke, he didn't sound miserable; in fact, his tone was light-hearted.

"Well, there you have it. The woman won't have me. She has good taste."

"My dear," the dowager said, "do you have any family you might have gone to stay with in London, say? Or another part of the country, that would explain your absence from the family home?"

"No, ma'am."

"Give it some thought," the dowager said, "on how this could be explained away. Or if I had any dear friends still active in society from the region..."

"If you could pay for my carriage ride home," Prudence started to say.

"Ahh, but, miss," he said as he stepped forward, "I thought you couldn't be separated from my daughter?"

Their eyes met, and Prudence found herself unable to look away. He was right, of course, that was the reason she had given. That was the reason she had clung to, refusing to go back home when he'd given her the first opportunity and the second. Yes, it was true that she cared for Harriet, but Prudence wondered if there was another reason why she'd chosen to stay with that man. Perhaps, although she didn't like to admit it to herself, she was quite pleased to be on an adventure. To finally be away from Alfriston. Away from everything she had ever seen. And if she was being honest, a chance to be with him.

She wouldn't drop her gaze, though. Blast him and his handsome green eyes, and the way his lips lifted at the edges, wanting to continue teasing her.

"Now I have your assurances, and your grandmother's promise, that Harriet will be well taken care of. She is reunited with her family. I—" Prudence struggled with the words. Her logic for staying with the girl had seemed so firm, but now it seemed less sensible. And the overwhelming danger to her reputation was also becoming clearer now they were back about society.

He took one soft step forward. "Yes?"

This annoyed Prudence no end. He seemed to know how to wind her up and had the power to get under her skin and to annoy her like no one else she had ever met. He even seemed to delight in it, she thought. And yet, all he had to do was smile, and she was ready to grin back at him.

"I have an idea," the dowager said. "Let us maintain that I travelled with my grandson down to... to... where were you kidnapped?"

"Sussex," Prudence supplied. She was conscious of Richard standing so close to her. Conscious of him, and how important he made her feel. It made her want to wriggle and run away from him. But if she were to do that, those feelings would pass, and she didn't want that; there was something most luxuriant about them. Feeling them twist in her stomach. Every time he came within a couple feet of her, she became conscious of it. A sort of increase in temperature that only seemed to affect her body.

"Very well. Sussex," the dowager continued, "and whilst in Sussex, I was taken ill and a very sweet young lady, you, my dear," she nodded her head at Prudence, "you offered to look after me, and we formed quite a bond, so much so that I begged you to be my companion. Does that not fit?"

"Better than any other scenario, although you have never had a companion in your entire life. Doing so now might seem a little out of character," he said.

"But I wrote to my father and told him about Harriet's...

about Lord Heatherbroke. Only about him. And I made no mention of Your Ladyship."

"I also supplied him with my address," he added. "So, the man would know where to find us."

Prudence looked at him then, despite her disloyal limbs. She had not expected him to be so gallant as to let her father know where they would have gone. It went against his own interests to protect Harriet.

"In that case," the dowager said, "I suspect we shall receive a call from a small party from Sussex. In fact, it will be within the next day or two."

"I don't know how my father will react," Prudence let slip.

"Well, you need not fear, our family has learned to take full responsibility for our actions," the dowager said.

The two of them started talking again, and Prudence resumed her seat on the sofa, watching them. She assumed, or at least felt certain, that the dowager's comment was well meant, but in truth, Prudence wasn't sure if she wanted anyone to take responsibility for her. It sounded a little ominous, or naïve. Because she was certain after hearing his proposal earlier, if one could even call it such, that she didn't want him to think of her as a responsibility. It would humiliate her to think that she had forced his hand or that he was trapped into the situation. *No*, Prudence thought, *I will need to work out for myself what I am going to do next.*

Supper, that evening, it was decreed, was to take place in everyone's own room. A young maid of about Prudence's age showed her up the stairs to her bedroom. Prudence watched the little ginger head bob ahead of her on the stairs. The maid appeared to be welcoming enough but did not make very much conversation. It gave her more time to think. They reached the first landing, and the girl led the way down one of the winding corridors, past several doors, before stopping.

"Here we are, miss." The maid pushed open the door to reveal the bedroom within. It was a pleasant room, lit with a soft afternoon light that gleamed on the surfaces and illuminated the handsome, four-poster bed, a neat writing desk, the little fireplace, and several other pieces of well-made furniture. It was decorated in a soft blue, with the carpet, counterpane, and curtains all in the same shade. "Your bag was brought up." The girl pointed to the case he had secured for her.

"Thank you." After the maid left, Prudence made her way across to the bed and flopped down onto it. Her forehead came to rest against the counterpane, and she sucked in steadying breaths. It had been a long day. Her mind kept turning back to the previous night. To that night. She had hoped that one brief experiment would satisfy her curiosity, but it hadn't. In fact, it seemed worse than ever; he'd lit a spark in her she had no idea how to quench. She hadn't been able to stop thinking about him.

She had a lot of sympathy for the Duchess of Woolwich; it would be far too easy to be seduced by Heatherbroke. Of course, Prudence admitted to herself, he wasn't even trying with me, but he had tried with the duchess. Imagine how enthralling that would be. She'd never considered desire as a sensation before, but now it seemed all that she could think about. It had gotten worse throughout the day and would occur at the oddest times.

Her imagination kept running away from her, picturing things that had never once occurred to her before. The idea of Heatherbroke—no, at least in her imagination she could call him Richard—that they could be alone together again. Not that it seemed very likely, but then again, wasn't that what imagination was for? She could paint the whole scene out in her mind's eye now.

She decided she would put them at a picnic, but one held late at night, in the moonlight in fact. She would be wearing a beautiful, pale lace dress, with puffed sleeves and a blue ribbon around her waist. She didn't bother planning what Richard would wear in too much detail. He always appeared to her eyes to be most attractively clothed, and in what appeared to be the most fashionable tan breeches, high boots, waistcoat, shirt, and jacket that she had seen in any of the magazines her stepmother kept.

So, they were on that picnic blanket in the moonlight, with the stars glittering down on them. This time it would be he, who kissed her. He'd start at her lips before moving to her neckline; then, perhaps he would try tugging at her dress a little. That was what she had wanted him to do when she had kissed him last. Her clothes had felt unnecessary. She had also wanted to rip away his clothes, too, so that she could see his chest. So that she could touch him.

Prudence found that she had rolled the counterpane around her. It was bunching now between her legs. She dragged it closer, to wedge it nearer to her core. It was a rather pleasant sensation, the firm way it sat between her legs. In fact, the more frequently she pressed down upon it, she found it brought both relief and a continued level of discomfort. Her whole body felt irritated; she needed to go running through fields somewhere or take a very long bath. But she wasn't satisfied.

So instead, she lay back down on the counterpane and gazed up at the domed material high above her. Well, she supposed she was always going to have to wonder what happened next between a man and a woman.

In the following hour, the food was delivered, and Prudence ate her fill. She went to see Harriet in the nursery with Miss Armstrong and wish the child goodnight. Miss Armstrong and Harriet seemed to have become firm friends after the terror of the robbery, the latter's bubbling sweetness melting whatever reserves the former had. As Prudence made her way back to her own room, she walked past a grandfather clock which told her that it was eight thirty. A little early, if one thought about it. She paused in the hallway, deciding what would be the best course of action for her to take. She was alone, in a huge house in the middle of a county that she had never been to before, surrounded by people she didn't know well. She didn't feel afraid. Perhaps she should have, but the older lady was comforting, the servants pleasant. And as for him… well… she knew him a little better, didn't she?

Prudence bit her lip. She supposed she could go back to her bedroom. She could lie down and try to go to sleep. But the truth was, she wasn't tired. Her mind kept turning back to her earlier question. What happened between a man and a woman? Surely, if she was ever going to find this out, looking in a grand library, that would be available in Brayton, was a good place to start. A good place for her curiosity to never be discovered by her father.

She could have asked her stepmother, but she didn't want to hear the woman's answer. Alternatively, she supposed she might have asked one of the married women in the village for a little more detail, but then they would only ask her why she wanted to know. Lastly, there was always Clara, who liked to pretend that she knew a great deal because she had two older, married sisters. But the truth was, Clara was just as ignorant as Prudence was. Prudence could not go through an adventure such as this and not come back at least a little more knowledgeable. If she were going to have a damaged reputation, she needed to leave Cumbria wiser than she had come to it, Prudence decided, as she pushed her way into the library. She had to know more. Her ignorance over how Harriet had come into being had left both of them vulnerable. She had always prided herself on being a fast reader. There were fascinating, brilliant books that her father owned which had told Prudence how democracy worked, how roads were constructed centuries ago, how the decimal point system functioned. They told the history of different cultures from the Byzantine empire to the Roman and Greek, but none of those books, written as they were for nomadic, bookish men, ever spoke of desire. Which was a shame because it seemed pretty important to Prudence.

THE LIBRARY AT BRAYTON WAS BEAUTIFUL. IT WAS CARPETED IN a mossy green colour, a fine contrast to the wooden shelving that ran the length of the room. Every crevice and every shelf was full of leather-bound books in various shades. There were ladders, too, because running about ten feet high around most of the room was a second level of books. The painted ceiling stretched high above her head. In fact, she thought, as she sank down into one of the cushy armchairs, if any place was going to be a solace to her in her confusion, it would be the familiar sights, sounds, and smells of a library. Even one as beautiful as this one.

Once she got her bearings and could understand how the library was arranged, she knew better how to start. It seemed obvious to begin with the sciences. Having found a book on the shelves that seemed to cover human anatomy, Prudence resumed her seat. The book started with the renderings of a man and a woman. She flicked through the pages, her cheeks growing warmer and warmer. She was not surprised that this sort of book had not been in her father's study. She looked at the bodies again; they were both stripped of their clothes, revealing everything. In all her imaginings of the moonlight and of Richard kissing her, it had never gone further than his shirt coming loose. Her mind had drawn a blank after that. Now she started to imagine more, and Prudence felt she was about to burst into flame.

She raised her hand to her mouth; it was very dry. She looked around the room. In the corner of the library, balanced on top of a handsome oak cabinet, was a decanter of what appeared to be red wine. Desperately flushed and bothered, Prudence got to her feet and went across and poured herself some wine. This wine, though, was far sweeter than anything she had drunk. It was rich and sugary, the most delicious she'd ever tried. She finished her first glass without noticing, poured herself a second rather greedily, and then glanced back to the science book on the chair.

"I will not allow you to defeat me," she said to the book.

Obviously, the book did not respond. The idea that it could, made Prudence laugh out loud, the noise reverberating in the silent house.

Deciding that it would be best to have a third glass to help her get through the rest of the contents of the book, Prudence sloshed yet more liquid into the glass and tripped as delicately as she could back to the armchair. She wriggled herself into a more comfortable position within its squishy confines, dragging her bare feet up onto the seat, and folding her dress around her knees. This was the same position she adopted in her father's study.

"That's better," she declared, as she propped the book open to better study its contents.

The page, detailing the elements of the male characteristics, confused her no end. Its instructions seemed to Prudence to be brutal and not at all similar to what she had felt when Richard had kissed her.

"That's not right," she said. "At least, I don't think it should be."

"What is not right?" came a masculine voice from behind her.

Prudence pivoted in her chair; in honesty, she hadn't been too surprised to see him. It was only eight thirty in the evening; he didn't want to go to bed. The idea of his bed, of him being in it, made Prudence blush.

"I wanted to do some light reading before bed," Prudence improvised. She was still a bit embarrassed about her refusal to his marriage offer.

Heatherbroke strolled forward. Once he had reached her chair, he plucked the book from Prudence's unresisting fingers. He flipped through the pages. One of his eyebrows lifted in a quizzical expression, and his mouth compressed into a thin line. "You do surprise me, Miss Pendleton."

"Well, you see, there isn't anything like this in my father's study."

"I would imagine not. Not to mention others that wouldn't be included, such as books of poetry, say, books that would tell you a great many things that I presume a vicar would not want his young daughter to know."

"But that's a problem, don't you see? How can I keep being so ignorant? It puts me in danger." *Of you*, she thought. But she didn't want him to know that.

"But I thought that was the whole point," Heatherbroke said. "I thought you just wanted to return to your little village and never leave it again. After the recent stress, involving a kidnapping and a robbery, I couldn't blame you. Embracing the idea of ignorance is bliss, no?"

"What made you think that?" Prudence leant forward in her seat as she spoke and knocked the wine over. It flowed across the carpet, the reddish liquid staining the soft beautiful green carpet. "Oh no," Prudence cried. "I'm so sorry." She dropped down on her hands and knees and started scrubbing the liquor with her handkerchief.

But Heatherbroke didn't move. Only after a minute did he, too, drop down next to her.

"How much of that claret did you drink?"

"Oh, I don't know. A glass or two," Prudence said. The stain seemed pretty bad to her.

He was so close to her now, which rather startled Prudence when she looked up and met his eyes. There was only a foot or so between them, and he was smiling at her. Reaching out his hand towards her and cupping her face between his fingers, they started moving against her skin, until one of them came to rest over her lips.

"Are you going to make a habit of this?" he asked.

"What do you mean?" Prudence felt inordinately slow in his presence. Perhaps it was the effect of his presence, or the wine; she wasn't certain.

"Well, no matter where I go at night, you seem to be there."

"It wasn't done deliberately," said Prudence. Although if she were honest with herself, she did hope that he might find her. She shook her head, dislodging his hand. She shouldn't let herself think like that. "But I don't understand," she said.

"What's that?"

Prudence got to her feet and moved across the library's carpet. It was being back in his presence once again. It rendered all the well-thought-out arguments she had a little fuzzy.

"What do you not understand, Miss Pendleton?" he asked.

"I thought," she said, "if I read about what happens between a man and a woman, then

I'd understand what happened between you and the duchess."

"Would that make you feel better?"

"It would at least be a comfort to know. I am tired of being so ignorant."

"I think a lot of men like their women to be innocent of those facts."

"Do you?" Prudence could not quite believe that she had asked him that. It had to be the wine, she reasoned; it had just given her an unusual sense of confidence in his presence.

Heatherbroke had unbuttoned his coat and taken out his handkerchief. He laid it over the spilt wine. He did not meet her eye and instead focused on the stain, watching the fine white linen soak up the red.

"I couldn't say."

"Why not?" Prudence took another step towards him, closing the distance. She would have loved to have taken one more step closer and feel his breath stir her dress as he gazed up at her. To be aware of him, and the scent that was his, woodsmoke, cigarettes, and whatever it was that made Richard, Richard.

"I think you should go to bed, Prudence."

"Why will you not tell me?"

"Because it is impossible to tell someone. Or it is possible to tell them the mechanics of the act, but the only way you will ever understand it is if you feel the sensation of lovemaking."

CHAPTER 13

It was so tempting to look into Prudence's innocent face and see the changing emotions there, as she watched him with curiosity. Her dark eyebrows drew down as she frowned, as she dwelt on his words.

"No, a sensation isn't quantifiable, not in a real way," she told him. She was bewitching, he thought, as she sat down on the carpet.

"There are feelings, emotions, that only one person can judge?" he asked.

"Well, I'm not going to find that in a book," she replied.

"At least, not in a science book."

Richard got to his feet; she was tipsy, he could tell. She seemed very relaxed with him and ever so trusting. The explanation was that Prudence seemed to have faith in him. That rather moved him. He offered his hand to help her to her feet. This, he realised as he held her hands, was a real challenge; being in her presence was intoxicating. Every time he was, he wanted to kiss her. Perhaps if he were to kiss her, he would convince her that he was serious in his proposal. "High time you went upstairs, Miss Pendleton."

Once she was on her feet, Prudence did not appear steady. Instead, she clung to his arm in a very dependent manner. "I'm sorry," she said. "I shouldn't have told your grandmother about the kidnapping. Sometimes, I do the wrong thing."

"We can all be guilty of that," Richard said. He was not going to hold a grudge against her. Especially given that Prudence was telling the truth. The realisation that she was honest had come to him in inevitable, undeniable waves, and now it beat against his mind. In a manner designed to torture him, not that he deserved better. He hated himself for not believing her before, and the guilt for mistreating her far exceeded any mistake he had made with Annabelle. "It was all my fault. I acted without thought, or rather with only one."

Her large blue eyes stared up into his. They looked so guileless and trusting that, for a brief second, Richard wondered if he could scrub away all his past, would it be worth it? That if she had accepted his marriage proposal this afternoon, would he be purged of his guilt? He wished Prudence had said yes. He had played out the idea in his mind, and it seemed like a happy enough conclusion. Was it worth washing away that sinful night with Annabelle for a chance with someone who was as sweet, clever, and as promising as Prudence was?

For just a few moments, he told himself it would be his greatest desire if that were possible. To have the simple, straightforward option, to be able to offer Prudence what other men could, an untarnished reputation. Then he looked back at her and knew that whatever else happened between them, she wasn't the simple option. She was brave and daring, and he was lucky to be in her company.

"Come on, you should go upstairs. You shouldn't stay here with me," he said.

But she still held on to his sleeve. The cotton of his shirt caught between her delicate fingers. "I don't think you've earned your reputation."

"No?"

"You're not a wicked seducer," she said, "since it was me who made a fool out of myself, not you."

He thought of her innocent kisses back in Derby.

She had taken a step back now, away from him. She swayed a little on her feet, her handsome figure unsteady as she tried to remain upright. This attempt lasted only for a minute before she went and leant against the table, propping herself up. "That's better. Yes, as I was saying, I don't think you're much danger to anybody. You are nothing like some of the moustache-twirling villains in one of those books. They are always obvious and not a bit like you."

"I thought you didn't read very many of them."

"No," she admitted, "but Clara talks about them all the time. She loves a good villainous character. It is always about ravishment and all that. It seems to happen a great deal. Clara reads them to me so we can be prepared."

"And that's what you thought I'd be like?"

"Well, yes," Prudence said, "after what happened. It seemed logical."

"Then why didn't you run away?"

"Because I couldn't leave Harriet. And then…" Here, she leant forward, still holding on to the table for balance. "Because I'm good at reading people, at seeing what they're like. And if you'd wanted to do that—that ravishment—to me, you would have done so already. It's not in your nature."

"Perhaps it only used to be."

"Or perhaps I'm not your type. I don't stir those sorts of emotions in you." She raised a finger and pointed at him. "Yes, that's it."

If only you knew, thought Richard. He bunched his fists to his side and let out an uneven breath. Prudence was the most beautiful girl he'd ever seen, and she stirred desires in him more than he ever thought possible. "You don't understand."

"Because it's about the sensation?"

"Because it's about that and it being mutual."

"How does one know when it is mutual?" She smiled at him then. Despite the fact that she'd had several glasses of claret, Richard felt certain she was flirting with him. It was rather endearing, of course, and tempting.

"Are you teasing me?" he asked, taking a step towards her.

Prudence stayed where she was, against the table, eyeing him confidently.

"I might be," she said, gazing at him with the most appealing look. "I realise that many people don't tease you. It doesn't go well with being a marquess. They might not think it's appropriate."

"But you disagree?"

"I think everyone should be teased."

"I suppose that's true." He had drawn within a couple of inches of her. Just to be near to her, was to be aware of the sweet, warm scent of roses that was at the essence of Prudence. Now the smell blended with the slight lingering fragrance of claret. A boozy and intoxicating blend. He reached out a hand and touched the edge of her dress. Just the edge, held between his forefinger and his thumb. It was part of the skirt, close to her hip. Her eyes shot up, and she looked at him. Between them, he could feel the tension, the raw, rubbing feel of a coiled spring which could be eased down or released.

"Do you want me to stop?" he asked.

"Stop what?" Her hands lifted and first came to rest on his forearms, almost like she considered dancing with him before she raised her hands higher and came to place them on his shoulders. "It's nice," she said, "having you so close. I don't understand why."

Richard's hands had moved to her waist, and he lifted her onto the table so she was sitting on the surface. Their faces were inches apart. He lowered himself and started nuzzling a slow trail of kisses along her jawline, listening as he moved along her skin, listening for her response. The breath hitched in her throat, and she let out a little moan. Her skin was soft cream and tasted like it was dipped in honey. He would go as slow as she needed him to, as delicately as he could, using all his willpower to stop himself going any further. "How does that feel?"

"Mhm." She had leant back.

When he glanced up to check on her, she was smiling at him through partly lowered lashes. She was such a stunning sight that Richard caught his breath. God, he thought, if he were a better man, he would stop. He reached out a finger to lift a piece of her hair, moving it off her face. The silken glide of her hair was so moving to him. The dark tress seemed to fit around his finger, and with his left hand, he slotted his fist amongst the beautiful strands, angling her face up once more and kissing her.

Prudence wriggled against him, pushing herself more up against his body, her breasts flush against his chest, her legs widening so that Richard could stand between them. Her hands lifted and wrapped around his neck, and she resumed kissing him, responding with a little start when he eased his tongue into her mouth.

"Do you want me to stop?" he asked, easing himself back a little, but not stepping away from her.

"This is what you meant about sensation?" She was still clinging to his shoulders. "Is this why people sin?"

Richard nodded. Her features were flushed with a delicate tinge of pink, visible even in the candlelit library. "Some people find they are unable to stop."

"I can see why." She giggled and then raised a hand to her mouth. "I shouldn't have told you that."

She was adorable, and Richard felt himself touched by her innocence. He was moved by her and wished more than ever she had accepted his offer. He knew he would never be such a cad as to take advantage of her. But he wanted her to say yes, yes because she wanted to, not because she was compromised. "Come on," he said, trying to take a step back, "I should—"

"No." She clung to him. "Was that all that happens?"

"I thought you had read that science book. So, you're now the expert, aren't you?"

Her eyes dropped from his, down to gaze at his lower body, and Richard felt himself stir against his breeches, becoming even more aroused. Each time he was near Prudence, he doubted that he could become any more attracted to her, but then she would look at him, as she was doing now, and it was overwhelming.

"No, it isn't everything," he said.

"Can you not show me?" She still held on to him, and with his patience and desire close to snapping, Richard stepped closer to her once more, wedging himself between her skirts, feeling her thighs part for him.

"No one," she said with a light sort of laugh, "will believe that nothing ever happened between us."

"So, you want to make it a reality?"

"If this is my one chance," she said, her voice bright and optimistic, although the bravery didn't quite reach her expression, "before I have to go back home and stay quiet forever, then why shouldn't I?"

Richard knew there was more to her statement, more to what Prudence had alluded to, but he doubted she would tell him right now. "Lean back," he told her.

"What?" She tilted her head to one side and frowned up at him.

"Do as I say." He returned his hands to her waist and eased her farther back, until she was lying flat against the table, her legs dangling down, unable to reach the floor. With one quick movement, he flicked her skirts up, exposing her long limbs which were clothed in cream-coloured drawers. Carefully, he ran his hand over her legs. He paused when he reached her hips, drawing his fingers over the cotton material, to linger where her sex was. She was warm under the cloth, and a little wet, and she lifted her hips when his hand nudged against her mound.

"What—"

"Stay still," Richard told her. She fidgeted and let out a strange sort of sigh, her breathing a little loud in such a quiet space. Again, Richard returned his hand to the slit in Prudence's drawers, and he eased the cotton apart, bringing the folds of fabric past her hips, down over her thighs, then over her knees and ankles, before it pooled on the ground. Her skin was soft, golden in the light, he thought, as he came to stand between her legs. Immediately, her hands flew to try to cover herself.

"I..." he heard her whisper.

"I thought you wanted me to show you what happens?" Her hands dropped away.

He stepped closer to her once again, so that the front of his breeches grazed against her sex. Then he leant down and started kissing her, moving lower to work his way from her neck to her breasts, to her stomach, kissing his way over her skin and through the dress. He reached around behind her dress and loosened her stays, the corset bunching open at the front and allowing him to pull the seams apart, exposing her breasts. They were perfect, small, and pink tipped, with nipples that darkened from the centre out. From this position, he reasoned, it would be possible to remove the dratted item, but it was enough that he could see her breasts. Tentatively, he cupped one, and Prudence lifted herself more fully into his hand. As he kissed her, Prudence held on to him hungrily. Richard stole back between her legs with his fingers, back down to her sex, parting it as delicately as he could. She shuddered under his hand.

"How does that feel?" He lifted his head to try to read her face, his fingers sliding around the little bud of her sex. He pressed in every now and then, before letting his hand graze lightly over the entrance to her sex.

"Hmm," she said.

His finger slid a little way inside her entrance, and Prudence's hips buckled. "More," she said, her hand trying to grab at his.

Richard eased his hand away. This would be some kind of torture, but Prudence deserved better than to live her entire life wondering if she could have made a better choice than him. Still, he could give her something to remember him by, without losing his soul. He could give her that, he thought.

With deftness, he lifted her once more, farther onto the table, hoping it would support both of their weight. As he moved her, she clung to him, her legs wrapping around his midsection. Her loose hair tumbled over them both.

"What are we doing?"

"This." Richard leant back and lowered himself farther down her body until his face was poised over her sex. In the faint light from the candles, he could make out the dark curls of her mound. They were in stark contrast to her pale thighs and the small slither of her pink sex. Parting the folds with his fingers, he started kissing his way, coaxing his lips over the shape of her clit, feeling her flex beneath him. She tasted delicious, as good as honey, the sort of elixir the gods in myths wrote poetry about, and just as intoxicating.

Prudence wriggled frantically, the beat and pulse between the pair of them undeniable. With her hands, Prudence started massaging her way along his shoulders, over his shirt. Her fingertips dug into the muscles of his back.

He pushed himself back and loosened his cravat, the silken material bunching and catching beneath his shaking fingers. Kissing her was more than Richard had imagined; this, being able to taste her and kiss her everywhere, felt like some sort of divine torture.

"More," she said, her head raised a little from the table. She looked dazed by his actions, he thought with satisfaction. He lowered his head once again and resumed kissing her. Using his fingers and tongue, he pressed shallowly into her sex, driving Prudence higher and higher with each lick. She fidgeted and wriggled against the onslaught, but Richard kept his free hand rooted on her hips, keeping her steady.

From deep within her throat, there came a strange sort of moaning cry that went on. Knowing that she was close to her release, Richard kept up the rhythmic movement of his tongue and fingers until he felt her body reach its peak. She quivered and gasped out his name before she stilled, completely spent.

He kissed her sex once more and then stepped back, turning away from her. She was so beautiful there, lying in what seemed to be perfect bliss, gazing up at the ceiling, that he was ever so tempted to undo his breeches and ease himself into her. He doubted he would have lasted very long. He shook his head, clearing the image away. No, she deserved better than that. *Besides*, he reminded himself, *you promised yourself that you wouldn't let another woman be hurt by your actions.*

Richard returned to the table and eased Prudence's skirt back down over her legs, before placing his hand around her back and bringing her into a sitting position. He saw a look of hurt surprise play across her beautiful features, before she glanced up into his face with a smile.

"That isn't everything, I mean, the book—"

"That is all that can happen between us." He stepped back and started to try to re-tie the dropped folds of his cravat.

Prudence had hugged her arms around her sides in a protective gesture. "Is that because of the duchess?"

"What about her?"

"That you're still in love with her?"

Richard grimaced. That was what a majority of people, including his own grandmother, had assumed. Why else would someone act as he had? Turning his back on Prudence, Richard crossed the room and went to his desk in the corner of the library.

He drew out a key and slotted it into a drawer, before taking out Annabelle's love letters.

Richard crossed the room to where Prudence was sitting. She had picked up her drawers whilst his back was turned. She had either clambered back into them or had hidden them. He handed her the letters.

"What's this?" she asked.

"They're... well, I guess you could say they're love letters."

"Ones you wrote to her?"

"No."

"Why don't you tell me yourself?" Prudence asked. "What happened? I assume these are your proof that you're telling the truth. That it was mutual. But I'd rather hear your version."

Yet again, Richard found himself surprised by her. She was turning down the evidence that would clear his name. Instead, she only wished to hear his version of events.

"I would guess," she added, "you've never shown this to anyone who might—"

"I've never shown them to anyone, but you."

"Go on then, I don't need the proof. Tell me what happened."

"After George's death," Richard started. It was hard to describe the state he'd been in, after witnessing George's fall. It was caused by a startled horse, something which was an everyday occurrence in Hyde Park. But not on that day. His brother was laughing over one of the Oxford Set's recent exploits and a planned trip up to Paris to fetch Woolwich back home, and in the next flash, George had disappeared from view, thrown down to ground by his loyal stallion.

"He was dead by the time I reached him," Richard said. Most of his friends had already driven off to the coast, so none of them were home, or around, when Richard needed them. A constable was found, and then the doctor, before the undertaker was sent for. Richard knew this must have happened, but he could not remember any of it. He had gone home and tried to write to his grandmother.

He glanced up at Prudence; she was watching him from her seat on the table with a mixture of worry and touching concern. "The news surrounding the death of the Marquess of Heatherbroke travelled with pace through town. My first visitor insisted on being seen."

"It was the duchess?"

"Yes." Richard remembered the young married matron, pushing her way past his butler, refusing to be sent away. She was the only woman amongst the Set and was therefore used to being listened to. Her bonnet was shoved on, and she seemed to be concerned for him. He recalled being touched that she cared enough to come. She had sent the butler out to get tea and hidden his whiskey on a shelf. She had held Richard's hands and gazed into his face. Only with hindsight, did Richard feel wary about the manner in which she had regarded him.

"My poor, poor Richard. I've heard about what happened from Lady Morris, and I just had to see you. And of course," Annabelle had said, her dark brown dress pressed against his feet, with her chin resting on his knee. He still remembered the feel of her breath on his hands as she gazed up at him. *"Of course, you are now the marquess."*

That thought had registered in Richard's mind before that moment. Now it seemed an overwhelming, herculean burden laid on his shoulders. There would be some people in the capital, even in his acquaintance or Annabelle's, who might think that Richard would be pleased at the turn of events. Now he was a marquess. Now he was wealthy with a title, land, and purpose. He would have given it all up to have George back.

"I hadn't thought of that," he had told Annabelle.

"No, of course, you hadn't, that isn't like you."

He was playing through the memory. He was recalling all the little things that Annabelle had said. Now he was older and more cynical, he recognised the mercantile gleam in Annabelle's eyes as she discussed his acquired rights.

"I must insist you have some tea," she said.

He would have preferred to have kept on drinking the whiskey. It seemed the only logical choice in such a situation. To drink until the day's tragedy faded, just enough for him to sleep. He allowed her to continue fussing over him. As much as he knew it would be better for her to leave, it was still nice to have a familiar, feminine presence with him.

He looked up from his memories and into Prudence's face; the contrast of the real concern and the sugary falseness of Annabelle now seemed a tell-tale sign. He was annoyed he hadn't spotted it all the way back then.

"So, she stayed with you," Prudence said.

"That's right, she stayed. The hours went by, and at first, I was grateful for the company. She... she always was very practical. She had a lot of things organised and helped me with that." Richard hated facing the weakness he had shown back then.

"I lost my mother," Prudence said, taking his hand, "when I was small. But I had my father to rely on throughout. You had no one."

"Does one always need somebody to help one get through such losses?" he asked. Unsure if he meant his brother, or his parents, maybe he meant both. He clung to her hand. It was such a solace to have her close. But his mind dragged him back to that fateful night.

"You know, my dearest, you were always my favourite amongst the Set," Annabelle had said.

"Phah." Richard remembered laughing at the idea of that and telling her, "Only as the delightful younger brother you could order around, command as you like. I am the pet of the group, the young idiot."

"Not at all." She had come over and grasped his arms, forcing him to hold on to her and gaze down into her pretty face.

She was perfection, he remembered thinking, but off limits. That way danger lay.

"*God, what nonsense, you could have had the pick of us on your come out,*" *he had told her.*

"*But not you.*"

"*Come now, Annabelle, you can't be serious.*"

In response, Annabelle had lifted her hand and unbuttoned a section of her gown, revealing the swell of her breasts. Her eyes had travelled to Richard's in open invitation.

"And you engaged in…" Prudence's voice trailed off, as she made a gesture with her hands, to indicate the act that Richard and she had enjoyed on the very table she sat on.

Richard smiled at her. "It was nothing like that, I can promise you."

Back in his study in London, all those years ago, the servants had retired to bed. One of them was sent with a message up to Brayton for the dowager. So, there had only been Annabelle, gazing up at him imploringly.

"*You have no idea what it is like between Jasper and me.*" *She reached up and placed her hand on Richard's face.* "*Or what I would do, were I given my choice again.*"

"*Woolwich is a good man,*" *Richard remembered saying.*

Annabelle took no notice of his words. She pressed herself against him; her hand had dropped from his face and was already starting on the buttons of his breeches.

"*I never said he wasn't,*" *she said,* "*but he doesn't look at me the way you do.*"

"So, you went further with her?"

"That is correct." Richard released Prudence's hand. It was a night he hoped would have no consequences. He'd received Annabelle's letters for three weeks afterwards. Richard had ignored these missives, embarrassed by his actions. It turned out that when Woolwich had heard of George's death and made his way to the French coast, bad weather had stopped him from crossing the channel for weeks. There, of course, had been Annabelle's undoing; she could not pass Harriet off as Woolwich's.

"When did you find out she was going to have Harriet?" Prudence asked.

"When Lynde, Verne—God, the whole bloody Set—all my brother's friends, well, they were supposed to be my friends too, when the lot of them arrived at Brayton…" He recalled the scene with painful precision. "Woolwich hates me. He'd let them all know that I had defiled his wife."

"She never denied that?" Prudence asked.

"She insisted I had tricked her. So, they cut me dead. Said I was not to return to London, not to address them again. Woolwich wanted to shoot me. It's thanks to Verne I'm still here."

"Why didn't you show them Annabelle's letters?"

"If they thought me capable of that, of doing that to a woman, then I never knew them," he replied. He had handed the letters to Prudence, and it felt like a release to have those envelopes in her hands. "Besides which, I didn't want Woolwich to go after Annabelle in her condition. She had lied to her husband, made him believe that I was the villain. I could at least let her have that."

"But it was a lie."

"Yes, a necessary one. No one was to know about the child. The duke wanted me to be tormented by it."

"But you found her?"

"Only thanks to a friend of mine."

The minutes ticked by, and Richard waited for her reaction. He had never told anyone the whole story before.

"I am sorry." Prudence pocketed Annabelle's letters and got to her feet. She walked over to him. She cupped his cheeks between her hands before she kissed his forehead. Then, she slipped from the library.

Richard watched her go. It had felt like a blessing, that kiss. He could feel it throughout his body, feel it reverberate through him, the loss of her. He wanted to call after her, for the consolation she offered, a sanctuary that he hadn't felt in years. But she had already left the room, and Richard had no choice but to sink back into the armchair and feel grateful for the brief moment of solace she had given him. Still, he reasoned, they had time, time for her to warm to him, time for her to see that marriage to him wouldn't be so terrible. He hoped this was true, as he was falling in love with her.

CHAPTER 14

Prudence awoke the next morning, determined not to feel guilty for what had happened the night before. It was too wonderful, too exciting, too exhilarating to be dismissed. And since Richard had not gone as far as the book had alluded to, that final last step was still hers to decide. The problem, Prudence thought, as she lay in bed, was imagining going any further with anyone but Richard.

Shaking her head with disgust at the idea of some other random man, Prudence sat up in her bed. From around the curtains, she could see the faint light of the new day.

As the dowager had said yesterday, it wouldn't be long until her father arrived. Surely, she reassured herself, the journey would have forced the vicar to soften a little. Prudence hoped more than believed this to be the case.

Yesterday, Prudence had only understood the dowager's loyalty. Now, having read the duchess' letters, she understood Richard's fear of betrayal and liars.

Climbing out of bed and making her way over to the little travelling case, Prudence selected some of the items that Clarence had chosen for her. They were all a little oddly sized, but with a few well-placed ribbons, it wouldn't matter.

Hastily, she pulled on the pale pink gown, the colour complimenting the dark waves of her hair and her English rose complexion. Prudence stared at herself in the mirror above the fire. She wondered how she would compare to the sophisticated duchess, who would know everything that was to be known about being a proper lady.

Except fidelity, a voice whispered with vehemence.

Prudence pursed her lips; after last night, who was she to cast any judgement on finding him desirable? In her mind, she painted the image of Woolwich as some terrifying vision of opulence, with double chins and an awful temper. The duchess had come alive in her love letters, and whilst Prudence might feel for the woman, she found she could not excuse their lies.

Deciding she would be best asking the dowager, Prudence made her way out of the room and down the corridor. She went first to Harriet's bedroom.

"Good morning, little one."

Harriet was playing on the floor with Miss Armstrong. The latter bobbed a curtsey and drew back to fetch herself some tea.

"How do you like it here?" Prudence asked, sinking into the floor next to Harriet and gazing at the drawing the little girl had painted.

Harriet said, "Richard said I can stay here forever and ever. That this house is to be mine."

"Do you like the idea of that?"

"It's very big." Harriet leaned against Prudence's side. She cuddled nearer and accepted the arm that Prudence wrapped around her shoulder.

"Would you like it if it were just the three of you?"

"As in Father, you, and me?"

"I will need to go home soon," Prudence said.

"Stay." Harriet wriggled closer to Prudence. "If I ask Father, couldn't you stay?"

"That wouldn't be appropriate," Prudence said.

"What does that mean?"

"I can't stay, even if I'd like to."

"Why not?"

"I need to go home and look after *my* father." Even to her own ears, it sounded weak.

Prudence shook her head. She didn't want to be a governess, not after the passion she'd experienced with Richard. She wanted more than that. "But I hope that I will be able to visit you, and when you're older, we shall meet often. I will also think of you as my fairy child."

In a desperate act to distract herself from another flash of pain at the prospect of separating, Prudence kissed Harriet's cheek repeatedly, and the little girl squirmed and jumped away, giggling at the attention. If only she could wave her hand and fix the situation, Prudence thought, but it was not like there was an easy solution to an affair, a ruined reputation, to an illegitimate child.

"Come, child." Prudence got to her feet. "Shall we go and explore your new home?"

Harriet jumped up. "I want to see the ponies."

The two of them waved goodbye to Miss Armstrong and made their way through the grand hallways of Brayton, discussing how long Harriet would have to wait until she could start learning to ride. It was her dearest wish, she declared. That, and to have a puppy.

"What would you like?" Harriet asked as she swung off Prudence's hand.

Before Prudence could answer, she became aware that they were being watched. Her eyes lifted from Harriet and searched the hall, seeing Richard at the far end. He was smartly dressed in a dark blue morning coat, with a handsome waistcoat edged in a little gold. It was striking against his sharp, masculine good looks. He looked so at ease, so in his own sphere, that Prudence couldn't help but envy him, in a place that was so his own.

Upon their entrance, he had glanced up, and he was now gazing at them with a mixture of curiosity and something else, something a little darker and more regretful.

"Good morning," Prudence called out to him. Part of her knew others might have reacted in embarrassment after what happened in the library, but she couldn't force herself to feel a certain way, and all she felt was happiness. Someone, perhaps it was Clara, or even Clara's mother, Mrs. Blackman, had once said, "Tomorrow's problems are just that, and can't be solved today."

Richard came towards them, laying down the notepad and stack of papers he'd been carrying. He dropped down to one knee before Harriet and grinned at her with the same excitable look she adopted herself.

"Did I hear someone mention horses?"

"Yes," cried Harriet, her loud voice echoing around the hall, bouncing off the handsome portraits and furniture that lined the walls. "Can I ride one? Oh, please."

Glancing up at Prudence, Richard raised an eyebrow, before saying, "How about we just greet them at first? Horses don't like to be surprised all at once. We could work our way up from there."

Harriet's excitement ebbed a little, but she nodded and followed after him. Tentatively, as he was worried that his daughter might spook, Richard reached down and took the girl's small hand in his. They looked so mismatched and created such a contrast, that it forced a strange sort of lurch in Prudence's chest, to see *her* girl with him.

"Aren't you coming, too, Miss Pendleton?" Richard asked. He had pushed open one of the side doors to the house and was about to walk out into the sunlight.

Prudence followed in their wake, hearing snippets of their

conversation, all of it focused on the horses. The grounds that they walked through were as handsome as the interiors of Brayton. The front lawns stretched out as far as the eye could see. There was a lake in front of the house that was dotted with floating lilies and, off in the distance, a small island that one could row to in the height of summer. Across the shimmering watery surface, Prudence could see herons and swans.

She had no doubt that Richard and his brother had gone fishing in that lake many times over the years. She could even imagine them swimming in it, but only when it was very warm. The pale blue sky was decorated with fluffy clouds playing across it, and in the far distance, Prudence could make out the shape of the vast, northern hills that surrounded them. The hilly lifts that were coated in sprouting browns and greens filled in the rest of the view, and their grandness put the Sussex Downes to shame.

She had read about this part of the world, had read about so many fascinating places, and had thought that those writings were the limit of what she would ever see. None of these pages did justice to such a landscape and being in this setting really was a luxury. But this was only part of the reason she'd felt so drawn to Brayton. She would have liked to think it was because of the overwhelming beauty of the house and grounds, but really, it had far more to do with the enjoyable, seductive and, as she was discovering, rather sweet gentleman before her.

"I find I must thank you for last night," Richard said after Harriet had lulled into silence and made her way off to look more closely at the lake.

With an uncertain look, Prudence stole a glance at him, but he looked sincere, his handsome features stilled and reflective. "Is that so?" she asked, feeling certain she should never have thought of him as sweet; that was a real mistake, and his curved, smiling lips were warning her so.

"Indeed." He grinned once more. "There are very few people I trust enough to discuss my brother with. So, I was relieved to have been able to... talk through the grief that occurred with someone who understood. I found it most helpful. The whole evening." The way he drew out the final choice of words convinced Prudence that he didn't just mean their conversation.

"I..." Prudence wondered how she should reply, even though she could tell that he was teasing her. She decided to be serious. "It is a comfort to discuss loss with someone who has experienced it, too."

"It is. I imagine you miss your mother every day."

"I have this necklace that keeps her with me. It is a remembrance of love, I like to think." Prudence touched the cross at her throat.

"You were prepared to trade it for Harriet's safety."

"For a person I love, it did not seem as important."

"I have never had the opportunity." He paused, glancing back at Prudence, saw her face, and laughed good naturedly, "No, please believe me. I have never had the opportunity to talk through the details of what occurred between myself and Annabelle, to clear my mind in that manner. I had no idea how useful it would be, to be able to lay it all bare, so to speak."

"Thank you," Prudence said.

"I find myself in your debt." He was gazing at her in a way that Prudence did not quite understand; he expected her to take his meaning.

Being so close to him, brought with it a mixture of the good and the bad, Prudence thought. Seeing the flecks of soft brown in his eyes that were now visible in the daylight, illuminating all the lines that composed his handsome face, a strong jawline and beautiful lips created an attractive visage, but it was also tormenting, as it was a face she did not wish to let go of. It would have been nice—no, more than that—it would have been heavenly to cling to his arm and walk through the sunlit, beautiful summery lawns, being teased and daring to tease him back. But the threat of tomorrow or the day after that, when she would need to leave, still lingered. Prudence dropped her arm from his hold and took a step back away from him. "I hope, Miss Pendleton, you did not regret—"

"No, sir."

"Perhaps you might feel comfortable enough to call me Richard, and I may call you Prudence? At least, when we are alone?" He looked at her with those large green eyes, and Prudence wondered how anyone could ever refuse him anything.

"No..." she said. "I don't think we should become too informal with each other. That would not be wise."

Heatherbroke nodded, and they walked in silence along the pathway.

They had rounded the corner of the estate, and only twenty yards away, was a handsome looking stable, with several horses being groomed outside it. At least three stable-boys milled this way and that, fetching the horses out and caring for the animals.

"Yes, I suppose I can see the sense of your words," Heatherbroke said. He paused, his free hand shooting out and holding on to Prudence's arm, bringing her much closer to him than before, so that his breath stirred the hair near her ear. The action made Prudence blink and quiver with the memory of last night. "I suppose that is sensible. You have no idea how tempting it is to repeat last night's... indiscretion. Or how delicious you taste."

Prudence's entire face flushed, and she felt herself wobble against him. Heatherbroke continued to hold her, pressing himself into her side, so she felt secure but also warmed by him. It was a dizzying combination.

The two of them waited together for Harriet to join them. Prudence was certain she could not step away from him. With a quick squeeze of her hand, Heatherbroke released her and went and scooped up his daughter.

"Shall you meet these wild beasts?"

Harriet waved her hands in the air, and Prudence smiled at the sight before swallowing down her embarrassment and following after them.

"This one is called Pegasus," Heatherbroke told Harriet. He lifted her up to stroke the bay's neck.

"Is that because he can fly?" Prudence had walked forward, close to where the pair of them were.

"Something like that. At least, when you ride Pegasus, it feels like that."

She moved away from the two of them. It was too easy, that was what Mrs. Blackman's statement lacked, Prudence realised. It came with no warning of what one might lose if they clung to the present day. Prudence forced her face to relax as she looked back at Heatherbroke and his daughter.

"Someone hasn't had their breakfast."

"Not hungry."

"Now that is a shame," Heatherbroke said as he picked Harriet up again and placed her on his shoulders. "Your great-grandmother has prepared something rather special for us. And I'm afraid that it does include food. Do you think you might reconsider?"

"What is it?"

"Follow me," Richard said. Every so often, Richard would pretend to stumble and cause Harriet to giggle. They walked, Prudence bundling up her pink skirts and laughing at how over the top Heatherbroke's movements were. They left the stables and cut through the edges of the woodland, weaving their way past the trees and hedges. It brought back memories to Prudence of the forests in Sussex. It missed only the sights and smells of Sussex, salt from the sea and the cry of seagulls.

Heatherbroke had kept walking, and Prudence continued on her way beside him, her thoughts in turmoil. She realised her rejection had come too soon, too abrupt, but how on earth could she let him know that? Whenever she glanced up at him, she saw that he was watching her with a sort of soft interest.

Around them, the scenery had changed. The lawn sloped downward at a slight right angle. Harriet had chosen to roll down it, whereas Richard offered his arm to Prudence. This time she took it. It was a comfort. Nice, to be close to him. It had been so earlier, but it was even more so now. She struggled to better understand why her father had shielded her so much, shielded her until she had monkeyed his words for her.

The slope had levelled out and revealed a rather stunning sight. It wasn't visible from the house, but to the left of the lake, tucked in by the shores, was a neat little Grecian building.

All of it was white stone and pillars, its roof gleaming in the sunlight. Sat at a table in the centre of it was Lady Heatherbroke. When she saw them, she raised her hand in greeting to them all.

"Is it like a picnic?"

Prudence found herself laughing at Harriet's question. It would be the grandest picnic she had been to. Laid out on a white tablecloth, was a delicate willow-pattern china tea set and delicious foods, strawberry tarts, fruit salads dotted through with gooseberries, currant buns, and freshly baked bread still steaming from the oven, or so they smelt, with cheeses, pots of jam and cream, and kettles of tea and coffee.

"What an idea of yours," Lady Heatherbroke called as she saw the three of them approaching. They walked up the steps to the Grecian temple.

"I trust you slept well, my child?"

"Yes, thank you, my lady."

"Now, I think, might be the best opportunity for us to collude."

"Is that so?"

"Oh, of course." The older woman helped herself to a healthy array of foods, whilst everyone else clambered into their seats. "You see, we must have a prepared version for when your father arrives. Besides, I feel I should know a little more about you, since you have taken such good care of my only great-grandchild."

Prudence wet her lips and, during the breakfast, let the dowager know all manner of things about her. From the village itself, to her dearest friend Clara, to her father's marriage to Mrs. Pendleton eight years ago.

"This is the Duchess of Woolwich's aunt? She is also your stepmother?" Lady Heatherbroke asked.

"That's right," Prudence replied, keeping her tone quiet and low so that Harriet, busy with the iced buns, did not seem to notice.

"And that is how your family, your father, came to be connected with..." The dowager paused as she mulled over her next choice of words.

Prudence drank her tea in order to fill the silence. Given the look in the dowager's eye, she was grateful not to be the duchess.

"And you have had no contact with any of the rest of your stepmother's family?"

"None, save for Harriet."

"For that I can only assume you must be grateful."

Prudence smiled. The woman whose letters she had pored through last night, who had acted with no dignity, so it had to be love. How much Prudence sympathised, how much she understood the woman's desperation. To be trapped in a loveless marriage and to think there might be the possibility of escape... no, she felt for the duchess.

Prudence caught Richard's eye. It was clear he was listening to their conversation whilst talking to Harriet.

"Why not take the child to paddle?" Lady Heatherbroke commanded.

Dutifully, Richard got to his feet and carried Harriet down to the shoreline, grinning at Prudence as he left.

With a gesture of her hand, Lady Beatrice dismissed the two maids. "I would prefer to talk in peace, child."

"Thank you, ma'am."

"Most women I know would have jumped at my grandson's offer of marriage yesterday.

But not you."

"No," Prudence answered. She did not want to dwell on that rash decision.

"Would you care to explain why not?"

"Why should we? Nothing untoward has occurred, and I have no desire to force someone's hand."

"It would be the best way to silence any gossip."

"Surely, you would prefer a grander match for Richard?" Prudence asked her question without thinking. The dowager smiled at the informal use of her grandson's name.

"Indeed, at one time that would have been my preference, and that was the aim for

George. We might have looked for a member of the royal family, say. But that was George."

"If George could marry a princess, why couldn't Richard? I can't imagine—"

"My dear," the dowager interrupted her, "I must say you don't do a very good job of convincing me that you are indifferent to him."

"I never claimed to be indifferent. I don't think anyone could be indifferent, but…" Prudence leant back in her chair and watched the father and daughter begin their first cautious steps into the water, each of them with identical looks of disgusted delight on their faces.

"But?"

"Well…" Prudence re-focused. Not on the dowager, that would be too much, but down on the floral china pattern before her. She swallowed, giving herself more time to think. "Well… I would think that once someone was aware of the situation, what has befallen the family, one could only sympathise."

"It tugged on your heartstrings?"

"Yes," Prudence said.

"And he told you what happened."

"Enough."

"Not enough to offend your modesty. That is the main reason we'd never get a grand match for him. Besides which, he'd need a woman who wouldn't mind Harriet being here."

"I do believe that any woman who got to know Harriet wouldn't turn her away."

"Easy for you to say," grumbled the dowager. "Not everyone is as loving as you. I suspect that's your father's good Christian duty shining through, rather than his wife's." Prudence made no comment and continued to eat her grapes.

The dowager leant closer and said, "I suppose he told you what the precious little duchess did?"

"Ma'am?" Prudence asked.

"Well," said the dowager, "that woman convinced her husband to chase Richard up here. Got all his dear friends to desert him in his hour of need. He was twenty-four." She let out a sigh. "I heard them accusing him of things he would never have done. I know he's kept her love letters. I found them months later."

From the water's edge, the continued talk and laughter rose, and Prudence almost wished she was over there, dipping her toes into the cold waters.

"She did it as an act of revenge, I think," the dowager said. "I saw her at the funeral for

George. Never have I seen a more besotted idiot."

"She hoped her husband would divorce her."

"Some women," said the dowager, "like to be the centre of male admiration. They aren't happy with their one season, and they want the attention to continue."

"But..." Prudence trailed off, wondering how, if Richard had acted in a different manner, he might have had everything, the beautiful duchess and Harriet. Whilst he might have lost some of the friends from the Set, should it have been risked? Divorce was an ugly word, but one some in the nobility might have considered.

"Don't you think he should have done it? Risk the scandal of divorce?"

"Not for a woman like that. Because if he had wanted to out her, he would have done so," the dowager said, after a moment's hesitation. "You must understand my resentment towards the Bradleys, towards all the duchess' kin, does not extend to you."

"My stepmother..." Prudence started to say, uncertain of what she was protecting, but nevertheless hoping to at least justify Mrs. Pendleton's actions. "I don't believe she knew all the circumstances. My stepmother did not even tell me who Harriet was. Beyond that, she was to be raised as a foundling."

"The child is best with us." The dowager got to her unsteady feet. Her wrinkled hand reached out with surprising quickness, grasping hold of Prudence's shoulder. "I know it hasn't been ideal. But perhaps some good can come of this."

"Beyond a dear, sweet child being reunited with her father?"

The dowager sidled them both forward, out and away from the table, and towards the steps of the little temple, angling them towards the water. "I did not mean for Harriet." She pinched the top of Prudence's hand and laughed at the look on her face. "Whilst it might not have been the most traditional of meetings, I'm a big believer that society does not always know best. Look at Woolwich and his wife. They were considered to be an example of a noble family." The two of them descended to the lawn, but still the dowager hung on to Prudence's arm. "I liked seeing the pair of you with Harriet if you must know. Richard was all for bringing her back and locking himself away from the outside world. But with you here..."

"He can't?"

"And that's a jolly good thing," the dowager declared. "If anything, you are confirmation that my grandson has made mistakes, but that they shouldn't define him. I think if you told him how you feel, he would be receptive."

The two maids, who were lingering on the shoreline, glanced back at her but did not come any closer.

Richard turned then, too far away to have heard them. He snatched up Harriet and waded out of the water, placing her on the bank with the maids before making his way up to where the two of them stood. The sunlight nestled in his brown hair, illuminating the lighter points and almost creating a sort of halo, Prudence thought, around his head. The fallen angel indeed.

"Are you telling tall tales about me, Grandmother?"

"No, only the honest truth."

"That can sometimes be too much to bear."

"The alternative, though..." Prudence trailed off before saying, "If the consequences can be born, then isn't the truth the best way?"

Richard looked away from her and out over the water, but Prudence was pleased to see that a faint smile lingered on his lips. If she were brave enough, she could tell him, she could hint to him... that she would be kinder, keener, if he were to ask for her hand again.

CHAPTER 15

As they prepared to make their way back towards Brayton Manor, the truth was that Richard could not remember a day that felt as lovely as this one. It had been such a long time, perhaps even going back as far as to before George died. The tightness in his chest had subsided, diminishing since he had found Harriet, and making it feel as if he could breathe again. He drew fresh air into his lungs, and with each intake, he was reminded of how crucial Prudence was to this contentment.

He'd been hoping to bring Harriet here, for her own sake, and to have her installed in the family home; a desire that was based on righting a wrong of the past. Watching Prudence moving alongside his grandmother, talking to Harriet and chatting to the servants, he saw how she had slipped into his world, how she made the imagined picture into a better reality.

It wasn't only that, though, Richard admitted to himself. There was also the undeniable beauty that Prudence possessed. Her bright blue eyes were so gentle as she spoke, her smile lighting up her face as she gazed at him. Her elegance seemed to permeate through all her gestures. It wasn't skin deep, though. He saw the small smile on her lips when she viewed

Harriet, or how she loved to laugh, and the kindness she showed to all those she met. Aside from that, there was also how she had reacted to him since their initial meeting. Not many women would have handled it as well, or with such vivacity, or strength of character. In short, it was impossible not to admire Prudence.

The only problem, as far as he was concerned, was she had turned down his offer of marriage, flat. He could hardly ask again so quickly.

The pathway snaked away, and Lady Heatherbroke and the child continued talking as they made their way along it. Harriet seemed to bounce next to the dowager. Listening, the dowager nodded down at the girl. It was a relief to see his grandmother like this. She had gone through so much in the last ten years, witnessing more than any woman deserved to.

"How does it feel to see them together?" Prudence asked.

Even now, meandering through the lawns, he could imagine dragging Prudence back inside and locking the doors. Pulling down that pink gown of hers and not letting her out of his presence until she was officially ruined. Given how she had moved and moaned under his fingers and mouth last night, wouldn't she be receptive? He glanced at her. The blasted woman seemed unflustered and calm, with a little smile on her full lips. God, he wanted to go further.

It had amazed him that he was able to restrain himself.

"You look very content," she said.

"Is that so?"

"Indeed. You are at peace. It is nice to see."

I would be more so if you had said yes to my proposal, Richard thought. He stopped himself. An idea had just occurred to him. Wouldn't Vicar Pendleton insist on them being wed? And Richard would raise no objections. It would be an unfair trick, she would say yes, and he could win her round?

"Only nice?" he asked.

"I should have picked a better word. I wanted to ask you something."

"Yes?" Richard replied. His mind was still focused on the shape of her body as it glided along the path next to him.

"I thought a little more about what you offered," she said.

Richard's chest contracted. He'd made her the offer of marriage without really thinking it through, more knowing that his grandmother had expected it. It had been made in the heat of the moment, but now, faced with the reality of her and the possibility of her staying at Brayton, that was something else. Yes, he knew it was all too sudden. Still, he wanted her to at least consider his offer a little more before her father insisted on it. He had come like a whirlwind into her life. Perhaps she wanted to return to simpler things.

"I didn't mean to be impolite. I should have done more—"

"I know I should have phrased it with more grace." The words came out of him. But they weren't what he wanted to say to her.

The woodland that they walked through offered them only a little shelter. He was conscious that his grandmother and daughter were walking close to them, which did not create a romantic scene.

"I did not want you to feel that you were being forced," Prudence replied.

Richard resisted the temptation to roll his eyes, as if he thought it would be so very terrible to be wed to her. Didn't she realise what sort of redemptive temptation she was to him? How much he would have liked to feel he was good enough for a woman such as her?

"I wouldn't want that, not in the least. To be forced into something so permanent. To feel one or both of us had been made to do something against our wishes," she replied.

"I should not have given you that idea," Richard said. "That wasn't kind of me. It shouldn't ever have appeared flippant. I would take such an opportunity with the utmost seriousness."

"Thank you." She paused beside a tree. "I know I am not a catch for a marquess. You could wed some duke's daughter or—"

Richard was about to reach out and take her hand; the idea was not formed in his head of how or what he should say, but he did want to reassure her that she far outshone any duke's daughter. To let his dear Prudence know that if she would accept his proposal, he would do his best to make her happy. That whilst he wouldn't use the term love, he would treat her with the greatest respect and affection. And as for their nights, well, he would make sure she enjoyed each and every one of them. But before any of this could occur, before he could even reach out for her fingers, there was a loud, ferocious cry from twenty or so yards off.

Close to the entranceway, near the front steps of the house, was a middle-aged couple who had descended from their carriage. They were staring around the place. Then Richard spotted that the man was wearing a collar. It had to be Vicar Pendleton, and what must be Prudence's stepmother and Annabelle's aunt, Mrs. Pendleton. The pair of them had spotted the picnic party, and there was an odd gurgle as they hurried towards the party. Both of her parents looked like a strange blend of fury and concern. They bustled and talked to each other, feeding their own outrage as they moved closer.

Behind the pair of them, Richard also saw Lord Lynde climb out of the carriage. His elegant figure followed after the older couple, crossing the lawn in their wake.

Prudence had moved away from the group and quickened her step as she collided with the Pendletons, their voices excitable. Mrs. Pendleton appeared to be crying, her voice moving up and down the scales in interesting directions, as she hugged her stepdaughter. This performance continued until the Cavendishs and the servants reached them.

Vicar Pendleton gazed around the group, his blue eyes paler than his daughter's. He found Richard and gave him a dirty look. "Are you Heatherbroke?"

"That's him," Lynde said. He had rolled up his sleeves, readying himself for the fight.

"You have manhandled my daughter and ward, you..." The vicar had reddened, and he looked like a disgruntled parrot, his fatherly face on the end of a long, wobbling neck. "How... how..."

"Father," Prudence said. She took hold of her father, at first giving the appearance of holding him up. "There has been a misunderstanding."

"I demand to know—"

"How like you, Heatherbroke, damaging one woman wasn't enough," Lynde said. He looked murderously at Richard.

With a wave of his hand, Richard sent the servants indoors. He would have preferred to send Harriet in, too, but she was now holding on to his grandmother's skirts and watching the interaction between the adults.

"I thought I said never to visit Brayton again, Lynde. What are you doing here now?"

"Well, I only told you about your daughter with the hope of resolving matters." Lynde looked away from Richard, and he turned his face towards Prudence. "Good morning, Miss Pendleton. I don't know if you know me, but—"

"You're Lord Lynde?" She curtsied.

"Miss," Lynde replied in confirmation. He made to move towards Prudence, but Richard put out his hand and stopped his one-time friend.

"Miss Pendleton is a guest in my home, you have no right—" Richard's voice was rubbed raw with anger.

"Strange way of coming by guests," snapped Lynde.

"Enough of this," the dowager piped up. "We have set it about that Miss Pendleton has come here as my companion. She has had a maid throughout the journey up here. I give you my solemn promise that nothing untoward has occurred. I would have thought that we could all agree this is the best solution for all. I should think that would be enough for everybody here. Now, may we go inside and take tea?" She put her hand out to Vicar Pendleton, grasping the man's arm. "As long as no one has gone around shouting to all and sundry about this interlude, no one need be the wiser."

"I would have that from Miss Pendleton's lips alone," Lynde said.

"God, no," Richard said, the fury of the statement surprising even himself. "You shan't be alone with her."

"Her reputation is safer with me than you," Lynde argued back, spoiling for a fight. His stance straightened as he angled himself away from Miss Pendleton and towards Richard.

"I can state to all present that nothing inappropriate occurred," Prudence said, still standing beside her stepmother. She looked like a handsome slim reed, being batted here and there by arguing voices. Her pale pink dress encased her, but Prudence's dark head was bent in submission. Richard had a sudden desire to let slip just one or two of their experiments, or even the roadside robbery, but then he caught her eye and realised he couldn't bear to embarrass or upset her. Even if it meant losing her. He had already done enough, and she would not take the protection of his name.

"Mrs. Pendleton, please allow me to escort you inside," Richard asked.

"I-I..." Mrs. Pendleton muttered. But she released her daughter's arm. Bowing, Richard also offered his other arm to Prudence. "Unless you want to wait with the carriage, you'd better come in too," he snapped at Lynde.

He turned away from Lynde and started talking to Mrs. Pendleton with as much kindness as he could manage. From behind them, there was an annoyed sigh as Lynde followed them inside.

Once in the house, the dowager took the vicar across to the sitting room at the rear of the building. It looked out onto the kitchen garden and had the best view in the morning, with its warm, fresh light. The maids had laid out a tea-set.

Richard walked the two Pendleton women in, depositing them both on the nearby sofa, before walking across and standing by the door. He wanted to give the impression, as much as he could, of being respectful. Although he couldn't help himself, his eyes kept drifting over to Prudence. It dawned on him now that she could be leaving him. Beforehand, he had been able to dismiss the idea, push it out of his head with ease, but now faced with her family, he knew she would leave Brayton, and that their brief idyll was gone.

Harriet sat between Prudence and Mrs. Pendleton, her little face moving around the sitting room, curiosity and excitement written into her expression. Even to a casual observer or to a small child, the tension was palpable.

"You're going to get away with it," muttered Lynde. He had entered and walked across to stand next to Richard. "You have the luck of the devil."

"Nothing happened," Richard lied.

"You may not be a friend of mine anymore, but you once were, and..." Lynde was shaking his head. His tone lowered further, and he said, "And there is no way in hell that you didn't at least kiss that woman."

Turning cold eyes on Lynde, Richard replied, "You are mistaken."

At last, Lynde looked away from him. "Well, that's good news then."

"Don't even think about it," Richard said.

"Calm down," Lynde said. "If you aren't going to stake a claim to her, someone else will."

"This isn't a game."

"You're right, and we are not in our youth anymore. We're all grown up, or at least we are meant to be." Lynde paused, and he accepted a cup of tea from one of the maids.

"She is not just some..." Richard managed to control his voice, but Lynde was smirking again.

Vicar Pendleton coughed. His voice, when it came out, was enriched with dust and cobwebs. Richard wondered how poor Prudence had survived and flourished into such a bright, luminous presence. He could not imagine a bigger contrast. "I think it best we go home."

"To London first, my dear," Mrs. Pendleton corrected him. "Lord Lynde has been kind enough to offer to drive us there."

"What about Harriet?" Prudence asked.

"I have been in contact with His Grace, when we were in London, and he has ceded to Heatherbroke's claim. He is prepared to leave Harriet at Brayton..." Here, Mrs. Pendleton's voice wobbled.

"Just like that?" the dowager asked, her tone speculative. His grandmother's cynicism mirrored Richard's own.

"Woolwich has said as much. Harriet will always be welcome in Alfriston. But we are agreed that her staying with her natural father is in her best interests."

"That's correct," Vicar Pendleton said. "We are happy for Harriet to have a home with us, whenever she might want to come back." The vicar gazed at Richard. "But I want *my* daughter home with me."

So much for Richard's hope that the man would insist on the proper course of action. So much for the old boot insisting on Prudence marrying him. Well, Richard thought, *I can try to tip the scale.*

"If it would comfort you, sir, I have offered Miss Pendleton my hand," Richard declared. "I would be honoured if she were my bride."

Mrs. Pendleton let out a little gasp at Richard's words. Everyone pivoted in their seat to look at Prudence.

"No," the vicar said, "my daughter is needed at home."

Richard heard the vicar, but his eyes were focused on

Prudence. Her gaze moved from the floor to Richard, and she gave him a faint, sad smile. She was so lovely, it robbed him of his breath. Richard had a hideous thought. Prudence believed his words had been a salve to his conscience, and none of it was more than a formality. But how could he say as much in front of everyone? *Besides,* his mind whispered, *you've no proof she cares for you.*

"In that case, since that's resolved," Lynde said, slapping his hand against his thigh. "I would suggest we leave as soon as possible. This will be somewhat difficult to explain, so the sooner we can be in London, the easier it will be to justify our absence. Besides, you owe me a borrowed set of horses, I think."

"Go and collect your things, child," Vicar Pendleton said, and it surprised Richard to realise the man meant Prudence.

Prudence got to her feet and curtsied to the dowager. "Harriet, would you accompany me?"

Harriet scrambled off the sofa and followed Prudence out of the room. Richard resisted the temptation to follow Prudence. The vicar and his wife looked across at the two of them.

Vicar Pendleton said, "I know that my God compels me to embrace forgiveness, but having met His Grace once, I do not know how—"

"If you would like to interview Miss Pendleton on your own, you may. But I have not deflowered your daughter. Nevertheless, I would be more than willing to wed Prudence."

"No." The vicar declared it again, with a firmness that seemed to surprise everyone in the room. In fact, the man seemed very angry. "I won't have her marrying a man such as you and moving away from everything she knows."

Lynde got up and moved across to the vicar, his hand coming to rest on the shoulder of the older man. "Surely, there could be worse sons-in-law to have?"

"I won't have her leave me." It was a strange utterance. Richard wondered if there was another reason why the vicar was so possessive of Prudence. Based on the look on the man's face, the vicar wasn't going to allow Prudence to lead her own life anytime soon. The poor girl.

Still, she doesn't seem to care, he reminded himself, *else she would have said something. She's had plenty of opportunities to.*

Unaware of the awkwardness, Lynde patted the vicar's shoulder. "We will be leaving in the next thirty minutes, in that case."

"That may well be for the best," Mrs. Pendleton said. "I would like to be in London for my niece's confinement."

Lynde bowed low to the dowager. "It was a pleasure to see you again."

"We must stop meeting so," the dowager bit back.

Lynde laughed. "Were you ever in London, I would be delighted to see you at Gratton's."

"You think to charm me with ices?" She laughed, but Richard noticed a little sparkle around her face as she gazed at Lynde, flattered by his boyish ways.

"We'll wait in the hall for Prudence." The vicar put out his hand and lifted his wife to her feet. He bowed to Lady Heatherbroke. His eyes seemed to pass through Richard almost like he wasn't there, and the Pendletons left the room without a backward glance.

"I suppose I should," Lynde made a formal handshake with Richard, brief and unfriendly, "I'm pleased that there won't be pistols at dawn." Lynde tried to crack a joke whilst he raked his hand through his dark blond hair.

Swallowing down all his more elaborate replies, Richard instead settled on, "Have a pleasant trip back."

With a step back, Lynde closed off his expression, all the kindness in his face fading. He walked across the handsome salon, pausing only to look back at Richard. He nodded, then he was gone.

As much as he was loath to admit it, Richard was touched at the sight of some kindness from Lynde. Shaking his head, Richard sank down onto the sofa opposite his grandmother. The dowager was staring at him, with a look he was unfamiliar with, a sort of inscrutable expression that spoke of emotions that she kept beneath the surface.

After a minute, she spoke, "Would it be fair to say I know you quite well?"

"Yes, yes," Richard said.

He could hear movement throughout Brayton. Steps through the building. It wouldn't be the servants. It would be Prudence, making her goodbyes to Harriet. Leaving. He refocused on his grandmother, on her sharp features, and the kindness that existed beneath her faded exterior.

"Did you ever see me criticise your dear father, my only son?" the dowager asked. She did not refer to the marquess often since his death.

"Not that I remember," Richard replied.

"Or George?" Her question surprised him. They so rarely talked of George, despite the fact that he was a constant presence in Richard's mind.

"No. I don't think so." Richard racked his brain.

There was a slam of the front door, and then a scratch against the parlour door before Harriet entered.

They would be making their way to the stables now, Richard reasoned as he smiled at his daughter. Harriet came forward and sat down next to him, her hands cradling something.

Lynde would not waste any time. He would want them to reach at least Lancaster by the evening. If she wanted to stay with him, she would have, she could have, she only had to accept his offer. He wondered if Prudence would have been satisfied with her "experiments," and if her curiosity was satisfied with what the two of them did together. Would it be enough to keep her sated until some lucky man swooped in?

"What do you have there, child?" Richard asked Harriet.

"Prudence gave it to me. She said it was for you."

"Give it here, then." Putting out his hand, Richard had no idea what Prudence could have given Harriet that would be so small.

In a show of reluctance, Harriet opened her hand, and Richard could see it was the small ruby cross that Prudence wore daily. It was the only tangible thing she had of her mother's. He could not believe she would leave it with him.

"She said you were to keep it. It was for you. But you can't wear it. Can I have it?"

Richard looked up at his grandmother. "Prudence loved this necklace." His mind seemed to be moving at a very slow pace, nothing quite made sense to him.

The dowager grinned. "Do not be some sop, you foolish boy, do you think she would leave that behind unless she loved you?" His grandmother let out a sigh, a funny, pained noise. "Did you ever tell her how you cared for her?"

"I offered her my hand."

"With as much style and kindness as if I were blackmailing you to make that offer. Get after her. She's in love with you, as much as you are with her," his grandmother snapped. "And if you're too proud, or whatever your reasoning may be, then you are a bigger idiot than I thought you."

Richard found himself on his feet, the necklace clasped in his hand. The sound of his grandmother's encouragement echoing in his ears, he ran from the house, through the hall, before hurtling down the steps of Brayton Manor. He was just in time to see their carriage disappear.

CHAPTER 16

The journeys to and from Brayton were, to Prudence's eyes, as different as one could imagine. The uneasy truce between Richard and herself had morphed as the minutes and miles ticked by into a delightful tension. It was the kind she had come to enjoy. With the exception, of course, of the roadside robbery. The tension spoke of an awareness dancing over her skin. She realised how much she'd liked the attention of his eyes on her. It brought on the start of a glimmering sensation which ran over her body. Now, she knew what the end result of that sort of excitement meant. But there were other, more important things that she missed about Richard, like how he asked for her advice during the journey, respecting and liking her knowledge, and how the pair of them had seemed so aligned, at least in Prudence's mind. If only... she kept turning her thoughts back to how he felt about the duchess. Was there something there, some kind of unspoken love or connection she could not understand?

She hoped against hope he would understand what leaving that necklace behind meant. She had said she would only give it up for someone she loved. Would he understand that? If only they'd had more time.

On the carriage rumbled, down muddy tracks and onto bigger, wider roads. All the unease within the carriage was still left to be broken; they did not venture to make conversation. Vicar Pendleton would begin on a subject, or direct a query to his wife, but no one else spoke until they reached Lancaster where there was to be a change of horses.

"Miss Pendleton, I know you are somewhat familiar with my family." Lynde had led Prudence away from the courtyard and inside a snug little inn with a handsome red brick façade. Prudence took a little relief at finding herself out of the carriage and able to stretch her legs. It was strange, Prudence thought as she looked into Lynde's well-built and strong face, how lucky and excited she would have felt to be with one of the most eligible bachelors in Sussex. How Clara would be envious. The Blackman sisters were ever eager to meet the handsome blond man who now stood close to her. A lord now, and when his father passed away, an earl. "I know my father has always held the highest opinion of the vicar."

"I was not aware you even knew of Alfriston."

"Of course."

"The inhabitants would have been pleased to have seen you about the village."

He laughed with a gallant boom, his firm jawline lifting as he let out his amusement. He took her hand and led her to a seat by the window, letting Prudence get comfortable as she viewed the courtyard.

"Sir," Prudence decided to cut through the pleasantries that it was clear Lynde would have preferred to continue with, "you have a very negative perception of Heatherbroke."

"I would have assumed you would have been likewise disinclined to admire his company. After what occurred."

"Nothing occurred. He behaved as a gentleman throughout," Prudence said. Those delightful, reckless, sensuous secrets of that night in the inn when she had kissed him so. And again, when they were together in the library. Those memories would remain hers alone. Hers to hold on to, whatever the future might hold. They were glimmering, golden moments that would light up any future dark nights.

Lynde had moved away from her. He was drumming his hand on the table. "Miss, your stepmother's niece, the Duchess of Woolwich, may well contradict this view of him."

"How well do you know Woolwich's wife?" Prudence's question made Lynde turn back and frown a little. His expression told her he wasn't quite sure how to answer that. She had stumped him, and it was clear to Prudence that Lynde did not like being put in that position. "After all," she continued, clasping her hands together and keeping her voice low, "whose character would you have vouched for, in your previous knowledge of them? Who would, in your experience, be more likely to lie?"

Lynde stopped. He looked very pained; he hated having to think on the topic.

"I know it is not easy," Prudence said sympathetically, "but it must be considered." As Prudence spoke, in bustled both Pendletons. Deciding now should be as good a time as any, Prudence wet her lips. It was not her secret, she knew, and yet keeping quiet was damaging a man who deserved better. Heatherbroke deserved to be treated like the good man that he was.

"I couldn't say," Lynde replied to her earlier question.

"I have never met Her Grace. But I have known Lord Heatherbroke for the last few days. I have seen the suffering their affair caused him, and the repercussions it has wrought on him. I have also had the opportunity to read the duchess' love letters to him." Prudence drew one from the pocket of her pink gown. It was one of the many gushing, love letters that Richard had entrusted her with. Well, he deserved to have his named cleared, and Prudence could at least give him that. Turning, she looked at her stepmother. "Francesca, would you verify Her Grace's handwriting?"

"Oh, my dear..." Mrs. Pendleton's tone was ever so shaky; she could not quite believe what was being asked of her.

"A man's good name hangs in the balance," Prudence reminded her.

Mrs. Pendleton took the letter, unfolded it, and glanced at the contents of the page. Her rounded cheeks flushed as she gazed at the sloping script and then stuffed it back in the envelope. "That is my niece's hand."

"As the note states, and there are several others like it," Prudence collected the letter, "Her Grace was very much in love with Richard. She was the one who pursued him. I have no doubt that, were Heatherbroke not suffering after the death of his brother, Harriet would never have been conceived."

There was a strained silence after Prudence finished her speech. Mrs. Pendleton had dropped into the nearest chair and was fanning herself, saying again and again, "Oh, my. Oh, my."

Lynde was pacing, his expression angry. The only person who was viewing Prudence closely was her father, a shrewd look on his countenance.

"Then, pet," Vicar Pendleton said, "why wouldn't he use these to clear his good name?"

"His damn pride," muttered Lynde. He stopped moving and looked at Prudence. "God, Verne warned me as much. But I didn't want to see it. I heard what he'd done with you... That's it, isn't it? He didn't want Annabelle to suffer?"

Unable to hold Lynde's gaze, Prudence looked away. She moved to her stepmother's side and took up the woman's cold hand. "I do not think that Heatherbroke will ever move to reveal this, but I want all present to be aware of what a good man he is, and how his honourable nature is not inclined to have hurt me."

"God, Verne was right," Lynde said.

"She's not a bad girl," Mrs. Pendleton whispered, clasping her stepdaughter's hands. "Just rather spoilt, perhaps."

Prudence returned the squeeze. "Don't fret, I have no doubt

that, should he have wished it to be known, Richard would have made it so. Everyone wishes to protect the duchess as much as possible."

"She's just so dear—" Mrs. Pendleton sighed, but her statement was cut off, with Vicar Pendleton's reaction to Prudence's use of Heatherbroke's first name.

"Richard? *Richard?*" the bookish man screeched. He, too, was flapping his hands. "What are you thinking, child? Talking of a man in that manner?"

"Father—" Prudence started to say, but she was cut off as Vicar Pendleton began to rant and rave. She was finally able to get out, "He risked his life to save me."

"What, when?"

Prudence flushed, recounting the highwaymen tale wasn't ideal, but needs must. "He came to find me when we were set upon by thieves."

Her father's pale eyes bulged, and he spluttered out, "Dear God. He was the one to get you into such a scrap."

"But dashing to rush out and save her—" Mrs. Pendleton added.

"I have raised you to be a good girl." The vicar cut off his wife. "To listen to my words, my advice, at all times. But no, no, you seem to have transformed into... into... well, really, child. You should know better than this. And as for the note I got from you, it seemed designed to cause as much mischief as possible. I have taught you better. What would have been the reaction to this in Alfriston, had we not kept it quiet? To think... to think..."

As he spoke, Prudence realised it was always going to be this way with her father. He was so scared, far too scared of everything, and perhaps, he always would be. But Prudence wasn't. She had shown her bravery; she had shown that she was keen and willing to embrace risks to experience life as fully as possible.

"Father." She cut him off with a firmness that surprised both of them. "I cannot stay with you forever."

"I need you at home."

"No, Father, you do not." He had kept her back, leaving Prudence with only wistful imaginings that led down garden paths, but never went any farther. Unlike Richard, who opened up so many possibilities, affection, desire that cascaded through her body until the whole room seemed to tilt, and... well, perhaps, one day there might be more. There might be real, honest, respectful love.

Prudence thought of Richard's look of surprise when she'd kissed him, how he'd read to his daughter, how he'd laughed at Lady Heatherbroke's rulings. He had such generosity of spirit, she decided. "I am old enough to go for a position as a governess if I so desire." Vicar Pendleton followed Lynde out of the room, muttering about viragoes.

"Now, my girl," Mrs. Pendleton said, once the door was shut behind the vicar. "You can tell me the truth. I saw that man..." She tutted, her cheeks jiggling as she smiled at her stepdaughter. "He didn't even steal a kiss?"

"Perhaps once," Prudence admitted, "but he soon came to realise that I was who I claimed, a very pious..." But words failed her, and Prudence found that she was crying and unable to explain why.

"Oh no," Mrs. Pendleton fussed, leaping up and patting Prudence's back. "Don't cry, don't cry."

She had no logical explanation for it, other than she was a fool to fall in love with Richard. She had thought she had approached the sensation of being around him very well. And whilst she would have liked to experience more with him, it was not that she missed the more physical side of their relationship. There was more to it than that.

She felt flustered and bothered, being away from him now. And she kept wondering if there was something she might have forgotten at Brayton. Her mind dragged her down the alleyway of wondering what would have happened if she had said she was

Woolwich's mistress? Would he have seduced her then, back in the inn, all those nights ago? Would she have wanted him to, as she did now?

Prudence dropped down into a free chair and let herself cry, the sort of self-indulgent tears she would have rather avoided if she could help it. Perhaps she should have allowed herself to be compromised, because at least then... at least then, she'd have known him more. She would never have forced him to marry her, but she would at least have the comfort of knowing what he felt like inside her.

Mrs. Pendleton, who had excused herself, returned with a cup of tea and news that the carriage was ready for the journey onwards to London. Sipping her tea, Prudence prepared herself to go farther south and away from Richard.

A day later, they reached London. Lynde hopped from the carriage as they passed around the edge of Hyde Park, wishing them well on their trip onwards to Putney. He added that he had work to do. Prudence watched him go. She had her doubts. She suspected he wanted to be away from the Pendletons and that his guilt over Richard had reached a breaking point.

Vicar Pendleton's sour face watched Prudence in annoyance. She could not quite work out if this was to do with his real resentment at the situation, or if it was at Prudence's recent revelation. Their dynamic of father and daughter had always been one where the vicar was in charge, with Prudence dutifully following behind him. This new change in Prudence, one that had existed in her for years, was now emerging. Her father didn't like this change.

"Please don't look at me like that," Prudence told him.

"I will look at you any way I please," Vicar Pendleton replied.

"Here now," Mrs. Pendleton said. "Doesn't the river look

pleasant tonight? Why, one can see for miles. Look, Prudence, don't you think that's the prettiest sight you've ever seen?"

Her prior self would have said something soothing to please her father. But now she wasn't quite so sure. London did look rather charming in the spring light, the trees in blossom, and the sunlight sparkling on the River Thames. There was a whole, wide world beyond Alfriston, beyond what her father wished to protect her from.

The carriage slowed outside a large Georgian town house that looked onto the river. This must be the Bradley family home, Prudence assumed.

"Dear Annabelle will be in residence. That is what my sister told me." Here, Mrs. Pendleton drifted into silence, her gaze riveted on her husband.

"There will be no mention of Harriet. Or anything that occurred in the last few days. As an unmarried woman, Prudence should not stay in residence here with such a person," her father insisted.

Both women ignored him. Behind them, the carriage took off. Whatever debates, and no matter how envious she might feel towards the duchess, the woman at least deserved to know that her daughter was safe and well cared for.

The Pendletons started to make their way through the garden and up towards the house, all of them holding on to their muted silence. If she needed to, she told herself, she could go to the Blackmans or even back to Richard. The idea brought a smile to her lips as Mrs. Pendleton knocked on the door of the Bradley town house. From deep within the building, a noise seemed to resonate, which sounded like it might be crying.

Mrs. Pendleton knocked again, more loudly, the door swung open, and the three of them entered the building with trepidation. The crying was louder now. They stood there in the hallway hovering and not knowing where to go.

"What's going on, Fran?" Vicar Pendleton asked as he pushed past Prudence.

"I don't know why you think I would know." Mrs. Pendleton reached out a hand to the banister, when from the top of the stairs, there appeared a young maid. She was wearing a blood-stained dress and carrying a pot of water in rather shaky looking hands.

"Who are you?" she asked.

"Where's Lady Bradley?" Mrs. Pendleton asked. "I'm her sister."

"Oh, ma'am!" The maid came down the stairs to the halfway point. Prudence thought that the maid couldn't be much more than fifteen. "The duke and Sir Bradley are away. They left abruptly, and everyone else was out but me... then Her Grace, they... Her pains came on all of a sudden."

Mrs. Pendleton rushed up the stairs, with Vicar Pendleton charging after her, neither of them waiting to hear the end of the maid's story.

"Here, let me take that," Prudence said, taking the water basin from the weary looking maid. "What happened then?"

"Her Grace's ma... her mother, I should say, was here, and I went for the doctor... but..."

"But?"

The maid looked in Prudence's face and let out a great sigh, tears running down her face. "She died. Her Ladyship, she died."

Patting the young woman's arm, Prudence reeled from the news.

"Go and make yourself some tea, and drink it slowly," Prudence told the maid. "No, don't worry, I will take this. Where is the doctor?"

"Upstairs, with Lady Bradley."

"And His Grace, the duke?"

Here, the maid coloured. "They fought," she said, "and he left the house. Please don't tell no one."

"All right," Prudence said as she walked across to the nearest table. She placed the jug down on the surface. "Your secret is safe with me. Where are the other servants?"

"It's just the small staff, Mrs. Malley and me. No one else is here, it being a Sunday," the maid said.

"You can go," Prudence replied. She had no great desire to go upstairs. But without another servant in the house, more hands would be helpful.

Prudence went up the stairs, locating her father and the doctor having a heated discussion on the first-floor hallway.

"Where's the blasted husband got to?" the doctor was asking.

"Could he have gone to his own residence?" Prudence suggested. Her other thoughts were less generous. They leant towards the idea that Woolwich had gone off drinking. Or worse, Richard had made it clear that Woolwich kept mistresses, so perhaps he had gone to one of them?

From behind the doctor, there was a constant crying noise, either Lady Bradley or Mrs. Pendleton.

"There aren't any servants available," Prudence said, although she suspected the doctor would already be aware of this.

"Lady Bradley assures me they should be returning today," the doctor said. "In the meantime, I must go and get a wet nurse."

"The baby," Prudence could not quite believe it, "the baby survived?"

"That is correct." The doctor gave her a weary smile.

"Father, you will go and find the duke," Prudence said. "Doctor, I will trust you to have a wet nurse here within the next three hours. I will take care of both the ladies."

Gratefully, the doctor nodded at her and moved off. "Thank you, miss."

"Well, I don't think—" Vicar Pendleton started to say, but Prudence cut him off.

"I cannot go looking for him myself."

Vicar Pendleton nodded and followed the doctor down the stairs, while she made her way into the bedroom.

She was grateful that Annabelle's body was covered with a sheet. Lady Bradley sat in the corner of the room, holding a little baby and looking like an older, war-torn version of Prudence's stepmother. There were two other people present, Mrs. Pendleton and a woman who Prudence assumed was Mrs. Malley. Looking around at the morose women, Prudence knew she would need to take charge.

"Lady Bradley, I am Miss Pendleton. We've met once, at your sister's wedding." Prudence spoke in a soft voice. "I'm going to take the baby."

"It's a boy," the older woman said. Her voice echoed. "He got what he wanted."

With great care, Prudence eased the baby out of Lady Bradley arms. The infant was red-faced, his face screwed up against the light. Prudence smiled down at him. It was too early to know if he would share any similarities with his older sister, Harriet.

"Now, Lady Bradley," Prudence continued, "the most useful thing you can do is to go and have a cup of tea, and then perhaps take a nap."

"I couldn't. I—"

"I insist," Prudence said. "Your maid will be brewing the kettle downstairs. Fran?" She turned her gaze on her stepmother. "Can you gather together any useful information on the undertakers?" At that word, Lady Bradley started crying again and was pulled out of the room by Mrs. Malley, who nodded at Prudence.

Mrs. Pendleton's expression was weary. "Oh, my child, I can't stand it. I thought the worst was behind us." She came forward and looked at the baby before she, too, started crying.

"You had better go downstairs, too, and please, when you have had your tea, send the maid or Mrs. Malley to me with some fresh milk," Prudence added.

Mrs. Pendleton left, and a minute later, Prudence followed her down the stairs and into the nearest salon. She had no desire to stay near the dead body. She tried to instead focus on the child in her arms. As she gazed down on his little face, she sent a silent prayer up to the heavens, to where she hoped the duchess would hear her: *I have held both your children in my arms. I will do my utmost to care for them both.* The maid appeared with the milk jug and a teaspoon, before disappearing up the stairs again.

It was here, in the position of the Madonna with a baby, that Woolwich returned to find his child and Prudence.

"Who the devil are you?" he snapped at the sight of Prudence.

"Hush," Prudence said, in a gentle, soothing tone, "he's just gone to sleep." She pushed the little jug of milk away onto the nearby table. She then fixed the man with a clear, blue-eyed gaze. "Are you Woolwich?"

The man blinked at her. He did not fit the image Prudence had imagined of him with his double chins and engorged gut. He was taller than Richard and lacked any of the refined handsomeness that she so adored. There were no angelic elements to Woolwich; he would have looked more at home in the ancient gladiator ring. He radiated ruthlessness. No, Woolwich was all muscle, blond hardness, and granite-like firmness throughout. He gazed at Prudence with a look of annoyed confusion, and for a second, Prudence feared he would have thrown her from the room were it not for the child she held.

"I am," he answered the stranger's question of his identity. "Then I have some bad news, would you care to sit?" "Spit it out," Woolwich muttered.

Prudence pointed to the chair opposite her. She had hoped not to be the one to deliver this news, but what choice did she have? He would know soon enough. "This is your son. I am waiting for his wet nurse. I regret to inform you that your wife died during the labour."

It was difficult to do justice to the wild, almost mad look that passed over Woolwich's face. A look of utter confusion, pain, and denial. He scrambled up, away from her, and looked prepared to fight the nearest person, to fight anyone who could take away the grief of this experience.

"No." He looked back at Prudence. At her muted expression, he dropped back to his knees and started to cry.

Reaching out a hand to a man she did not know, Prudence patted his shoulder. Still crying, Woolwich leant against Prudence, putting his head against her thigh. She felt his tears soaked through the material of her dress.

"There must be some mistake."

"She's upstairs. The doctor has gone for the authorities."

"And—"

"What the devil?"

Prudence raised her head at the familiarity of that voice. She gazed into Richard's beloved face. Her heart sang at his arrival. He must have understood what the necklace... what she was saying to him, without words. And he had followed her. He had found her in such a tragic moment. For a delicious stretch of seconds, their eyes met, and Prudence imagined pouring out her heart to him. How she had missed him, how she yearned for him, how she wished he would kiss her once more.

Richard's eyes, though, dipped and travelled down to look at Woolwich, still crouched next to Prudence.

"Get the hell away from her," Richard shouted. He reached out his hands towards the other man's throat.

Prudence closed her eyes and prayed for this day to be over.

CHAPTER 17

Richard didn't need to see much to further increase his hatred of Woolwich. It was enough to see him close to Prudence.

"Get away from her," Richard repeated himself. He didn't wait for Woolwich to move but strode forward and yanked the man up, not noticing Woolwich's wet cheeks.

"Richard," a feminine voice was saying, but he was too far gone. He hated Woolwich with a passion that burnt through reason. Prudence belonged to him, and if anyone—any man—considered her in anything other than a welcoming light, he would be happy to murder that gentleman.

"You would dare to make overtures to a young, unmarried woman?" he asked, pushing against Woolwich's solid chest, hating the man who had cut him off for years from his daughter. Who had removed his dear friends from his life when he needed them the most? Was that not enough? Let alone trying to win his way into Prudence's heart.

"Richard," the voice was firmer now, "look at me."

He turned and gazed at Prudence. She was looking rather wan,

213

but still, she was magnificent. In her arms, lay a tiny child, whose mewling pink face was balling itself up into a frightful cry.

"Hush," she soothed as she raised the baby up and petted it.

"What the hell are you doing here, Heatherbroke? As if this day hasn't got bloody bad enough."

"Whose child is that?"

"I wouldn't mind knowing that myself," Woolwich said.

"This is Her Grace's son," Prudence said. "If you two cannot be respectful around a newborn who has lost his mother as well..." Her eyes moved to Richard, hoping he would understand. At once, his fighter's stance softened, and he looked pained.

"My God. I didn't know." He looked in sorrow at Woolwich.

"The stress of knowing you had stolen her child hastened her demise," spat out Woolwich. He grabbed Richard, holding him up by scruff of his neck. "It's your fault."

The scene had descended to some seventh circle of Hell, and Prudence couldn't imagine a way that they would not come to blows. The baby had started crying, too, which made things much worse.

"Please stop, please stop," she said again, but only Richard seemed to be listening to her. The fight had gone out of him, and he put his hands on Woolwich's arms.

"I'm sorry, I'm so sorry for your loss," he said, his tone understanding.

"Don't you apologise to me. Don't." Woolwich dropped him and his eyes swung back to Prudence. "So, you know him, do you? Familiar with this creature, are you?" His tone was enough to tell Prudence what Woolwich thought of her, and his gaze swept over her body.

"Don't speak to her in that way."

"You're the village whelp who was raising little Harriet, aren't you?" Woolwich had put two and two together. His eyes were boring into Prudence now.

"That's right," she said.

"How romantic, a wild kidnapping, I've heard all about it," he said, his tone dripping with cynicism.

"We are both—" Prudence started to say, but Woolwich cut her off.

"Don't you worry. I'll blacken your name about town, my girl, so he won't think of coming near you." Stepping closer to Richard, Woolwich whispered in his ear, "I'm good at spreading rumours. Given your reputation, I don't suppose it possible for Miss Pendleton to be able to show her name in polite society again."

"Sir," Prudence spoke, "I hold in my possession damning evidence against your wife, which would liberate Richard from any ill-intentioned misdeeds he was accused of. My own stepmother has already vouched for their authenticity. I'm afraid that Harriet was conceived, at least on Annabelle's part, in love."

As Prudence spoke, she jiggled the baby up and down on her lap. He seemed to enjoy the movement, but even Prudence knew he must be hungry. It was then that Mrs. Pendleton entered the room; she had been waiting outside. She looked as tired as anything Richard had seen that day. "Now, will you both behave with the dignity that Annabelle and this baby deserve, and go find a wet-nurse for this infant?" Prudence asked.

"I don't believe you," Woolwich spat.

"Jasper," Mrs. Pendleton said, "my niece was many fine things, and I will not speak ill of the dead, but that love letter was written to Heatherbroke. He may have betrayed your friendship, but he never took advantage of Annie." She looked between the two men, sighed, and then went to Prudence. "The doctor has returned. He's given a sedative to my sister. I have

Mrs. Collins outside, waiting to begin nursing."

Prudence handed the baby up to her stepmother, whilst Woolwich sank down into a neighbouring chair. Mrs. Pendleton slipped from the room, carrying the child. Richard watched Prudence, and how she seemed to be handling this new twist. He gave her a sympathetic look, ready to say something about her retiring as soon as possible.

"Get out of this house," Woolwich said. He still made no move to stand or threaten Richard, but it was clear who he spoke to.

Prudence followed Richard out of the room. She caught up to him by the shallow porch steps.

"I cannot stay," Richard said. He was unable to stop himself from moving one curl of hair from her face. Then, once he'd touched her skin, he seemed unable to resist, bringing his hands around her waist and pulling her to him. She came to rest her head on his shoulder. Richard felt himself relax against her. This was why he'd hurried after her. This, this moment, was the peace he sought.

"How did you find me?"

"I was following not far behind, I lost you around Rugby… and then," Richard sighed, "well, Lynde was waiting for me at home. He gave me your direction."

He told her how it was a long, awkward exchange between Lynde and himself, where Lynde gave Richard a full-throated apology for his behaviour and how the Set were willing to believe the worst of Richard. They had been so desperate to believe both Annabelle and Woolwich, but they were wrong. Lynde then said his honour demanded that he let the rest of the Set know about everything.

"He was talking about the Set and them forgiving me, but all I wanted to know from him was where you had gone," Richard told her.

"What about your name, having it cleared?" Prudence was gazing up into his face.

"It doesn't matter to me. I have found two far more important things." Again, he brought his hands up and put the necklace back around her neck. Then his hands dropped lower and encircled her little waist, marvelling at the familiar rose scent of her and the way she swayed in his arms.

"Have you come to like being so solitary then?" she teased.

"The only person whose opinion I care for is standing before me now." It amazed him how easy it was for him to say something that he had struggled to vocalise before now. "I'm a fool not for realising earlier."

Prudence stepped away from him, taking his hand and leading him out into the garden at the front of the townhouse. Around them, the night's sky glittered with densely arranged stars. The sounds of the riverboats could be heard. Richard found himself rather disinterested in any of that, only caught on watching Prudence move through the garden. She walked until she found a small bench under the branches of one of the trees. Far off, the noises could be heard from the house. Woolwich, it had to be assumed, had taken over the running of the Bradley household. His voice could be heard echoing through the rooms, and Prudence was grateful that she was not inside.

"Should we—"

"I certainly shouldn't," Richard said, coming over and sitting down next to her. He reached out and took her hand. It felt cool and perfect to his touch, and there was an immense comfort in just holding her like this. But he still wanted more. Wanted to know what her answer would be if he asked her to marry him in the way she deserved. "Prudence, you must know why I came here."

"It wasn't just to return my mother's necklace?" She withdrew her hand from his.

"Ever since that night in the library, no, earlier," he began. Now, his certainty with words failed him once more. "I lied to you that night," he said.

"You did?" she sounded surprised and a little hurt.

"A lie of omission. I told you that that sort of lovemaking, you might experience with others. And whilst you might go through the motions," he hated the idea of that, so he added, "you would not feel as you felt with me."

"I don't understand."

"Lovemaking isn't an experiment, to be trialled as a doctor or a historian might." Richard spoke, conscious that they were in a garden and within view of the public footpath.

"Those feelings of connection, adoration, the joy that we experienced together..."

"Did you feel them with Annabelle?" she asked.

"No," Richard replied. The urge to stand up, to pull Prudence to her feet and kiss her was overwhelming. "I need you to understand that I have not come here with the intention of anything honourable. I have never cared a whit for that. I came to London with just one mission, and that is to marry you as soon as you will have me. I realised I needed your kindness, your strength, and your curiosity in my life. I need you."

Prudence made a strange sort of snuffling noise, which was far from her normal, elegant sort of expressions. She turned around on the bench to face him. She was crying; great, fat tears fell down her cheeks.

"You don't have to," she said. "I don't mind if I never get that again."

"What?"

"If I can only experience that with you, I will hold on to the memory."

Richard leant forward, brushing his lips against the sensitive skin on her neck beneath her ear. "You have no idea of what more I can show you." Prudence gasped. "What?"

"That was just the first course," he teased as he started to trail light kisses into her hair.

"There is a lot more to reveal to you."

Again, Prudence wriggled against him. "It can't happen here."

"No," admonished Richard. "As I said, we can't do anything more unless..."

"Unless?"

"Unless you agree to marry me."

She gave him a sad smile. "You know I won't say yes. I cannot marry you, unless," Prudence looked away, "unless I know you... you love me as a man should love his wife. You see, it really wouldn't be fair to either of us. I couldn't... and then..."

In delight, Richard started kissing her, swinging Prudence up in his arms as he did so. He lifted her clean off the ground. It was an admittance of her feelings, or as much as Richard needed to tell her.

"I love you, too, you perfect angel."

Prudence laughed once she was freed from his arms, then kissed him back.

"Is that a yes, then?" he asked. It was tempting to just continue kissing her, but he wanted a definite confirmation of her agreement to marry him before he continued.

"My father won't approve," she said. "Especially after I let slip about the highwaymen."

Holding her in his arms, feeling her breath against his shirt and her hair against his lips, Richard nuzzled the brown strands of her hair. If she or her father thought that the vicar's approval was something Richard sought, then they had another thing coming. He wasn't going to let some vicar's anger affect their happiness.

"Does that bother you, that he doesn't approve?"

"It isn't ideal."

"Sweetheart," he said, his hands dropping down to her waist, just holding her, letting himself get used to the sensation of it. "Do you think that your father would approve of any man you liked?"

Her blue eyes looked back towards the Bradley house, her expression conflicted. "It's complicated. He would like me to stay his daughter forever."

"He likes to have a say over what you do?" Richard guessed.

"He always has," Prudence said. "I don't think I saw how bad it was until now. Until I left and did something, or rather you, did something terrible."

"That kidnapping is going to haunt me through this marriage, isn't it?"

"It will be my winning hand," she teased him, moving away, and sinking back onto the bench. Her expression was still worried. "What shall I do?"

Richard was tempted to tell her to stop caring; Vicar Pendleton could go hang for all he cared. But he knew this wasn't a helpful sentiment for his prospective father-in-law, so instead he took both of her hands in his before he spoke. "I think we should go to Gretna."

"Again?" She laughed. "I had no idea how close we were to it before, when we were at Brayton."

"It seems, love, that we are doomed to crisscross this nation, searching for each other."

"I..." her tone was uncertain. She looked so indecisive, and selfishly, Richard thought he needed to press home his advantage.

"You won't be missed tonight. They've got enough to deal with. In some ways, we would just be underfoot. We could be at Leicester by midnight," he said, without really thinking through the journey, just wanting her consent to undertake it.

"You know I'd like to," she replied.

"Think of it this way," Richard said, pulling Prudence to her feet, "it'll be like another kidnapping, but this time we'll leave a note."

Prudence laughed and kissed his cheek. Her whole face seemed to be aglow at the idea. "Another daring quest, you mean?"

"With as many experiments as you like," he said and watched Prudence's eyes widen with desire. He doubted if they would make it to Gretna, without several stops along the way into whatever hotels or inns they could find. He needed her. He wanted her. What did the sequence of events matter, so long as the ring ended up on her finger? That particular thought reminded him.

"Here," he said, stepping back and drawing out from his pocket a square-cut diamond surrounded by pearls. It was held together on a delicate gold band that was one of his mother's favourite pieces of jewellery. "This was one of the few things I bothered to collect before I chased after you. It belonged to my mother. She would have approved of you."

Prudence swallowed but didn't move. Deciding he might as well do the thing properly, Richard dropped down to one knee before her. He raised his hand up towards her.

"Will you marry me?" It surprised him how nervous he was about her answer, despite everything. There was a pause, in which Richard started to worry; it knotted in his chest. Yes, she loved him. Yes, she desired him. But would she let the unconventional way they met, and her father's hatred of him, hold her back?

"This time," Prudence said, stepping forwards, taking the ring from his proffered hand, and slipping it on her left finger, "we will leave a real note, stating our intentions."

By the time the note was written in the drawing room, Mrs. Pendleton had roused. She saw the two of them together, saw the ring, took one look at the letter, and said she would take care of the vicar. She smiled at the pair of them and then said, "At least one good thing has come out of today."

With that blessing, Richard went for a hackney, which then took the pair of them across the river and up towards his Mayfair abode. They sat beside each other, asking and answering questions, but more often than not, drifting into silence. Richard was sure he could sense what preoccupied Prudence; it would be her nerves now that it was happening. It had to be a fairytale, as if at any moment Richard would vanish.

The whole journey, he held her hand and told himself that unless she was ready, truly willing, he could wait for the marriage contract. They would wait until they reached Gretna. Wait until she was ready. The point was that they were together. It rather shook Richard, he realised, to feel so dependent on another person, but the only sign he gave of this was to squeeze her fingers. He would be the perfect gentlemen, he told himself, and make sure, utterly sure, that she was happy. He owed her that much.

Once the hackney had dropped them off at his Mayfair residence, Richard bent and scooped Prudence up in his arms, carrying her up the steps to the front door.

"What are you doing?"

"Giving the impression that we're already married."

He thought she might protest, but all Prudence did was giggle. He was beginning to like this rather free-spirited version of her, the side he'd imagined and seen the occasional glimpse of.

The housekeeper ushered them inside with a knowing look, but Mrs. Wilson didn't say a word. Richard took the steps to the first floor two at a time.

"Won't we give the—"

"Never mind that," Richard said, reaching his own bedroom. The master bedroom. He never used the space, preferring to avoid this particular Mayfair room unless necessary. Now that he was to have a wife, well, then he shouldn't be shy of calling this place his own. It was a pleasant bedroom, with a beautiful wooden fireplace in the corner and large windows that looked onto the street outside. With care, Richard let Prudence go and walked across to the windows, pulling open the shutters and letting some fresh air fill the room.

"Won't we get cold?"

Richard stepped closer to her. Even through the threads of their clothes, so many layers of them, he could feel the heat of her body and could imagine the shape of it, the parts of her that his eyes hadn't feasted on yet. "I doubt it," he said.

Prudence flushed and stepped around him, making her way closer to the bed.

In great haste, Richard busied himself by the fire, starting it up by adding logs and paper, before watching the flames leap around the wood. "There we go. That'll help if you were worried. I only opened the windows to air it out a bit." He realised that he was nervous, as if he were the one losing his virginity, rather than her.

Richard looked back towards the bed; Prudence had shed her bonnet and her longish coat. She was just wearing the modest little white dress, with a simple ribbon under her breasts.

"I can't get this off on my own," she whispered, sinking into a sitting position on the bed. "None of that," he said, making his way over to her, "unless you're ready."

In answer, Prudence pulled him on top of her, pressing herself up against him. This time, she kissed him with a hungry passion, running her hands with vivid curiosity over his shoulders and back. Richard was comforted to know her lust wasn't aided by alcohol. Just good old-fashioned desire. The exact same desire that pumped through his veins.

"Hold still," he managed, rolling away from her and divesting himself of his coat and shoes. "You little wanton," he added.

Prudence smiled at him. Her beautiful mane of hair had lost its pins and was now tumbling loose down her back. Her dress was rumpled and dipped down low on her left shoulder, exposing the top part of her breast. She was visible by the faint rays of moonlight and the golden flare of the fireplace. These colours played across her features and the shape of her body. With a smile, Prudence reached out her hands towards him, and Richard did not quite understand how he could contain himself long enough to strip.

"Patience," he whispered as he pulled her close, kissing his way from her rich, full mouth, down along the line of her throat, before dipping his head lower to caress the top swell of her left breast. Prudence let out a little moan and arched upwards. God, he thought, she was so responsive. The dress beneath his hands tore as he tried to get to her skin, before the material gave way and revealed her undergarments, including the stays and drawers she wore.

"What will I wear tomorrow?" she murmured, her voice heavy with humour and what sounded like bemused lust.

"Don't let us worry about that," he said. His hand ran over her stays, pulling at them until finding the laces. With his free hand, he dipped lower, lifting and shifting her skirt up and away from her and revealing her long, shapely legs. She shivered as his fingers yanked away her drawers. "Cold, sweetheart?"

"Not with you here," she replied. Her hands started to move over his body now, tentative at first, drawing patterns against his exposed skin, running her palms over his shoulders, his back, before drifting them lower and towards his breeches, which he had kept on. He didn't want to undo them quite yet, and shock Prudence.

"Why not get under the covers?" he suggested.

Prudence got to her feet. She was magnificent, he thought, mightily pleased with himself. Her hair flowed over her shoulders, which covered her front, but the light from the fire backlit her, illuminating all her curves. Without even realising how seductive she appeared, she hooked her hands into her stays and dropped them to the floor, followed by the sheer slip of an undergarment she wore underneath. Now she was naked, standing there in front of him. The sight of her made whatever words Richard was about to offer stick in his throat. There were not enough complimentary things that he could tell Prudence, to do justice to the sight of her.

She scurried over to him. "Say something." Quickly, she

climbed into bed next to him; her haste and modesty seemed adorable as she yanked the blankets around her.

"You've quite stolen my words from me."

"All of them?" Richard nodded at her. Reaching again for him, Prudence pressed a few tender kisses to his mouth. "There," she said, "I will give them back to you."

Her hands then reached for his breeches. Richard scrambled off the bed. It was a delight, if a rather overwhelming one, to know that she desired him, too, as much as he did her. Prudence's eyes followed him, but it was her recent words of encouragement, of returning his kisses to him. Richard yanked off his breeches, pausing when he saw the expression on Prudence's face. She flushed when she saw the size of him.

God, he told himself ruefully, *don't go behaving like an untested schoolboy.* "Don't worry," he said aloud as he climbed in next to her.

Swiftly, he pulled Prudence over to him, angling his mouth over hers in a deep kiss, letting the feel of her lips and his tongue work on the magic that existed between them. The kiss was demanding and all consuming. Easing her back amongst the pillows, he lifted himself over her, gazing down at her, at Prudence in his bed. It moved him, seeing her thus, stretched out before him, all soft curves, smooth skin, and fierce blue eyes that demanded more kissing. He wondered if he would ever get bored of doing so. He doubted it.

He brought his body into contact with her, pressing his muscles against her skin, rubbing the points of her nipples against the hair on his chest, teasing her with the sensation. When Prudence moved to put her arms around him, Richard pressed himself closer to her, placing his thigh between her legs and bringing it up to press and hold against her mound.

She murmured at the rough movement, rubbing herself against his muscled leg. Richard bent his head and took her nipple into the cavern of his mouth, rubbing the pink point with his tongue.

His hand snaked down across her stomach, dipping past her belly button, over the flat contours, and down into the thatch of dark brown curls that nestled at the apex of her thighs. Prudence let out a whimper at the intrusion of his finger. With gradual care, Richard pushed deeper into her entrance, delighted with the way her muscles clenched around his finger. Her reaction to him was like adding fuel to the fire, and Richard had to pace himself to keep from just pouncing on her.

"How does that feel?" he asked, inserting another finger into her.

Prudence moaned under him. She was magnificent. Her eyes fluttered open, and she looked up at him. "More," she said.

"This may hurt a little, but I will be as gentle as I can," Richard promised her, kissing her forehead as he moved himself into position over her.

As if he needed any further encouragement, Prudence reached up and grabbed at his back, trying to pull him into closer contact with her. Slowly, with tentative care, trying to concentrate on keeping Prudence as happy as he could, Richard eased himself inside her, inch by careful inch. She was as tight as anything he could have imagined. It was a blessing that she was as wet as she was since it made the intrusion that much easier.

"More," she said and lifted her hips to meet his, slotting the pair of them together. It was like heaven for Richard. Whatever pain she had experienced was done. Or at least, her maidenhead was gone, and she gazed up at him, her eyes wide.

"Are you all right?" he asked, hoping she would tell him yes, and that he could continue. The urge to move his hips, to pound into her, was overwhelming.

"Yes," Prudence said. She frowned, her lovely face tensing as she wriggled under him.

Then she gasped. "That feels—"

"So bloody good," he finished.

Again, she moved, lifting and grinding her hips against his.

"Mhmm," she murmured.

Richard bent his head and resumed kissing her passionately, holding her body against his, and hoping that she felt the same intense wonderous feeling that he did. Just feeling her move, just looking at her, was intense and all consuming. Her body would have adjusted to his size now, he thought as it relaxed around him. So, he started to shift, with a mounting urgency that surprised him. It was satisfying to feel Prudence move and moan beneath him, as she caught on to the same tempo that had pulled him in, the beat of their bodies. As the movements grew wilder and wilder, Prudence let out a strangled shout, before Richard allowed himself his own relief. Collapsing down on top of her, his climax rocked his body. Cautiously, he lifted himself away from her, watching her face.

"How do you feel?"

"Really?" She laughed, the sound warming his heart. "Well, I can see why they don't put that in the science books."

He grinned and pulled her to him, holding her and letting their breathing relax. It would be a pleasure to keep her like this, her body flush against his own. Leaning over her, he kissed her forehead before rolling away, then went to the wash basin, returning to clean her up. Richard finished cleaning away the moisture between her thighs. It came away with a few drops of blood, proof of Prudence's lost virginity. Her eyes went to the rag, which she took from his hands and placed on the bedside table, before smiling at him. Needing no further encouragement, Richard climbed back into the bed and dragged her close to him. He covered her face with kisses, in much the same manner as Prudence had begun this whole experiment. She snuggled closer in his embrace, and the pair of them soon fell asleep, wrapped around each other.

CHAPTER 18

Never in her life, could Prudence remember sleeping nude. But if it was to become the new reality with Richard, she did not think she minded that much. There was something liberating about it. Freeing. It was also charming to find him curled up close to her, his arm resting on her stomach and his head nestled by hers on the pillow. She could hear him breathing, a slow steady sound of slumber.

She wondered what he dreamt of. Part of her had woken, worried about the things that were yet to be solved—her father, the death of Annabelle, how Harriet would cope with this as she grew up. But there was solace to be found in moments like this one and the family Richard and she would create together, that would ease both Vicar Pendleton and Harriet. Hopefully, all would manage to find joy in the coming days and years.

Prudence hoped it wasn't selfish to think like this; she had experienced so much new in the last week, falling hopelessly in love with the man who slept next to her. Whilst it was a whirlwind, this loving felt as natural as breathing. It didn't feel selfish or wrong, and no matter what anyone told her, she would never regret the passion or excitement that Richard had brought to her life.

Looking at him now, lying on his front, gave her ample time to gaze across his strong shoulders, following the lines of his back down to his bottom. Prudence suppressed a giggle. She'd seen drawings of male statues before, in many of the classical books that her father owned. But none had come close to capturing the curved shape of Richard's arse. She reached her hand out towards it and laid her palm on the warmth of his skin.

"Testing the merchandise?" came his sleepy question.

Prudence decided she did not care a jot for modesty anymore; Richard had called her wanton last night. He had claimed to love her curiosity. "Yes, what of it?"

"I'm very flattered," he said. He rolled over onto his back.

"So, you should be." She kissed his forehead, making him laugh. "Are we going to

Gretna today?"

"I don't think we'd make it today."

"Any excuse to continue debauching an innocent."

"Who, me?" Richard touched his chest in mock outrage.

"I'm afraid so. How will I punish you?" She reached out and tickled his chest, making Richard push her off her feet and forcing her to land down amongst the pillows. She had discovered last night that he was ticklish, yet another adorable aspect about him. Richard got to his feet in mock outrage and went across to ring the bell for breakfast. He pulled on a robe. There was a knock, and Mr. Wilson's voice could be heard on the other side of the door. Richard asked for their breakfast to be prepared, as well as the horses and the carriage sent for within the next hour.

"No, two hours, please," Prudence called out.

"Very well," Richard said to Mr. Wilson. Then he closed the door and gave Prudence a strange look. "Are you planning on lying in bed all day?"

"At least a little bit longer."

"Care for some company?"

"I would consider it."

"Very well." Richard dropped his robe back down to the floor, leaning down over the bed.

With an impatient noise, Prudence reached out to him, causing him to lose his balance and topple down next to her. "I'm not in a rush to go," she said to him.

"No, I can see that." Rolling over, Richard pulled her close, dragging her on top of him, hugging her body against his. It was satisfying that Prudence felt so small within his arms. He felt himself control his muscles and strength as he held her and she held him close.

Beneath her thighs, she could feel his member move and stir again. They had made love again, during the night, with slow, aching tenderness, until Prudence could not remember her initial stab of pain when her maidenhead had given way. Any soreness after her first time seemed like a distance memory now, driven away by the tenderness that Richard made her feel. She was more interested in experiencing yet more of the leaping, dancing crescendos that Richard wrought out of her body, with his skilful fingers, his tongue, and his sex.

"Now, my little love," he whispered to her, his hand catching and pulling her hair to better lift her neck, exposing the column, and kissing his way along it. "You will have to let me know where we are to go on our honeymoon."

There were hundreds of places Prudence would have loved to say, but she knew the one location she wanted to see more than any was one she had studied for years. "Rome," she said. "The Holy See and all," Richard teased.

"I would prefer to see the Coliseum. I have read about it so often," Prudence corrected him, her mind far more focused on the gentle graze of his fingers as they rubbed their way along her back. It produced in her the most soothing and stimulating blend that made her both want to lie still and twist her body out until the sensation had passed. She met Richard's eyes and gave him a hard look, which just made him smile at her. "But I have to see the Pantheon and the Sistine Chapel..." she insisted.

"Very well," Richard said, "and after that, onwards to Florence, a little less bloodshed and a little more art."

"And I have one other condition," Prudence added.

Richard shifted over her, teasing as he did so, with any movement, be it his legs or the occasional wandering hand that might brush against her sex. She wriggled again as his hands rubbed and held her thighs steady, holding her in place below him.

"What is it?" he asked.

"We will take Harriet with us," Prudence said. "I want her to know that she is part of our family. It is important to me."

As she spoke, Richard stopped moving. He gazed at her in adoration. "That is very generous of you," he said. "I would like if she came with us too."

Prudence felt herself dimpling at his compliment. Then she added in mock seriousness,

"But perhaps we could have at least one nursemaid with us, so we could..."

"So, we could?" His voice held the glimmer of a laugh.

"Sneak off and do this?" she suggested.

"This?" He kissed her. "Just this? Nothing more?"

"And this," she replied, running her hand down across his chiselled chest. Pausing before lowering her hand to his hips, she clasped his face between her hands. "Again," she said, against his lips.

Richard laughed. "Oh, please, but only since you insist."

This time he rolled her over, kissing her once more before grabbing one of the pillows and arranging it beneath her stomach, propping her up at an angle. Prudence felt a little perplexed, as this position was new to her. She felt somewhat soothed when Richard ran his hand down over her back, before lowering it to cup and hold her bottom. The feel of his fingers nipping into her flesh made Prudence squirm. His hand moved lower, opening her thighs wider, exposing her sex. Prudence wriggled, caught between desire and embarrassment.

"Don't worry," Richard said. His voice sounded taut with lust. He eased a finger inside her. The angle added a tension to the movement. He teased his way in, here and there, feeling as he did so, the shape and slickness of her sex. Prudence let out a little cry, and then she found herself biting down on the twisted sheets as Richard steadied her bucking hips with the reassuring grip of his hands. Keeping her backside steady on the raised pillow, he thrust inside her in one sure movement. The sensation seemed to penetrate more than ever before, reaching deep inside her, lifting and heightening all her senses and making her feel she was being carried outside of her body altogether. Then, Richard started to move within her in deep, powerful, twisting movements that triggered an almost immediate reaction. Prudence found herself crying out in desperation, until with one final movement, she slipped over the edge of the inferno. She was lifted higher than ever, in a burst of released tension. Prudence felt her body tighten around Richard's sex, clinging to his member, and felt it contract inside her, before he collapsed down next to her. A second went past, then Richard pulled her over to him. Prudence cuddled closer, before Richard muttered in her ear, "Perhaps I should have said three hours to Wilson, instead."

ON REACHING CAMBRIDGE THE NEXT DAY, THE PAIR OF THEM walked through the city. They had decided to take a slow route up to Gretna; after all, they deserved a little more time on their own. Richard had dismissed the Wilson servants who had been travelling with them, and Prudence and he meandered through the beautiful, classical streets, marvelling at the architecture. They passed married couples who did not seem as devoted as they were, who did not walk hands clasped, but it seemed so natural to Prudence. So that is how they moved, linked and at ease with each other. They made small talk, delighting in each other's sense of humour and their plans for the future.

"Now that Lynde knows the truth, and the other people in the Set, your old friends should be told too?" Prudence asked as they walked along the river, the steady stream of boats and rowers drifting past with golden beams of light hitting the water's surface.

"None of that," Richard said.

"But I think you should consider clearing your name."

"I would rather my name suffered in the moment, and that Annabelle's could be cleared."

"Why?"

Richard paused. His face contorted before he spoke. "I disliked all that she has done to me, but I cannot continue to do so. I have her child, and we must raise little Harriet to think well of her memory, rather than me cursing her mother's name."

"That wouldn't be fair?"

"No, indeed."

On the pair of them walked, whilst Prudence mused on his words, before she spoke. "That is very decent of you."

"Besides," Richard added, "if it hadn't been for her interference, and the Bradleys, why, the pair of us would never have met."

"If you had ever been in Sussex—" Prudence mentioned.

"I had no reason to be there."

"If I had come to London—"

"Then I fear that your beauty would have made you a diamond of the first water. I would not have had a chance to win your heart."

"What nonsense," Prudence said with a wave of her free hand. The sentiment was sweet and spoke of Richard's devotion, but she doubted it was very much more than that. Her eyes travelled over the view before her.

"Did you not see how Lynde flirted with you?"

Prudence dismissed this. "Of course not, I was far too aware of you. Besides, he was just funning me."

"If you had paid him the slightest bit of notice, I'd have had to knock his teeth out. And as for Woolwich…"

He referred back to the moment of comfort she had offered the grieving man. Richard seemed far more inclined to forgive Lynde than Woolwich. "He was heartbroken," Prudence said.

"That man does not have a heart," Richard snapped, "after the way he bundled Harriet about. I can forgive the rest of the Set. I was always the baby brother. Their loyalty was to George and to me, second. Besides, I am sure I would have acted in much the same manner if I had I been told that one of them had slept with Annabelle. But I will never be able to forgive Woolwich."

With as much patience as she could muster, Prudence squeezed his hand. "You should be the bigger man, given what he has lost. You should write to them, to Trawler, Lynde, and," she paused, "who are the others?"

"They're a motley crew."

"Getting up to so many wild adventures," she guessed.

"Don't let them encourage you. There's Lynde, who you know already. And Verne.

They are the two who told me about Harriet's whereabouts. Verne is the son of a high-ranking French marquis."

"How romantic," Prudence teased.

Richard rolled his eyes but pulled her against him, before carrying on with his list. "The others were a bit older, some of them served in the war. Trawler always gives the impression of being very serious, but he isn't. Silverton, he's always been mysterious. There were rumours that he has been a spy at one point. Verne."

"What about him?"

"There are rumours they both serve at His Majesty's pleasure. For the home office." "You kept track of them, even—"

"Even after everything," Richard said. "They were my friends. At least I liked to think they were."

The sun slid behind a cloud, so in an effort of lightening the mood, Prudence said, "Perhaps you're right."

"What's that?"

"I might have preferred one of the others."

Richard bent his head and kissed her thoroughly, regardless of the passing boats and watching matrons, continuing until her head swam.

"Do you still feel that way?"

"Well…" Again, he kissed her until she shook her head.

"Shall we?"

"Head back to the hotel?"

"What a good idea."

They lay in bed next to each other just a few hours later, both too tired to move much. Prudence roused herself to venture forth a question that was bothering her since the proposal.

"When did you know?"

"Hmm?"

"You chased after me. When did you know you loved me?"

Richard, who had his arms around her, quirked an amused eyebrow at her and then looked up at the ceiling. "Determined to know all my secrets?"

"I think I had better. Aside from helping you to raise your illegitimate daughter, I don't want too many more surprises."

"I wouldn't object to several surprises from you." Richard laid his hand against Prudence's stomach. "Whenever that might be."

A warm blush spread over her cheeks. She now better understood what occurred in order for a woman to fall pregnant. She felt more excited about the prospect of trying for one now, so long as it meant more illicit moments with Richard.

His hands moved around her back and hugged her close. "In answer to your question, I suppose it was from the first moment you spoke."

"Don't be ridiculous." She wriggled herself loose, then looked at him. "You thought me a jade."

"That didn't mean I didn't admire you."

"That isn't what I meant," Prudence said. "I want to know when you fell in love with me."

"Now, don't judge me too much," he said, as he adjusted her body more at ease against his. Prudence could have sworn that each ridge and muscle of his seemed aligned to stir her senses.

"Now I must know," she said.

"Well, it was my grandmother who pointed it out to me. I was too arrogant to realise it." He looked so sheepish and pink-cheeked that Prudence had to laugh. In boyish fun, Richard avoided her gaze until she caught his face between her hands and stared into his eyes.

"You ridiculous man," Prudence said.

"I know, it is quite something to still be needing one's grandmama to save one."

"I don't think of it like that," Prudence told him. She climbed on top of him, her legs wrapping around his midsection, looking down at him in consideration. "I think you have just come to realise the wisdom of women."

"Is that so?"

"Oh yes, of course." She leant forward, her breast pressing against his chest in a way that pleased both of them. "You are surrounded by us. You will have to do as we say."

In one flipped movement, Prudence found herself on her back with Richard pressing her down into the mattress. He leant forward and kissed her ear, grinning down at her wickedly as he started kissing her neck. As he did so, his fingers delved and played with the edges of her sex, tempting her with just the lightest of touches and making her giggle and moan.

"I suppose that doesn't sound too bad, being surrounded by you," he said. "Still, perhaps we'd better get to making a son, just to even out the balance a bit more."

Prudence tried to think of something witty to say, but at that moment, Richard pushed himself inside her, and all her cogent thoughts flew straight out of her head. The discussion, she thought, could be solved later. Or maybe they were solving it, in their own way, now.

※

ON REACHING THE MIDLANDS A DAY LATER, THEY HAD DECIDED to treat the journey up to Gretna with a much slower pace than the last time they had crossed the country, although both were keen to see Harriet again. Richard had said, and Prudence agreed with him, that it was important for them to have their own time. Still, they reached the Scottish town ready and willing to be wed. Gretna seemed rather romantic to Prudence's eyes, in the fresh spring day, as they made their way towards the chapel. There was birdsong drifting in from the passing gardens. The town had several smiling, nervous, but generally excited young lovers, who all were as willing as Richard and her to defy convention.

As much as there was a tinge of sadness as she paused before the little chapel, her mind turning to the people absent from the ceremony, when she looked over and saw how handsome Richard appeared in his dark suit, she couldn't regret how any of this had come about.

It was a brief ceremony, conducted with very little fanfare, in a small cramped little room, over the obligatory stone anvil, by a rather red-faced, droning Scotsman. Richard had managed to find a simple enough white rose bouquet for Prudence, but there was no veil or grand gown for her. Two preoccupied witnesses from another ceremony watched the pair of them wed, with matching granite-like expressions on their faces. In return, both Richard and Prudence had watched their service, no one acknowledging the visible bump in the other young woman's gown. A soft, dim light poured through the window, filling the room with a tawny glow, making the space seem like it might have been better suited for a Macbethian witch's scene. It hadn't mattered. It didn't matter to Prudence. All she had seen was the darling man before her, his green eyes warm with love.

"I'm sorry, my dear," Richard said as they made their way back through the town, past scurrying townsfolk and the occasional passing carriage, "if the ceremony wasn't what you imagined."

They continued down the street, their fingers linked together.

"I did see a lot of weddings conducted by my father over the years. In his parish church, with the stained-glass windows and the organ playing." Prudence leant in closer, the smell of his cologne enthralling to her. "And I always imagined my own wedding would have been something like that."

"Then I am sorry." Richard looked guilty, his lips twisting as he mulled on what she had said.

"No, don't be. This was perfect for us. I loved it. Because it was ours, just ours, we didn't have to share it with anyone we knew. What made it unique, was our presence, and that was the only thing that counted." They were nearing the rustic-looking hotel. They had rented a room last night and would be staying there for their wedding night. They had agreed that tomorrow, they would make the two-hour journey down to Brayton.

"But still... I would have liked to have given you some big high-society party with a grand dress."

"That wouldn't have been us. And anyway, who do I know in high society?" They made their way through the hotel and up to their private rooms. The idea of meeting his Oxford Set had caused a barrage of worry and concern on what they would say, let alone all their family relations.

As they made their way up the stairs, there came the shout of other guests. As much as Prudence had gotten used to hotel rooms over the last week, and as much fun as Richard and she had had in them, part of her was looking forward to returning to Brayton and having her own room, with her belongings in them.

Richard had assured her she would be able to send to Alfriston for them. She doubted Mrs. Foley would refuse to pack them. Although, as Richard had said, perhaps they should be thinking of their Italian honeymoon soon; yet another chance of the wider world for her to see.

"Well, you'd better learn all about society. You are now the Marchioness of Heatherbroke," Richard said as they lay down on their bed, curling in on each other and gazing into one another's eyes. Prudence laughed again; she would have married Richard whatever his title or lack thereof, but it was an odd sensation to have acquired such a position. From such a lowly beginning, she did not know how she would cope, but then again, it wasn't like Richard and she couldn't embrace the unconventional. That seemed to be their way. If needs be, she could always ask Lady Heatherbroke, although she doubted the old dear went much for conventionality. Prudence laughed as they looked at each other, and Richard stole a quick kiss.

"That doesn't sound very like me."

"How does Lady Heatherbroke sound to you? Something you could get used to?"

"Rather nice. I think so." It did have a nice ring to her ears. It was good, she thought, to be able to step outside of her father's name, to claim a new identity which would be hers alone.

It was not a rejection of her father, but more an embrace of her new persona.

"That's a relief," he said, pulling her closer for yet another kiss.

"Oh dear," she whispered as Richard started to nuzzle her neck, an idea occurring to her, overwhelming her with a flash of guilt but with no easy answer. She looked into Richard's familiar, well-loved face.

"What is it?" He seemed distracted, far more focused on removing the simple cream pelisse she wore which, once unbuttoned and tossed aside onto the floor, was less keen to engage in a sensible discussion. This was a rather nice thing, to feel as desired as Richard made her feel, but sometimes... Prudence held up her hand to stop him in his tracks.

"Pay attention," she said.

"Yes, miss, yes, wife. That will take some getting used to."

"You're the one who suggested that we wed."

"And I'm not regretting it for a moment." He tried to kiss her again, but Prudence held herself back, difficult though it was. "Although..." he added.

"What?"

"Well, you made for a more willing mistress than wife."

"That's not true." She swatted at him.

"Then what is it?" His tone was more sombre as he viewed her, withdrawing from her so he could be less tempted to continue divesting Prudence of her clothes. "Let me know so I can go at once and fix it and then continue with what we were doing."

"Harriet will be so disappointed not to be a bridesmaid," Prudence said. It was something that the little girl loved so much as an idea. A great society wedding was what she would have liked, with as many grand dresses and full veils as possible.

Richard sank back down onto the bed and rolled closer to his wife, murmuring words against Prudence's skin once he reached her. His breath stirred her even before he spoke. "Yes, I thought of that. But I think a puppy might answer just as well, don't you?"

Once more, Prudence laughed and let Richard continue to undress her, far too overcome with happiness to protest any further.

THE END

THANK YOU.

Dear Readers,

I really hope you enjoyed reading *The Marquess's Adventurous Miss* and that you are tempted to read the rest of The Oxford Set.

If you want to read the prequel and hear more about how the love triangle between Richard, Annabelle and Woolwich started, then do sign up to my newsletter to receive a free novella, *The Debutante's Duke*.

I so enjoyed writing these two feisty leads, Prudence and Richard, and how heads over heels they fell for each other. The novel is set in an area of England close to where I grew up, and I really love the Sussex countryside for its rich history.

I love to hear from readers and can be reached on my social media platforms below –
www.instagram.com/ava_bondauthor/
www.twitter.com/AvaBondAuthor
www.avabond.co.uk

THANK YOU.

www.facebook.com/AvaBondAuthor

And if you would like to write a review that would make me so happy!

Read on for a sneak peek of the next in the Set, *The Lord's Scandalous Mistress*....

THE LORD'S SCANDALOUS MISTRESS. SNEAK PEEK.

Eastbourne, Sussex, December 1814

As a young matron of good birth, pleasing looks, and in a respectable marriage, Mrs. Isabel Hall was an important member of Sussex society. She expected to lead out the matrons at various public balls, attend the theatre in her family box, and contribute to the local charity collectives. But what she had never expected was for her husband to stumble through the doorway of their home, covered in blood, in the middle of the night.

Pierre Hall staggered into their house at ten-thirty, just as Isabel was locking up for the night. The front of his shirt was soaked crimson. He collapsed onto the hallway floor as soon as the door was closed behind him.

"Mrs. Gilbert!" Isabel screamed, the shock hitting her hard. She ran forward and was joined by her housekeeper.

"Let's get him on the sofa, ma'am." Isabel and the housekeeper dragged him into the front room, a stain of red coating the carpet.

Whilst Mrs. Gilbert went for hot water and sent the butler for the doctor, Isabel held Pierre's hand. It was an odd scene to play out in one's drawing room, a space where she would have entertained her mother-in-law or other matrons of the town, where gossip and the latest fashions were discussed. Never had their drawing room housed so much drama.

"I'm done for, wife," her husband said. His colour was very weak, it was true, but Isabel, who was always praised for her practicality, ignored his terror. With tentative movements, he jerked himself forward, and more out of instinct than true matrimonial duty, much less love, Isabel kissed his clammy hand.

"Tell me what happened to you." She had no idea what might have caused such an injury to her husband. Perhaps he'd been set upon by bandits. Pierre was a businessman, and the impression she had always received was that he was rather stuffy and straitlaced ever since their first meeting at her father's office. He liked to maintain that everything was orderly and correct, from how he never paid the servants a shilling more than they were owed to how he refused to dance on any occasion. It was not good practise, he said. Eighteen months of marriage to Pierre had not changed her initial view of him, nor deepened their connection, sadly. She was fond of him; she forced herself to be. Isabel was sure that Pierre felt something towards her.

"I'm going to die." His breath was laboured as he pawed at his front.

"Stop that," Isabel begged him. She was scared he would make things worse.

He raised his puppy-fat face to hers. His grey eyes were bloodshot. "You need to do something for me. Promise me that you will. Promise."

"If it's within my power," Isabel said. The desperation on Pierre's face was scaring her. As yet, there was no sign of the doctor. How long would it take the butler to cross the streets of Eastbourne? It wasn't the largest of places…

"James… He's a good boy, really," Pierre said, referring to his wastrel younger brother.

Isabel kept her face emotionless. Her views on Pierre's younger brother were not polite. To her mind, James Hall was the worst sort of man.

"He got mixed up with the wrong sort, with the Wareton Gang." His voice dropped lower, and Isabel crouched closer, down on the floor beside the settee, nearer to Pierre.

"What did he do now?" They were so close they were almost sharing the same breath. Isabel could smell blood and what she suspected was vomit.

"You need to help him."

"Please stay calm," she begged. She doubted his fear would help.

"It'll damage all of us," Pierre said. This time his voice was reed-thin as if his breathing had been affected. Isabel could not claim much knowledge of medicine, but she knew that if the injury to his chest had affected his lungs, Pierre wouldn't be able to breathe. And then he was right; he would die. Her eyes went to his face, and her panic started to mount.

She leaned closer. "What has your brother done? You have to tell me."

"There's money involved. He took some... bonds and the like. They're..." Pierre's voice was wobbly, jumping from word to word.

The front door of the Halls' townhouse was thrown open, and in marched Mr. James Hall. Pierre's dratted younger brother. He fancied himself a rake-in-training. At least that was the impression Isabel had always gotten of him. Getting to her feet, Isabel crossed to her brother-in-law.

"Tell me what happened to him." She tried to keep the desperation out of her voice; she did not like being vulnerable in front of James.

"They're going to hang me." James's normally arrogant expression was gone, and he looked as white as a sheet. For the first time, James appeared older than his big brother. Isabel could feel herself growing angrier with the pair of them.

"I burnt the paperwork," Pierre said.

"One of the men made away with the rest." James collapsed into the nearest armchair. "I can't go after him. They'd know it was me." He rubbed his eyes, then lowered his hand as he surveyed the drawing room. "She could go."

Heaving himself up as much as possible, Pierre looked at his wife. "Do you know the Hurstbourne estate?"

"Yes, of course." Isabel was familiar with the grand home, a good ten or so miles away from where they were in Eastbourne. It belonged to the great family of the district, the Earl of Hurstbourne, and his famously glamorous and beautiful children, Lord Lynde and Lady Viola. The estate was also close to her own maiden family home in Alfriston, so she had grown up in its shadow, hearing all about the stunning Lyndes.

James scrambled up and grabbed Isabel's hands in his own. "You have to intercept the man. Cut the blackguard off as he's making his way to the magistrate."

"What? I cannot. He will be miles ahead of me." If the man had set off straight away, he had a definite advantage. If the man rode as fast as he could, he'd be at the estate in two hours, less perhaps.

"He's injured," wheezed Pierre. "He doesn't know that you'll be lying in wait for him. He'll take the main road. He'll think—" He paused to cough, and Isabel noticed more blood ooze through his fingers. "You can catch him if you leave straight away. Go the back route."

"Don't be a coward." James's fingers dug into Isabel's small wrists as he pulled her close, away from Pierre. "You don't have much choice; he's got something on all of us. Including your father. Yes, that's right, your precious Mr. Blackman's involved too."

Isabel had turned and looked back at Pierre, but her husband seemed past caring. He turned his face away from the pair of them, and his skin was sweaty and pale in the firelight.

"The incriminating documents will be in his travel bags," James said. "You'll need to steal the papers back from him before he can get to the earl. He's the local magistrate." He made the last point as if Isabel was an idiot when she knew all too well the power the Lyndes wielded in the area.

"I can't," Isabel whispered. If it involved shooting someone... She shuddered at the idea of it. "But won't he have such a head start? Besides, I should stay with Pierre." She crossed over to crouch down beside her injured husband. After his outburst a moment ago, Pierre had fallen back amongst the cushions, all his colour gone. Tentatively, Isabel dabbed at his mouth with her handkerchief.

"Nonsense," James said, drawing closer and dropping to his knees to intimidate her by his presence. "If we are to survive tonight, it's down to getting those papers back. Now, my girl, you'll take the quicker route to the estate. You've got some time. The earl is elderly; there's a chance he won't be woken until morning. The problem is if his son is back for Christmas. Never mind that." He fixed her with a brutal stare. "You need to lie in wait and shoot the officer. It's better you go, far less suspicious than me going. We can lie and say you're abed if they come to check on us."

From the pocket of his velveteen jacket, James pulled out a heavy pistol, which he pressed into Isabel's hands. It was cold to the touch, and the feel of it chilled Isabel down to her toes. She knew, then and there, that she could never fire it at another human. Unable to bear it, she scrambled away, across the salon and towards the door, but James was quicker, cutting her off.

"But I—I've never fired a pistol," she said to James in desperation.

Pierre swore.

"We're counting on you," James said. "It's a new design. Just point and aim. Then shoot."

Isabel shook her head. She couldn't do it. James pressed

himself closer, leaning forward and whispering in her ear, his breath heavy. "Your father could lose everything for this. Your whole family will be damaged, and then what will happen to you… as a widow?"

Isabel looked into James's face. He wasn't lying. He seemed to know that Pierre was done for. His eyes narrowed on her as he saw that he had hit upon a nerve—her desire to protect her family.

"Very well," Isabel said, feeling as if she was entering a battle without knowing what the war was for.

Twenty minutes later, Isabel was riding through the countryside late at night, dressed as a man, with a pistol in her hand. She did not much fancy her chances of success. She wasn't familiar with smuggling. She wasn't familiar with business in any of its forms; it wasn't considered ladylike. She had been kept ignorant. Nor was she familiar with what her husband had been up to on this fateful night.

The irony might have made her laugh if she wasn't so scared.

"Dear God, keep me safe," she muttered under her breath.

It was madness, she kept telling herself. Utter and complete madness. Perhaps, it might have been more worthwhile if it had been done for love. But she wasn't in love with either of the Hall brothers. No more than Pierre was in love with her. She knew he wasn't, or he wouldn't have sent her out here on her own. It was being done for the love of her family. Then again, she thought ruefully, her father had married her off to a man she didn't know, so what good had familial love done her?

Isabel straightened in her seat. Her bottom was sore. She had never ridden like a man before. Her nervous stomach had settled, so she was at least wide awake. The cold of the night and the dread of James's threats kept her so. Great wintry gusts of wind were driving across the flat marshes, digging into her back. She would have liked to have stayed in the house to wait for the doctor, but there wasn't time. Both Pierre and James had insisted on that. They'd insisted that she be out of the house and on Pierre's horse as soon as she was dressed in his clothes. She wore his oldest suit, strapped to her with a belt. If anyone in polite society saw her now...

With a strangled laugh at the idea, Isabel slowed her horse down. Up ahead, the road widened and split. One route led towards Alfriston and all the sights of her maiden family home. It would be familiar. Comforting. Knowable. Secure. It was so tempting to run back there and hide, but she knew the truth would come out, and then what would the rest of them face?

Never in her life could she have imagined that she would end up in this position. And the lulling promise of an Alfriston welcome called out to her. But she had her duty first, which was to save her family.

Would the paperwork in that officer's bag expose her family and have them out on the street? How far would it stretch? Just to the Hall or wider still? Would it stop at her sister Agnes's marriage to Mr. Miles? Ruin Thomas's budding legal career? Humiliate her father and mother to all of society? Would she dare fire the pistol? She had her doubts, but perhaps she could hold him at gunpoint and get him to hand over the papers. As if she were a highwayman. *Stand and deliver.* Yes, that might work.

Isabel nudged her horse onwards, taking the pair of them farther away from the temptation of her family home and towards Hurstbourne Manor.

The great house was much talked about in Sussex society. It was agreed upon that Hurstbourne Manor was one of the most picturesque buildings in the county, if not the whole of England. Since the Blackmans were in trade, they had only been invited to the public Yuletide ball that the Lyndes had held when the countess was present. But that was many years ago before the great scandal that had engulfed the Lyndes, and never in all her six years of being 'out' had Isabel been invited to the great manor. Agnes, Isabel's sister, had always hoped that they might see the Hurstbourne heir, Lord Nicholas Lynde, during one of their trips to the local assembly rooms. Something about that name conjured up flights of fancy in Isabel's mind. Even on this December night, during the fear and terror of the last few hours, Nicholas's name seemed to stir something in Isabel's mind and awareness in her body. Back at the house, James had mentioned him in passing, and Isabel had struggled to control herself.

It was a girlish infatuation. You must focus.

In their youth, Agnes and Isabel had imagined that when Lord Lynde was down in Sussex, he might dance with one of them. Sometimes locals claimed that he visited the estate for hunting. Once, Lady Viola Lynde had been at the Brighton Assembly Ball, but her older brother had not been in attendance. Viola had been the belle of the ball, glistening in the centre of the room in a shimmering ivory dress, but nevertheless, Isabel had left the evening disappointed. The gossip sheets wrote about Lord Lynde and his daring friends, nicknamed the Oxford Set, and their exciting exploits. But Isabel liked to go further and focus just on Lynde. Imagining everything about him. About his strong jawline, his slim but handsome physique, how he boxed at Kingston's, how he was thought of as the quintessential Corinthian gentleman, the most gallant of the Oxford Set. It was written about in coded language, but Isabel had summarised as much. In her most girlish and silliest of moments, Lynde had been a true Adonis to her.

One of the sketches of Nicholas had even been part of a ritual that Isabel conducted whilst at school. But that had been over twelve years ago when Isabel had only been sixteen. Her girlish fascination would not help her now. She needed to make sure that

Lord Lynde's father, the Earl of Hurstbourne, did not receive the officer because that would mean...

It was dark. She blinked. Only the moon and stars guided her, and whilst her knowledge of Sussex was extensive, she did not know the grounds of the Hurstbourne estate. She slowed her horse to a brisk trot, sitting up in her seat to gaze this way and that.

She had to decide whether to enter the grounds and wait for the officer's arrival or linger outside the property. Slowly she edged the horse onwards, past the entranceway to the estate. The gates had been left a little ajar, but there were no lights on in the gatehouse. An oversight, she told herself. But one that might work to her advantage. All she needed was his bag. She didn't want to kill him. If she could startle the officer's horse, the soldier would be thrown off, then she could get to the bag without anyone being hurt. Provided the fall didn't do any serious damage to him.

Isabel climbed down and secured her horse to a nearby secluded tree with this idea in her mind. They would not be visible from the road. Hurrying forward, Isabel located a large branch and then crouched down amongst the trees and bushes near the gatehouse, waiting for the officer.

The woods were dark and dense, letting very little light in from above. The gatehouse was likewise gloomy, although presumably, this was just because it was so late at night. Occasionally the moon swung out from behind the clouds and gave Isabel some idea of her surroundings. But at least it wasn't raining.

Crouching down on the woodland floor, Isabel rested her back against a tree and let out an unsteady breath, her emotions threatening to overwhelm her. As a distraction, she rubbed her arms against her sides, bustling from one foot to another to keep warm. She wished James had given her his greatcoat because the slim jacket that belonged to the stable boy was not very covering or as thick as her husband's. She would freeze, she thought, as she huddled amongst the bushes of the estate.

Isabel was close to giving up hope and had lost track of time when she heard the unmistakable sound of an approaching horse. This had to be the officer, and she readied the branch she would use to trip the horse and rider. For a second, she thought she could hear multiple men talking, but she ignored the idea. Perhaps he was drunk and speaking to himself. Thankfully, the moon came into view, and Isabel could make out the solo rider approaching through the soupy darkness. Something about the set of his jaw and body, visible even in the dim light, spoke of authority. He rode through the gate.

She sank low to the ground and jabbed the stick out, catching his horse between its legs. The horse lurched to one side, and the rider was thrown off. This was better than using a pistol.

Isabel hurried forward and grabbed the horse's reins, forcing herself to ignore the yelling of the fallen man. If he could cry out like that, he must be fine. Her hands moved over the large horse until they alighted on the saddle bag, and she started rummaging through it. But the moonlight was not *that* good. She would have to settle for removing the bag from the horse altogether. Her hands shook as she struggled to loosen the straps.

Click.

A strange noise came from behind her, and Isabel spun round.

"What the blazes?" Five feet away from her was a tall man. He had his pistol raised, moving with a pace that shocked her. She caught sight of his glowering gaze and little else. His intense eyes were striking, deep and shockingly blue, visible even in the moonlight. He had the sort of immediately pleasing face that sucked the breath out of her lungs; she felt dizzy with it.

Maybe that's the fear. Glancing around, Isabel knew there wasn't time to get back to her own horse. She would need to make a break for it, regardless of how much of a criminal it made her. Out through the park, jump the low edges at the end of the estate, and then make her way back to Alfriston. That was her only choice.

Isabel took off running, the saddle bag flung onto her back. She'd always been fast as a child, but now that she was wearing trousers, it made her footfalls quicker. She darted into the safety of the dense woods, the man following in hot pursuit.

෴

Continue reading The Lord's Scandalous Mistress here.

ABOUT THE AUTHOR

Ava Bond has been a fan of regency romances since discovering Georgette Heyer on her grandma's bookshelf—especially *Faro's Daughter*, *Regency Buck* and *Devil's Cub*.

She studied Literature at university and has been writing since her early twenties. Ava lives in Scotland with her husband and small cat, Gwendolen.

www.avabond.co.uk

ALSO BY AVA BOND

THE OXFORD SET SERIES

The Debutante's Duke (prequel)
The Marquess's Adventurous Miss
The Lord's Scandalous Mistress (forthcoming)
The Spy's Elusive Wife (forthcoming)
The Viscount's Reluctant Bride (forthcoming)
The Duke's Rebellious Love (forthcoming)
The Rogue's Brazen Lady (forthcoming)

Printed in Great Britain
by Amazon